DATE DUE			
APR 19 '78			
NOV 1996	HOW INDEF		
MAY 1997	HPL		

Leather, Edwin
Vienna elephant.

THE VIENNA ELEPHANT

THE VIENNA ELEPHANT

EDWIN LEATHER

DODD, MEAD & COMPANY
New York

Printed in the United States of America
by The Haddon Craftsmen, Inc., Scranton, Penna.

1 2 3 4 5 6 7 8 9 10

Library of Congress Cataloging in Publication Data

Leather, Edwin.
The Vienna elephant.

I. Title.
PZ4.L4388Vi [PS3562.E2613] 813'.5'4 77-22320
ISBN 0-396-07507-X

TO TERENCE RATTIGAN,
friend and counsellor,
whose courage is a constant inspiration

1

KRONACH is a small German country town tucked away in the northeast corner of Bavaria, a few miles from that flash-point of central Europe, the spot where the West and East German and Czech frontiers meet. Ordinary, pleasant enough little place. Always was, still is. Though not fought over or bombed, by the end of World War II it was shabby and exhausted. Every able-bodied young man and woman had been conscripted and sent away years previously "to serve"—many of them to die for—their Führer. The old men and the women, as in thousands of other small central European towns, had carried on as best they could, spending their days running the farms, shops, a timber mill, a furniture factory, and three or four little engineering works that turned out bits and pieces for the German armed forces. With a sense of despair, they'd tried to fulfil the unreasoning and often impossible orders imposed on them from above; then, when they'd failed, they listened patiently to the rantings of itinerant officials. They had spent their nights in cellars and on the wooded hillsides while their houses vibrated from the constant din of American and British bombers thundering over their heads en route to the obliteration of more important targets.

When the fighting had ended in May 1945, there was little spirit left in them beyond the primitive human urge for survival. They did what they could, with broken-down machinery and no fertilizers, to produce enough food and warmth to sustain life, and they awaited with peasant-bred fatalism whatever their conquerors had in store for them. As things turned out, Kronach was luckier than many other small towns. What General Eisenhower had in store for them was No. 886 Bomb Squadron, of 306 Bomb Group, United States Army Air Force.

Northern Bavaria, in itself a lovely part of Europe—a rich farming area, harmless and domesticated—has been a cockpit of violence and war since the beginning of European civilization. It is at a crossroads for warring powers. Perhaps it was simply malign fate running true to form that one of the many unforeseen results of the Yalta Conference in February 1945 was to draw the line dividing the American and Russian zones of occupied Germany just north of Kronach. To emphasize their respective rights and privileges, both American and Russian commanders all along the line decided to maintain major troop installations as near the border as possible. Among those maintained by the U.S. Army Air Force was an ex-Luftwaffe airfield sandwiched in a salient between Coburg and Kronach and the new zone border, just north and west of the town. It seemed convenient. Both the town's buildings and its railway yards were comparatively undamaged; it was strategically located for the collection of war material—and for that longed-for day of repatriation.

While millions of Americans, British, and Canadians could not wait for that blessed day, there were a few exceptions. One of them, Staff Sergeant Alben Franklin Gleason, had served with No. 886 Squadron since they had landed in England in the fall of 1943. When he had first been told by the commanding officer that, as a key man in the outfit, he would be among the last they could let go, Sergeant Gleason had been an angry man. He was also a resourceful man; by the time they moved into Kronach in August of 1945, the "Gleason Plan" was quite clear in his resentful and none-too-scrupulous brain. It was a simple plan: "To hell with the Army Air Force; if the bastards won't let me go home, from here on I'm working exclusively for Gleason." Once he began to realize that every additional month of "working for Gleason" in Kronach could be highly profitable, he even worked well for the Air Force—sure, he wanted to go home, but there was no rush.

Back home, for Gleason, was Jersey City. He had been well known in a number of circles there before the war. By profession he was a pawnbroker and, in a modest way, a successful one. He developed good contacts in a highly specialized market. The police had not been sorry when he'd been drafted into the Army Air Force. Once there, his knowledge of handling jewelry, watches, and optical equipment had made him a natural for the technical services, where his deft fingers and agile brain rapidly became expert on bomb sights, gyro compasses, and assorted gadgets vital to getting an airplane somewhere near its planned target. The flying officers did not like him, but they knew the equipment Gleason serviced would not let them down. He was too fat and needed a hair cut, but when he said a bomb sight was accurate they trusted him.

After mid-September 1945, most of the aircraft that

took off from Kronach never came back. Army vehicles poured in from all over the American Zone, unloading what the Air Force considered valuable or secret equipment, which was checked, cleared, crated, and packed onto big transport planes for transfer to French or English ports. The planes then refueled, and headed straight across the Atlantic for home. The workload dropped, and the unit was reduced to a skeleton staff of key men. That suited Gleason fine—there were that many fewer busybody officers around who might inquire just what it was that kept him so busy. There was always the master sergeant. He was a bastard in Gleason's somewhat limited vocabulary, but they had always had a live-and-let-live, hands-off understanding. All through that autumn and winter he had worked hard, come and gone as he pleased, used the army vehicles assigned to his workshop as he pleased, and continued to supervise with meticulous care the work entrusted to him.

He had not only continued, but redoubled his efforts to contribute to the social life of the sergeants' mess. He may have been a surly sonofabitch so far as anyone senior to him was concerned, but he had a special talent for being the life of the party with everybody else. And for Gleason there was only one kind of party; it was called poker. He was "banker" and had been brought up to be an expert one back in Jersey City. In October 1945 the American papers had run a story about an Air Force sergeant who had filed an income tax return for $23,000 on gambling winnings. Public reaction was mixed: some said he was patriotic, others crazy. Gleason just said, "Piker."

Gleason's plan had always required a terminal date, and U.S. Forces Headquarters in Frankfurt had decreed that it should be March 20, 1946. At 0900 hours March 21st, No. 886 Squadron was going home. Eight months of carefully planned and executed hard work was going to finish on March 20th; the first phase of Gleason's postwar rise to fortune had been carried out; on that night it would be completed.

It was a dirty night, which suited him fine. The hideous weather—wind, sleet, and snow that drove everyone else indoors—was just what he wanted. It was dark before he sat down to supper in the mess hut. The poker game had been wound up three nights ago and as he had always "invested" his winnings on a weekly basis, he had been able to complete his banking business quickly. No one would notice or care if he slipped out after dinner tonight. He pushed away his empty coffee cup, lit up his usual White Owl, pulled up his coat collar, and went off to his bunk. The stinking weather was great from a security point of view, but it made the job in hand tougher.

Gleason reached his billet, where he piled on every sweater he had, two pairs of thick wool socks, and topped it off with his heavy leather driving coat. Still, he knew from his night work these last few weeks how tiring a cold wind could be.

He came out of the billet, puffed contentedly on his cigar, and took a good look round. No, there was nobody about that he could see. He sauntered over to the conveniently parked van, Heavy Utility (Personnel)—a HUP—in military jargon, and climbed in. He stepped on the starter without first turning on the lights. Despite the bitter cold, the badly worn engine started first time. Smart idea leaving a heater in it till the last possible minute.

Gleason drove slowly, without lights, around the two big main hangars. His eyes were now fully accustomed to the dark, and he knew every inch of his planned path. He passed behind a long row of converted B-29's where they were parked fully loaded awaiting the morning's take-off.

The only light to be seen anywhere came from a window in the back of the master sergeant's office. Gleason chewed on his cigar and muttered, "That stupid horse's ass. Still sittin' there fillin' in useless lousy paper as usual." But it was nice to know where he was. Gleason puffed contentedly, turned right around the ammunition shed at the end of the paved tarmac, sliding as quietly as the van could move up to the shed marked "Scientific Instrument Repairs. Keep Out." That was where he had been king these last eight months, and there had never been a more possessive and conscientious autocrat. No one touched anything in Gleason's domain without Gleason's permission and under his supervision.

As he came to a silent, coasting stop outside the sliding doors of the shed, he cast an eye over his right shoulder and noted with satisfaction that the back gate of the compound was still wide open. He had reckoned correctly that no one would bother to check it tonight.

He got out quietly, leaving the gleaming cigar butt behind him in the cab. The big door moved aside smoothly and silently on its well oiled track. He made no noise audible over the moaning of the wind. He drove the van straight inside, right to the far end of the unlit shed. Just as the wheels stopped rolling he heard a crunch on a board at the back, right where he had put it. He switched off the engine, climbed down, stubbed out his cigar, and shambled back Indian fashion to shut and lock the big door. He knew he was quite invisible inside the shed.

He peered through the glass panes beside the door. No one in sight. No light, no movement anywhere. There was a truck parked by the corner of the ammunition shed. Nothing unusual in that. That was where the military government boys were going to set up their office—there was plenty of security in that building.

He was glad to get the big door shut against the bitter wind. What a filthy night! He chuckled.

Close observation had taught Gleason that, tough as they were, the Russki border guards only two miles away didn't like lousy weather any more than anybody else. Things had been quiet around here since General Wheeler, on instructions from Eisenhower's headquarters in Frankfurt, had ordered the abandonment of Runway 18 back before Christmas. The general was damned mad about it—it made trouble for the ground control crew and was hell for the pilots. When the wind was blowing from the north, which it usually was all winter, it was damned dangerous landing those clapped-out old tugs on Runway 27. But Runway 18 had to go—the circuit for approach and take-off crossed over the Russian Zone border at 700 feet, and to the Russians that mattered. They regarded such over-flying by their erstwhile "allies" a violation of Soviet air space that was contrary to the Protocol of the Potsdam Agreement and an intolerable insult to the prestige of the Red Army.

Tough luck on the control crew and the pilots. It suited Gleason. Since the "violations" had ceased four months ago and the real hard winter had set in, the heroes across the creek had calmed down a bit. No one had heard a shot from over there since early January. Though the checkpoint on the Autobahn was still as heavily guarded, the atmosphere was less aggressive. More important to Gleason's operations, the Russians were now only patrolling within half a mile of either side of it. All secondary roads had been sealed off with barbed wire and concrete blocks. Cross-country patrols were few and far between, and careful examination through binoculars had shown they were always carried out at exactly the same time and along the same route. Gleason sometimes wondered how people who were chronically and nearly hysterically suspicious both by nature and by order could be so damned unimaginative.

As he made his way, moving his overweight bulk with the care of a slinking cat, a glance at his watch showed him it was just ten minutes to eight. There wasn't much left in the shed—the last batch of equipment and the men who had sorted and packed it had left for Cherbourg in six squadrons of Dakotas on one of the few days in January when Runway 27 had been usable. Since then his entire staff had consisted of two Dutch labourers who had been freed from a nearby prisoner-of-war camp and, for reasons of their own, seemed in no great hurry to go home, and one scared young buck sergeant. Since the kid had had the bad luck to be posted to the squadron on the 4th of May, just as their last operational flight was landing, the master sergeant had taken an instant dislike to him and rode him unmercifully. No, Gleason had nothing left to worry about now.

All the machine tools, testing equipment, and massive files of records and forms and specifications and amendments to specifications which the Air Force gloried in had been packed into the stripped-down B-29's and were now just awaiting the 0900 order to take off for Le Havre. What remained were mostly broken empty packing cases, bashed-in oil drums, a bench of badly worn hand tools, and other junk that Gleason had persuaded the station adjutant was not worth lugging all the way back to some midwestern stores depot. There were a few things Gleason had reckoned might come in handy at the last minute—and they had. Just what was useful for what and exactly which of the litter of old cases were not empty was no one's business but Gleason's.

He had made sure there was still electric power available, too—against orders. He opened the back doors of the van right onto the pile of junk and broken timber. He took a hooded mechanic's inspection lamp from under the back seat, hung it on a bracket well inside the van, and carefully threaded the cord back to a power socket on the wall. He adjusted the lampscreen so that only the faintest glimmer broke the solid blackness, shining out onto the pile at exactly the spot he needed light. Swiftly and silently he started to work his way through the debris. He knew exactly where the full cases were that had to be moved tonight. They were well buried. Gleason was gambling the foundations of a fortune against five to ten years in a military prison, and he had calculated every risk to the last decimal place, just the way he always calculated his banking risks in the poker business. That was why he almost never lost.

It took him nearly ten cold dreary minutes to get into his target area. The first two cases came easy; he lifted each one and placed it very gently into the back of the van. The third one was a little more difficult, a little too heavy. Maybe he had been a bit greedy? Forgotten how much some of this stuff weighed? As he went to lift the case, starting to puff a bit, his left hand slipped and ripped along a nail sticking out of a broken board. He swore to himself. The glove was ripped across and blood started to ooze through the wool. He squeezed his wrist for relief. It didn't hurt much. He thought of the priceless contents of that case. He certainly could not repack it now, and he had no intention of leaving it behind.

His mind went back to the ordeal of five nights before, when he had crawled on his belly within a few yards of the Zone border, got in through a window of the barn on the abandoned farm through which some genius had drawn the Zone line, and then lugged that case three hundred yards back again to the woods on the American side. The moon had suddenly broken through while he was right out in the open. Always fearful lest there be an unscheduled Russian patrol about, he had lain there panting, sweating despite the intense cold, feeling as though somebody had just shone a spotlight on him.

Nobody did. Nothing moved. After ten agonizing minutes, he had started to crawl again and reached the shelter of the woods in safety. Once he had that case in the van—the last one he had had to crawl for—and started the last journey back to the scientific instrument storage shed for final packing and delivery tonight, he had heaved one mighty sigh of relief. He had been damn clever to choose that abandoned old farm right in the middle of No Man's Land as his own private warehouse. No one else had ever tried to go near these battered old buildings—the trigger-happy Red heroes were just too close. Only Gleason had seen that they were just far enough away, too.

He got the third case into the van, placed it carefully down, and took off his gloves to examine the cut in the light of the inspection lamp. Just a skin break. Damn, he thought, it would have been better to pack seven cases and distribute this weight a bit more. Unloading and carrying this one up three flights of narrow staircase wasn't going to be any picnic either. Cases four, five, and six were not so heavy, but it took him ten painstaking minutes to work his way to them through the carefully arranged rubbish. The cold was now beginning to seep in, especially on his damaged hand. He noted he was ten minutes behind his carefully planned schedule. Not serious; she'd wait.

Then there they were, six wooden cases, each one meticulously packed and sealed. He had taken the utmost care with every parcel to ensure that no damage would come to it, either in transit or during the many months—probably a year or more—it would have to lie in its secret storage space. That had been the riskiest part of all. The one part he could not do alone. Could he trust her? He had worried for months before concluding that he had to. There was no choice. The way he had described it to her, it was a great deal for her, too—he offered the ultimate prospect of her getting away from the disaster that was Germany to start a new life in that Eldorado, America. Of course he had made love to her in the process; he reckoned she knew as well as he did this was strictly a business deal. But it was going to be a long wait. Suppose some other G.I. came along in the meantime and offered her a better proposition? Too late to worry about that now.

No, ten minutes was no great problem. He sat down in the back of the van to light a cigarette and enjoy the last chance he would have for a long time to gloat over those cases. He had "invested" over $40,000 in their contents —all his poker winnings since the squadron left Suffolk. Nobody knew better than he that the prices he had paid to some of those poor, terrified, broken-down D.P.'s for the goods he bought were daylight robbery. She had taught him early on in the game that the best sources of supply were ex-members of the German armed forces themselves, especially if they had ever had anything to do with the Gestapo, S.S., or various other gangster groups of the Nazi party machine.

To avoid the war criminal dragnet, countless thousands of Nazis and collaborators—and many others as well—had to acquire a new legal identity. Papers. What mattered were those precious papers. And fear, until they got them. Many of the bigshots made it without much trouble; if they could commandeer transport and gas, there were plenty of routes open that winter through the anarchy that was war-torn Europe, down to Spain and some North African ports. After that, all they needed to reach South America was enough money and a bit of luck. Simon Weisenthal in Vienna was still weeding out that lot. The smaller fry had to shift for themselves on foot and, as usual throughout its history, northern Bavaria was a crossroads for refugees moving in many directions.

Gleason was only one of many to appreciate the value of the market presented by so much human misery. Once he had worked out a reliable formula for laying his hands on the right papers, the word got round the Nazi underground network in the area and the customers came to him. Not to the camp, of course. Even Gleason did not reckon the officers' intelligence that low. There were other, easier and pleasanter means. Coburg was only ten miles away. A nice, sleepy old town, left behind by history, its railway communications completely destroyed by bombing, it was of no use to the military. Gleason found his girl there. Looked after her. Finally took her into partnership. As senior partner, his job was to keep the money rolling into the poker bank, bargain with the suppliers, and plan for the final disposal, the pay-off. The girl in Coburg arranged the contacts and provided the rendezvous.

All that winter there seemed to be an endless flow of human flotsam struggling to make its way westward to safety, real or imagined, who needed what Gleason could supply. It was amazing how many of them had some treasure to sell. Their only hope of evading an Allied prison camp lay in those magic papers—legal identification, a ration book, some kind of travel authorization—and the new legal money. U.S. dollars could buy anything. Nobody asked where you got them from, and Gleason handled more cash than the squadron paymaster, a thought that gave him ceaseless pleasure. The destruction and chaos that prevailed throughout the whole of central Europe in the immediate postwar era made looting a way of life.

News of the "business" travelled along clandestine channels from Austria to the Rhine and as far south as the Italian border. Many big operators were caught, but no one ever squealed on Gleason. The Allied military police and security authorities were too overwhelmed with bigger problems.

Gleason enjoyed his brief gloating. He'd got his breath back. He stubbed the cigarette and packed up ready to move. It was just a quarter past nine. A dark and stormy night, and all was well! He surveyed the junk pile. There were no tell-tale signs of his eight months' work. The odds were nobody would enter the shed until someone came to tear it down.

Gleason walked quietly back to the sliding door and very carefully slid it open a couple of feet. He stood there listening and looking intently. Everything was just as it was when he had entered. The sky was still completely overcast; the wind had perhaps dropped just a little. Occasional snow flurries still gusted, obscuring visibility. The roads would be slippery, he reminded himself. He opened the door just enough to let the van clear it, walked back, got in, and switched on the ignition. Barely in time he remembered not to turn the lights on, too. Damn fool! He took a deep breath and shook himself before gently slipping the van into gear. Just inside the shed door he paused again, listening and searching. Nothing moved anywhere. Nothing but the wind and snow. The truck that somebody had left by the corner of the ammunition shed with its back end toward him stood right where it had been before. That damn fool's engine won't start tomorrow morning, he thought. Now was the moment. He eased the gear shift into low, made a wide left turn, careful to keep on the tarmac, drove slowly through the open gate, and turned south on the main road.

There wasn't a light in sight for a mile in either direction. After a hundred yards Gleason accelerated a little and put the van into second. The rear wheels skidded three feet. The lousy surface was as treacherous as a rattlesnake. He kept his speed at fifteen miles an hour and finally turned on the head- and taillights. He was on his way. Nobody had seen him.

2

BUT somebody had seen him. A beefy, swarthy man with a toothbrush moustache who had been planning his program for tonight just as carefully as Gleason. He had never had a good opportunity to look into that junk pile Gleason guarded so closely, nor had he bothered to investigate what kept Gleason out so late after the poker games every night. He had known for months just enough about Gleason's operations to figure out for himself what the end result must be. The only unknown was when; now he knew tonight was the last time possible. He knew a girl or two in Coburg himself. Coburg was a small place, and girls will talk, however careful they may think they are being.

The instant Gleason's van was through the gate and turned south, the man's dark, muffled-up figure leaped down from his hiding place in the military government truck parked by the ammo shed. He ran round to the front, threw open the door on the driver's side, and climbed up. Another man and a girl were sitting there, shivering. The man on the seat made a gasping noise that might have indicated anything. The girl said nothing.

"Get the hell over!" the moustached man growled, and pushed the other two across the bench seat. He jammed his foot down on the starter and the big Mack five-tonner started with a powerful growl. He backed onto the tarmac, turned right, and headed straight for the gate. Like Gleason, his eyes were well adjusted to the darkness, and he didn't need lights at this point. He went through the gate and turned south just as Gleason, half a mile ahead, put his lights on.

As the Mack passed the end of the airfield fence, its driver switched the lights on. They were on the open road now; sooner or later Gleason was bound to notice there was another vehicle behind him. Why shouldn't there be? Traffic was not that rare around here these days. Just take your time, and keep your distance. Keeping his right hand firmly on the wheel, moving in second gear to maintain maximum precaution against a skid on this ice-covered potholed excuse for a highway, the man took a cigarette out, lit it, and took a heavy, self-satisfied drag. He opened the collar of his heavy leather driving coat and loosened a bright red silk scarf. Now that everything was going just as he had planned it, he too relaxed for the first time. He knew there was no turning off the highway for another mile, so he could afford to take his eyes off the dim red taillights of Gleason's van for a few seconds.

The other man and the girl sat quite still and said nothing. For different reasons, neither wanted to start a discussion at this moment.

The driver glanced down at the silent girl sitting beside him. He had learned that she had brains to match her looks. Most German girls in their early twenties had been hauled off to work in factories; overworked and underfed since 1943, the roughness of their skins, the sallowness of their complexions, and the state of their hair had aged them long before their time. Yeah, this baby must be smart, all right. He gave her one of his hard, gruff smiles, which was the closest to approval or affection he ever showed for anybody. She smiled back, and that was pretty flinty, too. Nobody spoke.

He snapped his attention back to the taillights ahead of him. Any second now, he thought. Gleason had his last real chance just a hundred yards farther down the road. Damn fool, even if a smart crook.

Hey! That was it. He'd turned right, just where expected. No doubt about it now, he was heading for that farm house north of Coburg.

The driver watched Gleason's van take the corner in a slide. Don't ditch yourself here, you damn fool! The Mack slowed down to a crawl. Let Gleason get to the cover of the woods before he could tell they had turned, too. The moment for action was getting closer.

There were no farm houses or lanes along this stretch; even if Gleason realized now that he was being followed, it was too late for him to do anything about it. Slowly the Mack drew closer. A hundred yards was just about the right distance at this stage of the game. The pursuer saw the van start to put on a spurt of speed. By the way the van started slithering and skidding all over the road, it was clear Gleason was getting worried. Those lights slowly gaining on him might belong to some farmer who lived on the other side of this lonely woodland. He would soon know for sure.

Gleason reached the vee junction. He had always planned to take the north fork so he might as well stick to it. He pulled the steering wheel slightly to the right, found a somewhat firmer surface where the trees grew right along the edge of the road and prevented the snow from drifting across it. He pushed the accelerator down just as far as he dared—the way the rear wheels kept skidding and slipping he dared not try to go any faster. Even if it was only a Kraut farmer, he didn't want to have to ask anybody to pull him out of the ditch now.

The driver of the Mack was enjoying himself. He had thought it all out. He knew every inch of the road. This lane stretched for three miles without a single crossing before it joined the main road from Coburg north to the Zone border. Both drivers also knew very well that in that three miles it wandered northward, and for over a third of that distance it ran parallel to the Russian Zone border —within fifty yards of it. The Yalta planners had thought that the river shown on their maps would be a natural barrier. Both drivers knew what the planners had not—that the massive Allied bombing of Nuremberg had caused such a diversion of the waters of the river Regnitz that this tributary river was now no more than a creek. And it was frozen over solid. For quite different reasons, the closeness to the border was meaningful to both of them.

The Mack was gaining on the van at an ever increasing pace. The way the van kept sliding about over the rough track made it obvious that Gleason was now a frightened man. "Great," the pursuer muttered to himself. He was now less than fifty yards behind and gaining every second. Another half mile, right along the bank of the frozen creek, and the Mack was smack on the van's tail. The driver revved up his engine, double clutched, shifted down into low gear, and then put his foot down on the accelerator. It was right here that the line of trees fell back away from the edge of the track, and there was a rough, meandering ditch on the north side of the road. He held the wheel tight and got himself into position in the middle of the road; he was only two feet behind the van. Then he gave one final vicious jab down with his right foot, pulled the wheel a fraction to the right, and hit Gleason's van with all the force that a 350-horsepower engine could give him. The van lurched crazily to the right. Gleason's frantic efforts to pull to the left sent him into a skid; the Mack dropped back a couple of feet and then rammed him again. The van spun round through ninety degrees and went nose down straight into the ditch. The right front wheel hit a rock and buckled. Gleason crashed onto the steering wheel and his breath was knocked out of him. The engine roared, then stalled; steam poured from the smashed radiator.

The Mack, under full control, braked fast and came to a stop just a few feet in front of the wrecked van. The relentless driver cursed with satisfaction, shouted at the man and the girl not to move, and jumped out.

In the van Gleason struggled to catch his breath. Dazed and frightened, his only thought was to get out. Who was the maniac in that Mack? He grasped for the door handle and, by putting his whole weight against the buckled piece of metal, managed to push it open just enough to tumble out into the snow and mud. He staggered to his feet and felt the nausea rising in his throat. He looked up straight into the face of a man whose fierce expression left no doubt about his intentions. Gleason tried to cry out, but the words were lost in a choking splutter. He felt himself seized around the neck by strong, eager hands and hurled back against the van door. The door window smashed as his head hit it, and he fell bleeding to the ground in a shower of broken glass. As he tried to stagger to his feet, a well-aimed boot smashed into the side of his head. He crumpled senseless to the ground.

The same boot roughly turned him over so that his face pointed downward into the snow and mud. Whether he was dead or not made no difference. He certainly would be before morning. On that stretch of road in this weather, it might be days before anyone came along and found him.

The man in the red scarf moved fast round to the back of the van. He knew just what to look for. He wrenched the doors open.

"Here! Come here. Quick!"

His companion climbed hesitantly out of the truck—he certainly didn't appear to be briefed on this operation. Whatever he had expected, he looked surprised. So did the girl. They had heard the glass shatter, but from where they had been sitting they had not seen Gleason at all.

"Open up that tarp!"

"But—"

"Open that goddam tarp!"

The other man got the point and quickly clambered up the icy, mud-covered back of the truck. None of them knew what was inside those crates, but red scarf knew enough to be sure his night's work would pay off. His powerful arms grabbed the first case that came to hand.

"Put these in the truck," he shouted and handed up the case. "There's plenty more."

Up they came, one at a time. Only one of them had been damaged in the crash. There wasn't time to examine it here, but it looked as though nothing more than a corner had been crushed and the top burst open. The whole job only took five minutes. The girl sat in the cab weaving her own private thoughts and never moved.

Some ten hours later, on the morning of March 21st, what was left of No. 886 Squadron loaded up the last of their belongings and paraded in No. 2 Hangar for muster. Everyone was present except for Sergeant Gleason. The adjutant conferred with the master sergeant. Nobody had seen him since dinner last night.

One tired young soldier suddenly thought with a shock, So that's who was in the van! Well I'll be a sonofabitch!

He didn't say anything. He couldn't. Another thought crossed his mind. "Dear God," he muttered to himself, "I hope they don't search our kit."

The sky had cleared temporarily and the cross wind dropped to 15. The forecast was still threatening. The lieutenant colonel who led the B-29's put it fair and square to the adjutant that his orders were to take off at 0900, weather permitting. It did, and he was taking off exactly at 0900. With his whole squadron. If one lousy staff sergeant had gotten drunk and couldn't get back to camp last night, the hell with him. He would be on charge for sleeping out of camp anyway. Leave him to the military government boys to deal with.

At exactly 0900 the whole squadron took off. No. 886 as a unit ceased to exist, like the hundreds of others whose job in Europe was finished.

Two days later the military government officer in charge of closing up the base and handing it over to the local German authorities received a visit from the police inspector at Kronach. With great respect and deep regret, it was the inspector's duty to inform the Herr Major that a farmer had found a wrecked USAAF van in a ditch a mile from his home. The body of a man was lying beside it.

In due course the appropriate personnel records unit in Washington was notified that Staff Sergeant Alben Franklin Gleason, while making unauthorized use of an Army Air Force vehicle on the night of March 20th, had skidded off the road, and was found lying beside the vehicle two days later. Death was recorded as due to exposure and loss of blood. They notified the next of kin and closed the file.

3

THE great baroque library of the Hofburg Palace had certainly seen better and grander evenings, but few in this century more auspicious for Austria than that of March 20, 1946. It was similarly favorable for a number of those who moved quietly about, chatting, sipping glasses of champagne—which most of them had not tasted for long, bitter years—nodding their heads in learned discussion or excited naïveté at the magnificence of the Habsburg imperial crown jewels. These were on display to an invited, privileged few for the first time since Hitler had stolen them in 1938, only to promptly bury them in an abbey vault in Nuremberg.

Many pieces of the priceless collection were older than the English or the Russian crown jewels, and probably rivalled in age only by those—rarely seen by common eyes—in the Vatican. In order to frame the display with a worthy background, much of the superb gold-plate dinner services, Sèvres china, and elaborate epergnes—also fresh from their wartime refuge in the salt mines at Alt Aussee—had been brought up from the Silberkammer. It was a glittering spectacle such as no one present had seen for years.

The idea of holding this party had originated in the fertile brain of Foreign Minister Karl Gruber—or of someone in his office—who had the great idea of using the recently, secretly returned Habsburg inheritance to create this first occasion for official "fraternization" with the Allied forces of occupation.

Miraculously most of the historic Hofburg had missed bomb damage. The world-famous library, though shabby and worn, still bore ample evidence of the past grandeur of the Empire. Dr. Gruber suggested, and President Dr. Karl Renner readily agreed, that the display of Austria's hereditary treasures in such a setting might combine just the right mixture of pride and humility, poverty and hope, and provide a tactful conversation piece to oil the squeaky wheels of relationship between occupied and occupiers.

Relations between the four occupying powers themselves were far from easy by March 1946. The total lack of cooperation by the Russians with their recent allies over innumerable matters, large and small, had already laid the foundations of the Cold War. The new Austrian administration was far from sure of itself. The political leaders of the Allies, Truman, Attlee, and Stalin, meeting at Potsdam in July 1945, had accepted the principle that Austria had been "liberated," not conquered. The provisional government of Dr. Renner had been quickly recognized by most other European governments and by the United States. But no one was at all sure just where to go from there. Everyone knew there had been Austrian Nazis, and that there were plenty of skeletons lying around waiting to be discovered. The evidence to stoke the fires of fear and suspicion was unavoidable and everywhere—in the newspapers and in the very streets and buildings themselves.

The roots of the March 20th party lay in the odd fact that Hitler had been born an Austrian and, as a frustrated and rejected young artist, had suffered his years of greatest humiliation and poverty in Vienna. He hated the city and everyone in it. Within a few weeks of the Anschluss, his vivid imagination devised a peculiar form of personal revenge. Some unknown historian conveniently dug up a decree of 1348 wherein the Holy Roman Emperor Sigismund III had ordered that the imperial crown jewels of that paradoxical and amorphous institution over which he temporarily presided should be kept in Nuremberg. The decree had never been carried out and for nearly six hundred years had lain forgotten. Many pieces in the Hofburg vaults in 1938 had not even existed when Sigismund had been laid to rest among his ancestors in Innsbruck. No matter. Since the crowning city of the Holy Roman Empire had been Aachen, there had always been some northern Germans who believed they had a claim to them. On Hitler's personal order the jewels were immediately seized by the Gestapo and carried off to Nuremberg, "the Party City," where they lay buried until nearly the end of the war. Troops of General Hodges' U.S. Seventh Army captured Nuremberg on April 16, 1945. Most of the royal treasure was found safe and sound in the ruins of a medieval abbey.

The five most important, symbolic pieces known as the Imperial Insignia—the crown of Charlemagne, orb, sceptre, and the two swords of state—were missing. Their recovery had taken Lieutenant Walter Horn, U.S. Group, Allied Control Council for Germany, on one of the most fascinating and mysterious investigations that body ever undertook. When Horn first arrived in Nuremberg to interrogate the Nazi officials who had had charge of these historic objects, Stadtrat Frier and Stadtrat Schmeizner, they had told him that Oberburgermeister Liebel, with two S.S. officers sent from Berlin, had removed the Insignia at Himmler's personal order. Liebel had later committed suicide. Rumour circulating among S.S. prisoners had it that the mystic symbols of Germanic authority had been sunk in Lake Zell in Austria, where they were destined to become the Holy Grail of a perpetual, fanatical Nazi resistance movement. On August 4th, after some days of questioning and nights of solitary confinement, Frier broke down and confessed that this was just another Nazi pipedream. On the 7th, Frier and Schmeizner led Horn and a working party to a vault eighty feet below the Paniers Platz, where they unearthed the five priceless objects safely packed in four copper containers.

This happy outcome was the result of an order signed by General Eisenhower on December 29, 1943, instructing his army commanders that Civil Affairs art advisers were to travel as far forward with the fighting troops as possible. He ordered the formation of the Monuments, Fine Arts and Archives Sub-Commission of the Allied Control Commission—commonly known as MFA&A, a joint British-American group which spent three years scouring Europe—except Austria, which for these purposes was left solely to the British—for the loot that Hitler, Goering, and their subordinates had "bought" or were "safeguarding." Even at 1945 prices the total value ran into hundreds of millions of dollars. The American 3rd Army under General Patton had discovered the biggest treasure ever found in the salt mine at Alt Aussee, but that was run from Munich, not Vienna, and most of it was Austrian government property put there by the Austrian authorities to avoid the bombing.

In January the Habsburg treasures from Nuremberg

and Alt Aussee were returned to Vienna in perfect order. Not a single diamond, emerald, or gold plate was damaged or lost. They were formally transferred to the custody of the new government, and on March 20th they were on display for the first time since Hitler's act of blatant and, apparently, pointless theft—he had never even gone to see them.

The party was a great success. Although the weather was foul, one of Dr. Gruber's aides had miraculously managed to commandeer firewood and coal. The ornate baroque stoves in the library were relit for the first time in three years. This comfort, rare for those times, and the champagne, which both the German and Russian armies had missed hidden deep in the cellars of the Sacher Hotel, rapidly produced a thawing of frigid behavior on the part of many guests. Though the Russian officers present, rigidly correct and in full uniform, kept pretty much to themselves, their chief, Lieutenant General Blagodatov, the Soviet member of the Inter-Allied Kommandatura for Vienna, was the life of the party as he basked in the unaccustomed sunshine of his Allied colleagues' thanks and congratulations. He agreed he merited such acclamation; admiring precious jewels was all very fine, but nobody but he, Blagodatov, could have donated forty kilos of caviar to the party. Forty kilos! So much had not been seen outside the Kremlin since Churchill and Roosevelt had met Stalin at the ill-fated conference in Yalta.

Politicians, senior civil servants, leading members of Vienna's indestructible cultural and artistic life, were celebrating the renewal of friendships that had been fractured by the years of holocaust. All the important people were there, all the easily recognizable faces. And a few who were not. One of the things that contributed most to the success of Dr. Gruber's party was that many of the most influential guests—the American, British, and French officers—were not so easily identified when seen for the first time in civilian clothes. They had made a tacit agreement to leave their uniforms behind. They appeared in Vienna for the first time as welcome and willing guests, not the symbols of an alien, imposed power. The gesture was much appreciated.

While the great men and their acolytes clustered round the historic crown of Charlemagne, the magnificent gems of the imperial crown, the flamboyant baroque table settings and robes of cloth of gold covered with rich embroidery, one of the smaller cases on the east side of the room was absorbing all the attention of two men. Both were obviously intelligent and cultured, but equally obviously of no particular importance since no one else in the crowded room paid the slightest attention to them.

The older of the two had the unmistakable air of a scholar: stooped of shoulder, untidily stuffed into an unpressed and nondescript old blue suit, a crumpled collar, and a hopelessly askew tie. He was balding on top, with a wispy gray fringe all round his bulbous head, and with large thick glasses that indicated eyesight badly strained in youth. He had a permanent pensive, benign smile—one of those men who look the same from age thirty to seventy and, in his case, giving the general impression of a gentle but prematurely decaying cherub.

The younger man was all of six feet, lean and muscular, with a pointed jaw, wide forehead, prominent Roman nose, and deep-set blue eyes that sparkled with humour and enthusiasm. His bearing was unmistakably military, though he limped badly and walked with a cane. His bristling moustache proclaimed, almost aggressively, his Britishness.

The objects holding their rapt attention were several sets of knives, forks, spoons, and assorted bits of useful tableware—saltcellars, pepper mills, and sugar shakers. The older man was experiencing an alternating cycle of delight and shock at the comments of the younger. He was amazed by his younger companion's knowledge. While all the great men present were excited by the brilliance of the royal gems and the sheer baroque grandeur of the overpowering epergnes, urns, wine jugs, and candelabra, the young British officer did not need to be told that they were nineteenth-century silver gilt. One of these solid gold eighteenth-century fruit knives, used by the great Empress Maria Theresa herself, was worth more, both aesthetically and in cold cash, than any five of the other pieces put together. Any connoisseur would have spotted that, but this young man also knew that they had been made in Antwerp in 1752 and given to the empress by the Duke of Alba as a present on her fortieth birthday. Though the elder man was born Viennese and had helped put the exhibition together, this detail was news to him. He was delighted. He was even more surprised to be told that Alba had paid three thousand ducats for them, which was too high a price for that time in the speaker's personal opinion. He was openly shocked by the throw-away line, "I know a man in Rio who would give ten thousand dollars right now for any single piece of them." It sounded so very un-British!

The young man's speech was also very un-British. He spoke German like a native Viennese. It was all most intriguing. The two had met quite by chance at the beginning of the evening, when it immediately became clear to both of them that their interest in the party was artistic and not political. Nor, at first, was it at all personal. Professor—it sounded like Kallen-something-or-other—met what appeared to be a typical British officer called Major Um-oh—it didn't sound like anything. Neither of them dreamed of asking for a second hearing. For over an hour they richly enjoyed each other's observations. The professor was especially interested in the Herr Major's tale of how Charlemagne's crown had been discovered and returned. How on earth did the Herr Major know Lieutenant Horn? He didn't say. The professor told the major how the staff of the Kunsthistorisches Museum, only in the early stages of putting itself together again, had been called in to set up the exhibition. It came out quite by chance that the professor was Jewish and owed his existence to the fact that he had been teaching in America at the time of Hitler's takeover, and had very understandably stayed there. When President Renner indicated that the time had come to end the festivities, they said good night happily with a perfunctory, "Do hope we meet again one day."

Professor Max Kallendorf went back to his temporary abode in the apartment of his wife's cousin in an unfashionable little street across the Donaukanal. The more he thought about it the more intrigued he became. By breakfast next morning he was so intrigued that he determined to track down his enigmatic companion, find out who and what Major Um-ah was. It was not difficult. A look at the list of the British guests, which a Foreign Office official made readily available to him, a chat with a British officer of the Control Commission whom he already knew, and a twenty-minute tram ride were all that was necessary. He found his quarry at the British headquarters in an office under the grand staircase at Schönbrunn Palace, just inside the public entrance on the west side. According to the sergeant-of-the-guard on duty, this room was the office of Monuments, Fine Arts and Archives Sub-Commission, Civil Affairs Division, Control Commission for Austria (British Element). Schönbrunn seemed a perfectly logical place for such a body to be housed. The full name and style of the young officer was shown as Captain

(Acting Major) the Hon. Rupert Conway, M.C., seconded from the 3rd Battalion of the Royal Welsh Fusiliers. After the usual cross-examination and form filling, the professor was allowed to see the Herr Major. The two men rapidly became inseparable friends.

4

"OH, Charlie! For the thousandth time, not on the cardinal's doorstep!"

Charlie, rebuked, cocked his head to one side and gazed nonchalantly around with quizzical eyes and uptilted nose that clearly implied, "Oh, all right, but just to please you, not because I have to." He lowered his right hind leg and sauntered across the street to one of the inevitable piles of rubble that have surrounded St. Stephan's famous cathedral these past too many years. The Welsh terrier, like all the inhabitants of 5B Stephansplatz, was nothing if not civilized. The man turned round from the cardinal's door, number 8, and sauntered back to his own, 5B.

The front of number 5B was entirely taken up with a large window and an iron-clad wooden door with a brass handle. The window, always immaculately polished, was of plate glass and bulletproof. Behind it on the morning of Saturday, March 20, 1976, were a large silver bowl of yellow tulips and, standing on an easel, a picture in a gold gilt frame. It was a beautiful and ethereal "Madonna with Cherubs" by Zanobi Machiavelli, a Florentine painter of the fifteenth century. Its mystery and its price were enhanced by the rarity of the little-known artist's work. Callers of sufficiently prosperous appearance could learn that the proprietor was prepared to discuss parting with it for something above four hundred thousand dollars—also that he was really not awfully keen to sell. In the middle of the window in plain gold capitals was the terse message: CONWAY WIEN.

Conway had never considered adding such qualifying phrases as "Dealer in Fine Art" or "Rare Pictures." From the day he opened back in 1950, he had relied solely on his own brain, experience, and reputation to do all the advertising he would need. It had only taken two to three years to justify the decision. Eventually he had opened a gallery in London and one in Chicago. The relaxed, confident middle-aged man on the doorstep now discussing hygiene with his dog had a totally possessive air about him that would leave the dullest observer in no doubt that this must be Herr Conway himself. Like anyone in Austria who had ever attended a university, he was known locally as Herr Doktor Conway. Only back in Britain, where he had been born but spent very little of his life, was he still listed at the Fusilier's depot in Cardiff as Major the Hon. Rupert Conway, M.C., having won the Military Cross at the battle of Monte Cassino in March 1944 and being the son of an English lord—or, more correctly (he was always articulate on this point) a Welsh one. Conway senior had been a diplomat, and they had spent most of their lives circulating around the capitals of Europe, except for a stint in Washington from 1923 to 1926, from which the young Rupert and his elder brother never quite recovered. Nor did they ever try. Their adored mother had been Viennese, with a strange mixture of Austrian, Hungarian, gypsy, and Jewish ancestry.

Rupert now was fifty-six. An inevitable thickening of the torso had not masked the broad, athletic shoulders; the face was a little fuller, the hair a little shaggier than that far-off and fateful evening at the Hofburg thirty years before. The "Herr Major" moustache had long since disappeared—Alexie, the only real love of his life, had objected to it from the first. The limp was still noticeable, but the cane seldom used. Success and a built-in love of life had changed the eager young officer to an urbane, immaculate, but not foppish man of the world. Insistence on exercise and fresh air at every possible opportunity had kept an essentially city-bound sophisticate in reasonably robust health. Romantically minded middle-aged female buyers frequently told their like-minded friends that Rupert Conway was "debonair." Only one misguided lady from Milwaukee had ever described him as "cute." It was one of the few sales he was glad to lose.

Having prevailed upon Charlie not to desecrate the doorstep of his friend and neighbour, Cardinal Archbishop Koenig, he turned his attention to the ritual—and with him it was a constant ritual—of lighting his pipe. In turning his head inward, away from the breeze, his eagle eye spotted one drooping tulip in the window. Automatically he made a note to remove it when he came back from lunch. He took a deep puff, turned to rest his eyes on St. Stephan's soaring steeple, forever reaching up to find its God. He never failed to find it inspiring. He was well aware that many in the cynical, cosmopolitan world he inhabited sneered at such thoughts, though fewer nowadays than ten years ago, he found. He had been born with them and had no intention of ditching them, even at fifty-six. He looked and felt exactly what he was: a man perfectly at peace with the world, content but unassuming about his obvious success, minding his own business on his own doorstep, momentarily enjoying the first touch of spring to reach Vienna after a hard, snow-laden winter. His lightweight fawn Burberry coat was getting its first outing, and he was hatless for the first time since last October.

Spring had arrived one day early in Vienna; the promising sun was pouring straight down Kärntnerstrasse and just beginning to drive out the damp, winter air from the alleyways and courtyards behind the cathedral. He glanced at his watch. At that moment the door of number 5B opened again and out stepped a handsome, smartly but simply dressed woman. He enjoyed the company of pretty women. Why shouldn't he? But he was a romantic at heart and an earnestly faithful one at that. His adored Alexie had died in childbirth in a Vienna hospital in 1951, only a year after their marriage. This woman was his cousin. She was nearly twenty years younger than he was, but they had been each other's favourite kissing cousins since they first met at her widowed mother's modest New York apartment when she was only nine years old.

Her name was Sandra Fleming, born Andrassy in a small village in northern Hungary, the youngest of the four children of the local squire and Rupert's aunt. At thirty-seven she was still pretty, well-groomed, desiring, and desirable. Her character, like most people's, was a blend of what heredity and fate had made of it—the gaiety and panache of the old Hungarian landed families from which she had sprung; the terrible years of hardship and suffering of her early childhood when, first the Iron Guard, and then the Nazis had hunted down anyone with a trace of Jewish blood; and finally the down-to-earth, practical upbringing by a widowed working mother in a New York suburb, the final haven of the only two members of the family to survive the successive calamities of wartime.

All her life Sandra had had to be practical, which for one of her parentage and tradition, was not easy. Her inherited intelligence had led to a good American college, where she majored in fine arts. She'd worked for twelve years in an interesting though minor job at the Metropolitan Museum, and when her mother died in 1972 she had made a disastrous and short-lived marriage to a man called Alex Fleming. Her still-attractive aristocratic face, with its wide sensuous mouth and deep-set large brown eyes, in repose still betrayed the scars of so many unhappy years. The childhood of constant flight and terror could never be totally erased from memory, and the divorce itself had been about as unpleasant as a man-become-alcoholic-and-brute could make it. She thanked God they had never had children during their few tempestuous years together. When her beloved cousin had written, saying that he needed a trained archivist to help in his now substantial international art business and offering her the warmth and security of his home, she had fled to Vienna on the first convenient airplane. The last three months had awakened a happiness she had seldom experienced.

Sandra returned Rupert's smile of approval and shut the door behind her. He took out two keys, strong and intricate-looking instruments that were attached through his right trouser pocket to a stainless steel chain fitted snugly but comfortably inside his shirt and around his waist. All his suits, which he bought in Vienna, not Savile Row, were specially cut for the purpose. He carefully turned both locks, one to seal the door with three separate and separately operated bolts, the other to activate the burglar alarm system. The installation was elaborate, but it cost less than it saved him in insurance premiums on the contents of Conway Wien. Vienna is probably the least crime-disturbed city in Europe, but in recent years art robbery, forgery, and blackmail have become an international big business. Conway was not a man to take unnecessary chances; he had been taught to be cautious. He returned the keys to his pocket casually, but with every movement carefully calculated and practiced to a foolproof and unforgettable routine. Charlie, finished with whatever it was he had had his eager heart set on and having run out of new and interesting smells, ran back impatiently to his boss and gave him a look all serious dog owners instantly recognize: "Hurry up, man; I'm waiting for my lunch."

Rupert took Sandra's arm and they walked unhurriedly through the courtyard, paused to enjoy the latest exotic displays in Herr Schonbichler's windows—in Rupert's view the only glamorous grocery store in the world—crossed Wollzeile and entered the short, narrow Durchauss leading to Herr Figlmüller's remarkable restaurant.

Sandra was of the opinion that Rupert had been putting on weight. She said teasingly, "I'm sure you chose your apartment solely because it is midway between Figlmüller's and Fenstergucker."

"Certainly not. Ungrateful girl. My motives are always aesthetic." They walked a few more paces. "But you've got to admit, their food is damn good."

"I can never understand how someone who insists on eating at L'Aiglon and the Pierre when in New York, eats nothing but sausages when at home."

"I repeat, my aesthetic taste. Did you ever eat better sausages? Washed down with more appropriate wine?"

"They're good, I'll admit."

"Besides, it's my Conway blood. My Welsh nonconformist ancestors revolt at the idea of unnecessary extravagance."

"Except when you feel like it."

"Except when it's necessary. There are few people rich enough to buy what I sell who have sufficiently refined taste to appreciate the delicacy of Hans Figlmüller's sausages."

Although he had earned a good living most of his life, Rupert was not a rich man. Riches were required to become one of his clients; wealth was a responsibility he never wished for himself. And it never troubled him, one way or the other. On the rare occasions throughout life when he found his bank balance reaching unaccustomed heights, he always managed to solve the problem painlessly by buying some fine objet d'art that happened to catch his fancy, then presented it to the relative, museum, or church that happened to head the list of his affections at the moment. It was an amiable and harmless habit for a middle-aged widower with no dependents to think about. Just once—and nobody but he and Max knew this —he had given an absolute little gem of a "school of Bellini" picture to a stunning young opera singer who had temporarily caught his fancy. Perhaps the fact that this lovely miniature canvas was entitled "Virgin in Glory" had been the cause of the lady's lack of suitable appreciation. At any rate, the experiment was never repeated.

They entered the world-famous little back-alleyway *Heuriger*, exchanged the usual effusive greetings with Hans and Gustav, who ushered them with solemn ceremony to Rupert's usual table and presented the wine list and napkins with respectful flourish. The menu was scrawled on a blackboard. When he was in town for the weekend, Rupert liked to lunch there. Saturday was the only day of the week Figlmüller's was not jampacked with tourists. And regular customers who were always appreciative and always paid cash—one of Rupert's Welsh principles—were entitled to special dignities. In this case the treatment extended to Hans and Gustav turning a blind eye to the presence of Charlie under the table, a presence in total defiance of Vienna's hygiene regulations. You couldn't get more special than that.

Ordering lunch at Figlmüller's never presented Rupert with any problem. Whatever rare and special variety of sausage had been created that morning was washed down with the relevant wine, in this case a carafe of refreshing Gumpolds from a vineyard outside Gumpoldskirchen owned by one of the numerous Figlmüller family. Rupert knocked out his pipe, and Charlie settled contentedly at his feet, well knowing from years of experience the delights soon to be surreptitiously passed down to him.

Sandra removed her soft brown flowered Jacqmar scarf, tossed out her luxuriant, long dark hair, and brushed it back over her shoulders. After three months in the security and comfort of her cousin's home, she was beginning to relax for the first time in years. The strained, hunted look that lurked in her dark, flashing eyes, and sometimes made fine, hard lines distort her quite beautiful smile, was slowly fading. She was happy—and just a bit tired.

"Have a nice time last night?" Rupert asked gently, extending his hand to light her cigarette.

"Mm, yes. Great fun. But I am tired."

"Not surprised. Why don't you stay home and go to bed early some time?"

"I know. But there is so much to see. You forget, I haven't ever seen Vienna like this before."

"You mean you didn't know Tommy before," he teased her.

"Well, yes, I suppose I mean that, too." She paused, sipped the wine, and gazed musingly into the glass. "Rupert, tell me honestly. Am I letting Tommy rush me too much?"

"My dear girl. What a question! Are you serious in such a short time?"

"No, no." There was a note of anxiety, even fear, in her voice. "Not serious. The scars from my three years with Alex haven't healed yet. But I've never met anyone like Tommy before, and he is charming."

"That's what half the eligible females in town thought until you came on the scene."

"Oh come! He must have many younger and more exciting girls to squire around than I am?"

"Maybe he thinks it's time to settle down?"

"Oh no, I hope not." A touch of anguish in her voice this time round. "I like him very much, but it's too soon, I'm not ready for any romantic entanglements yet."

Gustav produced the sausages, rich with the smell of garlic and melted butter. Hans refilled their glasses. Rupert beamed benevolence on the whole scene.

"Besides, I still don't really know anything about him."

"Maybe you know all there is to know. He is naval attaché at the United States Embassy."

"But that's ridiculous. He's a commander in the U.S. Navy, covered with medals and obviously extremely intelligent. Austria hasn't had a navy for fifty years. Why would they send a first-class man to liaise with a navy that doesn't exist?"

"Ah, well, that thought does occur to a number of people from time to time."

"He can't be in disgrace—the ambassador and Mrs. Buchanan think the world of him."

"They do."

"So he must be the head of the CIA here."

"Shhh. Not so loud. This place is riddled with Russian spies!"

"Now you're being ridiculous again," she said with mock petulance.

Rupert chuckled. This scenario was one he knew well, as he and Commander Tommy Thompson, USN, had been kindred spirits ever since the latter's arrival in Vienna nearly four years ago. It was a long time indeed to leave a first-class officer in what appeared to be a dead-end job.

"Tommy does a lot of interesting things, certainly, but I'm sure he's not one of the cloak-and-dagger boys. A lot of things go on here now, you know. The International Atomic Energy Agency is here; that Arab mob that keep getting themselves kidnapped—what do they call themselves, the Organization of Petroleum Exporting Countries—UNIDO, MBARC . . . You name 'em, we have 'em!"

Sandra laughed. "MB . . . whatever it was? Who are they?"

"Ah, that's us. That's where the British and Americans and Germans all talk to the Russians."

"What about?"

"About MBARC, of course. See if I can remember it. Mutual Balanced Arms Reduction Conference—I think that's it."

"That sounds like a good thing."

"Oh it is. Great. Lot of nice chaps. Trouble is the Russians don't pay one damn bit of attention. This is where East and West meet, though. Keeps men like Tommy busy. Vienna is once again one of the world's most intrigued-in capitals."

"Well, I suppose so. It's all a bit odd, I must say."

Rupert felt a cold damp nose pushing against his sheer silk sock, and a small whimper came from under the table. A large hunk of sausage was slyly passed down.

"But you do enjoy his company?"

"Yes, very much. I never knew a sailor could know so much about music and the theater and art. He's a positive encyclopedia. He even explained that weird piece of Bartok's last night."

"Ah, the A minor. Strange music, isn't it. Scherjinski

finds meaning in it Bartok never knew was there. Must have been an interesting evening."

They both resisted the fullsome blandishments of the attentive Hans and Gustav. "No, thank you, thank you. Just two coffees, please."

Rupert lit Sandra's cigarette and cut the tip of his cigar.

"So what else is new?"

"New? Oh, yes, there was something else I was going to tell you. For the first time in my life last night I actually saw a pink elephant."

"Pink elephant! Good Lord, you really are going to the dogs."

"No I'm not. It was a real pink elephant, all made with precious stones. You would have been interested."

Rupert put down his coffee cup very deliberately, very unhurriedly, but his eyes had the look of a mature hound who has suddenly and unexpectedly scented a fox.

"I am interested. Very interested. Pray continue."

"Well, it was . . . about . . . oh . . . thirty centimeters long." Although he had lived on the Continent most of his life Rupert still had to do a quick conversion into inches. About a foot.

"Beautifully carved. Some highly polished stone. Not exactly pink, I guess. A sort of quartz, mottled red and white. But the general effect was pink."

"Sounds like chalcedony," Rupert murmured, with that special murmur he always used when instantly coming to exactly the word that other people were still grasping for. Some people found it a most irritating habit.

"And it had diamonds for eyes. Big ones—at least two or three carats each, I should think."

"I'm extremely interested." Rupert very carefully lit his cigar. Good Havanas were not cheap in Austria, though cheaper than in London, and deserved to be treated with respect. He wafted a puff of smoke to the ceiling and meditated on it. A close observer, which Sandra was not, would have found his piercing eyes scarcely compatible with the languid, humorous repose of only a moment or two ago. He fixed her with a stare that would have done credit to a Grand Inquisitor.

"Where was it made?"

"I think the man said it came from Russia."

"Mottled red and white? Overall effect pink, right?"

"Right."

"Eyes were diamonds—two to three carats you said?"

"Right."

"And eyelashes? Did it have eyelashes of filigree?"

"Yes, it did."

"Gold filigree?"

Sandra had not been subjected to one of Rupert's professional cross-examinations before. It made her feel quite nervous.

"Yes . . . I think so . . . it looked like gold."

"And the head was on a spring so it moved up and down, right?"

"Right." She was now feeling quite alarmed. "You know it?"

With every question Rupert's manner and style of speech became more concentrated, more penetrating.

He pondered into the mellow smoke cloud of his cigar again and thought out loud.

"Mottled pink. Siberian chalcedony. Diamonds and gold filigree. It must have been Fabergé. Was it Fabergé?"

"I don't really know. I've seen Fabergé pieces in the Metropolitan Museum, of course, but it's not really my line. It certainly could have been."

"Where did you see it? What was the man's name?"

"Sorry, Rupert, I wasn't paying much attention."

"But you must have known where you were?" She had

never heard him sound impatient with her before.

"Let me tell you. After the concert Tommy took me to the Imperial for a drink. Then we met some other American friends of his. You know how it is, everyone was Bill and Charlie and Mary—I really didn't get all their names. Then this man asked us all to go back to his apartment for a drink. Jake, I think. Yes, they called him Jake. So we did, and he had this elephant."

"This man, Jake. Was he Austrian or American?"

"American. Some sort of art dealer. I think he said he had only just come to Vienna—to buy. Yes, I remember now, definitely. He's been living in Paris—or was it London?—and just came here recently. Said he didn't know anybody and wanted to meet the American community. He made quite a fuss about meeting Tommy. Wanted to be invited to the embassy. All that sort of thing."

"So Tommy would know his name?"

"Well, if he didn't, he could soon find out. He knew everyone else there."

Rupert almost brusquely waved for Gustav to bring the bill. Sandra looked at him uneasily. The abrupt form of questioning was almost accusing. She felt as though he were saying to himself, how dare you not know the man's name! And everything else about him while you are at it! The mundane act of paying the bill and exchanging compliments with Gustav momentarily broke Rupert's concentration. His shrewd eye quickly caught Sandra's strained expression. Years of studying faces of expectant buyers had taught him the telltale signs of mood changes.

"Come, my dear. I'm so grateful to you. This is most interesting. We must go home and look up your pink elephant. I have a feeling he may be quite fascinating." He was his usual, urbane, courteous self again. Charlie discreetly shook himself back to life and they left.

Rupert and Sandra sauntered arm in arm back up the

Durchauss and across Wollzeile. But Rupert's brain was far from drifting aimlessly about in the postprandial haze to which Sandra had been quickly propelled by the return of his customary gentleness. His early years at a spartan English public school and his wartime experience had not only taught him the value of the traditional British stiff upper lip but, much more important, had trained a tightly disciplined mind, which whenever required could completely overpower his genial, slightly self-indulgent appearance. This was another paradox in his complex character which practice had taught him to exploit whenever it suited his purpose. The game leg, which ruled out hurrying in any case, coupled with the cult of the pipe, had been woven into a pattern of habits whose sole purpose was to give their owner time to think.

As they turned into the courtyard, Sandra looked at him quizzically. "Now what are you thinking about?"

"I have been thinking about elephants. Oddly enough, at that precise moment I had shifted to swans."

"Swans! Why swans?"

"Did you ever meet my old friend the last bishop of Bath and Wells?"

"Must you always talk in riddles?"

"No, it's not a riddle. He is a very wise man, and he once told me a very wise thing. 'Rupert,' he said to me one day, 'take a lesson from the swans in my moat. Always keep calm and serene on the surface, even when underneath you are paddling like hell!' "

"Is there something very special about my elephant?"

"I'm not sure. Yes, I am sure. There must be, but I don't remember just what it is. You know who Fabergé was, of course?"

"Court jeweller to the last czar. He made all those fabulous Easter eggs and all that."

"Right. In the years before the First World War he was

the most fashionable maker of objets d'art in Europe. Among other things, he specialized in jewelled animals. You know Queen Mary's collection in the Victoria and Albert? He was very popular in Vienna, too. Your mother must have told you that Grandfather Eisenbath had a superb array of them."

"Gott in Himmel!" Like Rupert, Sandra seldom swore. He always said he preferred words with more syllables. When they cursed, it was in a variety of languages. "You think it belonged to him?"

"No, I'm sure it didn't. The list of his pieces is written in my memory. But I know I've seen it somewhere. There must be a clue in my old MFA&A files. Somehow or other I can just hear it shouting at me, 'Help, I'm Viennese, too.' "

They had reached the door of number 5B. Rupert went through the key routine. As he bent forward to turn the big locks, he paused a moment to admire the lovely Machiavelli in the window, as he had done every day for months. Another offending yellow tulip was drooping out of the silver bowl. He made a mental note to tell the faithful and tireless Frau Hauptmann to have them all replaced.

They passed inside and he repeated the locking formula. They walked the length of the narrow gallery—Rupert still insisted on calling it a "shop"—flanked on one side by five large early nineteenth-century English seascapes and on the other by a glittering array of seventeenth-century ikons recently brought from Istanbul. At the back were heavy mahogany doors leading to the offices, and a baroque staircase climbing to the balcony behind which lay Rupert's apartment. He unlocked the door and stood aside for Sandra to step into the small interior hallway. It was simple, elegant, but like everything associated with Conway, entirely masculine. A selection of English, German, and French newspapers cluttered the marble-topped console table, together with two pipes, and a large tin of tobacco. The ormolu and crystal chandelier was French; and on one wall hung three sets of stags' horns, shot by his father in the Vlachenwald many years ago. Across from them hung a portrait of a beautiful little fair-haired girl wistfully twisting a red ribbon around her hands, Rupert's grandmother, Julie Esterhazy aged three, one of the last portraits ever painted by Franz Xavier Winterhalter. The stags' horns served a strictly utilitarian purpose, carrying a bewildering assortment of hats, canes, and umbrellas.

He helped Sandra off with her coat, hung up his own, and stood hesitant for a moment, his hand still on the door. He was on the point of asking her to go down to the archives vault and start rummaging through the MFA&A files when she yawned and stretched and turned toward him with a resigned, tired look. It could wait till Monday.

"Just one thing, my dear."

"Mmm . . ."

"You're seeing Tommy tomorrow?"

"Yes, it's his turn to attend one of the ambassador's farm lunches, and Mrs. Buchanan very kindly asked me along."

"Good. Just ask Tommy one thing for me, will you?"

"Jake's full name."

"Yes, but rather more than that. I must get my hands on this elephant. Ask Tommy to fix it, please?"

"You want him to steal it!" Rupert's cryptic remarks constantly surprised her.

"No, no. Not yet, at any rate. I just want to see it. Ask him to get me invited for drinks. As soon as possible. Okay?"

He gave her an avuncular, affectionate kiss, and she went happily off to her room to sleep. Tommy's nocturnal energy took a bit of keeping up with.

5

BY 9:15 Monday morning—indecently early in any self-respecting art dealer's establishment—everybody who worked at 5B Stephansplatz was bustling. Everybody except Rupert himself, of course. On Sunday, after having walked the few blocks to the Dorotheergasse, where he attended the eleven o'clock service at the Evangelische Kirche, he had lunched alone at Hotel Sacher and then spent the whole afternoon and evening reading, researching, thinking. He had found a picture of the pink elephant in Bainbridge's standard work on Peter Karl Fabergé. His Monday morning program had been carefully thought out. The book was open on his desk.

Tommy had told Sandra what little he knew about the man who owned, or at least possessed, this unusual object. His name was Jacob Schwarz, American, about fifty, an art dealer of sorts who kept an office in New York but now spent most of his time wandering around Europe buying, either on his own account or for other American dealers.

He had been living in Paris for a time, but recently had moved his base to Vienna, where he had taken an apartment at 61 Reisnerstrasse, just across from the Italian Embassy. That was all Rupert needed at this stage.

"Here we are," said Rupert and handed Sandra the superbly illustrated volume of the master jeweller's creations. "That your elephant?"

Sandra looked at the double page spread, fascinated. Among the array of pictures of diamond-encrusted ikons and cigarette cases in gold and enamel adorned by precious stones were a lion in rock crystal, a frog made of jadeite, and a pink elephant. Siberian chalcedony, mottled red and white, two large diamond eyes with incredibly fanciful eyelashes of gold filigree.

"No doubt about it," she said.

"Good. We're on the right track. Turn over the page and you'll read its remarkable story."

Sandra read: "In 1898 one of Fabergé's most famous workmasters, Hendrik Wigstrom, was commissioned to make two elephants in blocks of Siberian chalcedony, which, though not rare in itself, was seldom found at that time in sufficient size to satisfy the buyer's somewhat eccentric requirements. The eyes are each of three-carat diamonds of the most perfect texture, with eyelashes of gold filigree, which was one of Wigstrom's special talents. The heads were mounted inside the bodies of the animals by means of an intricate spring mechanism made of twenty-two-carat gold, and of such delicacy that the slightest motion caused them to nod up and down."

She started to read the next paragraph, let out a slight gasp, and then read aloud. "The reason for this order, unusual even for Fabergé's exotic clientele, was that the buyer, Prince Ivan Stirislavski, whose family coat of arms centered on a red elephant, had fallen in love with twin sisters."

"What a character he must have been!"

She read again, "One of the elephants, which was in a private collection, disappeared during the Second World War. The other can be seen in the Winter Palace at Leningrad."

"Disappeared from where, I wonder?" Sandra mused.

"From the private collection of old Karl Meulheimer. He lived in a beautiful *Schloss* near Eisenstadt, right on the Hungarian border. I knew I had seen it sometime somewhere. He was a close friend of grandfather's. I found my MFA&A notes in the files. Took hours, but I finally pieced it all together."

"What do you think happened?"

"There are many gaps, of course. White Russian refugees after the revolution brought what treasure they could out of Russia. Some relative—or even a servant—of the Stirislavskis probably brought it to Vienna in the early nineteen twenties. At some stage they sold it, and as with many other fine pieces, poor old Karl bought it for his collection."

"What happened to him?"

"Huh. Need you ask? He was rich, highly intelligent, Jewish. Just like grandfather Eisenbath."

Sandra shuddered. She knew only too well what the Gestapo had done to their grandfather.

"Within a few months of the Anschluss the Nazis started confiscating all property of anyone they didn't like, 'safeguarding' they called it. Hitler and Goering had their own private gangs of official art looters. If you were a Christian, they bought what they wanted at their own price. If you were Jewish, they just 'safeguarded' it and murdered you when they got round to it."

"But didn't your MFA outfit get it all back?"

"A lot of it. Most of the great West European collections, especially the French ones. All the Rothschilds,

Seligmans, Leo Furst, Alexander Hauser, David-Weill—hundreds of millions of dollars worth. But from the Viennese Jewish families, hardly anything. The von Rothschild brothers' pictures were found in the salt mines at Alt Aussee, their magnificent libraries at Graz, but few of the minor collections were ever discovered."

"Somebody looted the looters?"

"Depends how you look at it. Linz, in Upper Austria, was the key to much of the operations. You remember, Hitler was born in Linz; he intended to make that unlikely town the art capital of the world, to his own eternal glory."

"Yes, I did read something about it, couple of years ago. . . ."

"Albert Speer's book. Hitler ordered Speer to start drawing designs for the place way back in 1938. That is why most of the stuff the Nazis walked off with was stored as near Linz as possible—along the Austrian-German-Czech border. And that is just where the great men at Yalta decided to put the Russian Zone border."

"Weren't the Russians in MFA?"

"No way! In this operation, the Cold War started the day our conquering forces met up."

"You mean to say they never cooperated?"

"Never. We returned everything we found that had been looted from Russia—there was plenty of it. Only two lots came our way. I remember Humphry Brook did a fantastic deal—swapped half the czar's library we found at Graz for the contents of Schönbrunn which they had. The second was when Baroness Alphonse von Rothschild personally stormed into Hungary and removed a whole trainload of family treasures right under the Russians' noses; it's all in the Kunsthistoriches Museum now. But, other than that, nothing. The Russians weren't interested. All inquiries met a stone wall. They were always too busy

—never knew anything about anything that we wanted. Have a look at this file." He handed her a thick, battered brown cardboard file held together by elastic bands. On the front appeared the word "Weesenstein."

Sandra very carefully removed the elastic and started to browse through the torn and faded sheets, many of them scarcely legible.

"Where's Weesenstein?"

"In southeast Saxony, the Russian Zone. Hitler's private cultural army, the Sonderauftrag Linz, was run by a museum curator named Hans Posse who worked from Dresden and Munich. When the Allies started bombing German cities really badly, Posse moved his record section out of Dresden to Weesenstein. Just as well he did, really, although we found copies of most of his archives. Very thorough people, the Germans. They catalogued everything they took—photographed most of it."

There was a buzz from the office intercom. Rupert flicked the switch and a small voice said, "Commander Thompson on the line, Herr Doktor."

"Oh, right, Mini. I'll take it." Sandra's eyes turned a shade darker and a degree warmer, which did not escape Rupert's notice. She appeared to concentrate on the Weesenstein file.

"Morning, Tommy. How's the fleet this morning?"

"Fine thank you, Rupert. All in full sail. Sandra told me you wanted to meet this character Schwarz."

"It would be most convenient, my dear Tommy. Can the U.S. Navy deliver?"

"Naturally. All signed, sealed, and delivered. We're invited to drinks tomorrow at six."

"Good man. Can you come here for a briefing before we go?"

"Yeah. Sure. Matter of fact, I think that's a good idea. It wasn't all that easy."

"Mr. Schwarz was reluctant to entertain me? I hope you didn't have to call in the CIA?"

"Not quite. But he didn't exactly jump at you. He's the first American art enthusiast I've ever met who clearly did not much want to meet you."

"Good."

"Good? Why good?"

"Too early to say, Tommy. Maybe he has something on his conscience. Anyway, thanks very much. Sandra, five-thirty here tomorrow, and drinks with friend Schwarz. Okay by you?"

"Wouldn't miss it for the world."

"Sandra says she thinks she can just put up with you for one more evening, Tommy. Right, old man. Many thanks. God bless."

While Rupert made notes and Charlie snored happily in his own private office chair, the only scruffy piece of furniture in this temple of good taste, Sandra thumbed slowly through the file. After several minutes she looked up.

"To revert to Weesenstein."

Rupert smiled encouragingly. "A subject of limitless fascination for me."

"Long lists. Many names here. Grandfather's, his friend Meulheimer, others I vaguely remember. Did the Russians find their treasures in Weesenstein?"

"Not quite that easy. The *Schloss* itself was more of an office, record, and sorting center. But all the area south and east of there, right through into Poland, is honeycombed with old mines, many of them unworked for centuries. And oddly enough, there were a number of obscure villages in the area that were never touched. I've always been sure that's the area to look. Heinz and I blundered in there before the fighting ended and got damn near shot by our comrade allies."

"Heinz Burgmann? Where did Heinz get into this?"

"Oh, that's too long a story. I just captured him."

"Rupert. I love you in the best way a grateful cousin could, but sometimes your habit of speaking in riddles is exasperating."

"Sorry, my dear. Briefly, Heinz and I were both wounded at Monte Cassino, he with the Austrian Army, I with the British. Then my company took him prisoner. We were in hospital together. When General Alexander had the extraordinary good sense to send me to MFA&A in Vienna, I conscripted Heinz as my driver. He's been with me ever since. Indispensable fellow. Part of the family."

"I see. So did you steal these papers from Weesenstein?"

"Fortunately there was no need. I told you—the Germans were meticulous record keepers. They kept many copies. Those came from Reger's files in Munich."

"I'm not even going to ask who Reger was."

"A Viennese, I'm ashamed to say. One of Hans Posse's righthand men, close friend of Seyss-Inquart, the Austrian Nazi leader, and one of the worst anti-Semites in the whole shooting match. He was in charge of records for Sonderauftrag Linz in the last years of the war. His files and records supplied the Nuremberg trials most of the evidence of Nazi looting."

"But not where grandfather's treasures were hidden?"

"Alas, no. He wasn't important enough to men like Posse and Reger. It was from collections like his that they feathered their own nests. But if you look at page fifty-six, where I've put the mark . . . that's it . . . Objets d' art, late nineteenth century, Russian . . . got it, there's friend Schwarz's elephant again. Can't wait to get my hands on it!"

As if to break the tension, he reached for a pipe. The two outstanding objects on his wide, Sheraton mahogany desk were a photograph of Alexie in a silver frame, very lovely and very peaches and cream in a very English way, and just a little bit pregnant—taken only a few months before she died; and a china bowl any museum would have been proud to own. White ground with red, pink, and yellow flowers, it was Chelsea Red Anchor made in London in 1756. This collector's item of rare beauty served admirably to hold an array of pipes. He stuffed a medium-sized bulldog with his favourite tobacco, known for some obscure reason as 123 and blended by the Lewis family of St. James's Street, London SW1 since 1787. He exhaled vigourously and muttered into the smoke, "Tomorrow night, tomorrow night . . ."

6

ON Tuesday, March 23rd, at exactly five-thirty, Commander Tommy Thompson with the punctuality to be expected of all graduates of the U.S. Naval Academy, walked into the hall of Rupert's apartment. And at a quarter past six Rupert's feline English Jensen slid silently to a halt outside the apartment block marked 61 Reisnerstrasse, in Vienna's fashionable third Bezirk. They went up in the elevator to the apartment across the front of the building on the sixth floor. Their ring was answered by a self-conscious white-coated waiter, obviously hired for the occasion. There were already half a dozen people in the room, Austrians and Americans, sipping an assortment of drinks and gossiping amiably.

The man who was obviously their host detached himself from the group and came to greet them. He was affable and polite, even likable, but he had an air of being a little uncomfortable. He was a slim, balding man, with outsized ears, dressed in a dark blue business suit and wearing a tie too garish for Rupert's taste. His face was heavily lined and his complexion pallid; he had a quick, nervous way of speaking. The loose folds of skin on cheeks and neck told Rupert his host had once been much heavier. He didn't look exactly unhappy—*apprehensive* was the word that stuck in Rupert's mind. Sandra thought the man probably had ulcers.

Though it would seem obvious that the one subject he and the famous Rupert Conway had in common was art, Schwarz showed no inclination to talk about it. He seemed preoccupied, conducting a seminar on international affairs; he was most anxious to know just what Commander Thompson thought about the recent terrorist murder of the Turkish ambassador in Vienna. And did the CIA think that the American ambassador was in danger? Tommy replied assertively that he had no idea what the CIA thought about the risk to Ambassador Buchanan, but that in his experience in Manila and Madrid, he had always found the CIA men to be dedicated public servants who deserved better support from Congress and the American press than they usually got. A lady from Greenwich, Connecticut, said she entirely agreed—some of her best friends were CIA men, and two of them had gone to Annapolis. A banker from Innsbruck proclaimed that Kurt Waldheim was wasting his time at the United Nations. Furthermore, had he, the banker, been running Austria instead of Chancellor Kreisky, the Palestinian guerillas would never have been allowed to get away with the kidnapping of the OPEC ministers and officials. He was about to explain how when someone changed the subject.

Rupert, sipping a solitary scotch and soda, was scrutinizing every picture and ornament in the room. Good stuff, certainly. The man has taste, I must admit it. But that awful tie! The pink elephant was an obvious centerpiece on a marble-and-gilt Louis XVI console table, but it is a built-in habit with all art dealers never to go straight to one's quarry. Rupert had learned in the army the old wise dictum that time spent in reconnaissance is never wasted. He had time. He wandered across to admire a lovely French impressionist landscape by a good, but minor painter of the Barbizon school. An enthusiastic lady from St. Louis who had just found out who he was latched onto him. They exchanged greetings; he lit her cigarette while she clutched his hand.

Then more people arrived.

"Beautiful paint texture," Rupert said. "So delicate."

"I just love these Italian paintings," the lady said.

"French," Rupert murmured.

"Now isn't that interesting," she said. "Of course you know all about painting, they tell me."

"They don't tell you aright," Rupert replied. He knew when and when not to be modest. "But I do happen to know about this one."

The lady took another swig—not a sip—of her martini and gazed into Rupert's somber blue eyes with a look that said almost out loud, "My husband's back home in St. Louis."

"Tell me more."

"Delighted. It's by a man named Pierre Bezot, who painted with Cezanne, Corot, and all that lot. But he died quite young and missed becoming famous. This used to be in Edward G. Robinson's collection."

The lady obviously was more stimulated by movie stars than artists. Rupert was edging her gently but firmly toward the console table, but the lady showed signs of misunderstanding his movements. He caught Sandra's eye, and she took the hint. While Schwarz was instructing the waiter to refill his guests' glasses, she sauntered over to the table and said, "Oh, Mr. Schwarz, I was so fascinated by this the other night. Do tell me about it." She said it with convincing innocence.

Schwarz gave every appearance of being perfectly at ease with Sandra. Perhaps it was just awe in facing up to Rupert's international reputation that made him seem nervous in his presence. Or was it health? He reminded Rupert of an ex-football player who had had a serious operation. One would never have guessed he was an art dealer.

"It is lovely, isn't it? I've handled a lot of Fabergé's work in my business, but this one I just couldn't part with."

Rupert somehow gracefully shed the lady from St. Louis and seemed to glide alongside Schwarz without perceptible movement.

"How interesting, Mr. Schwarz. I do agree with you. But why is this so special?"

Schwarz's tired gray eyes betrayed a hint of caution.

He looked down at the elephant, "Well . . . uh . . . well . . . it's a kind of mascot, one of my first really good deals . . . you know . . ."

Having secured the initiative, Rupert proceeded to press.

"May I pick it up." It was a statement, not a question, and without waiting for any response he did pick it up. Enthusiasm overwhelmed any pretence at good manners, although he was examining another man's property in his own home. Out came his jeweller's eyeglass, and he turned the beautiful carving over carefully in his hands. Schwarz looked anxious; the others standing near, fascinated.

"Yes, here we are," Rupert said, oblivious to the impression he was making. He had his glass close up to a tiny mark on the bottom of the animal's left hind foot. "Here we are. H.K. In Fabergé's code that was the mark of

Workmaster Hendrik Wigstrom. Beautiful, beautiful."

He put it down with elaborate care. Others moved in closer to examine it, to watch the head nod smoothly up and down. Schwarz looked relieved.

At that moment the waiter came up and in a stage whisper said, *"Entschuldigung, haben wir keinen Gin mehr, mein Herr?"*

"In der Küche—auf der Schrank—unterste Brett."

The waiter returned to the kitchen for more gin from the cupboard under the sink.

Rupert seized his opportunity. In his most clipped, sophisticated Viennese uppercrust accent, he said, *"Das ist ein sehr seltenes Exemplar. Darf ich fragen wo Sie es bekommen haben?"*

That pierced Schwarz's man-of-the-world image right in the solar plexus.

"Whoa, slow down, Mr. Conway. I can order drinks in German and pick up a girl, but I haven't got used to the Viennese accent yet. My German doesn't really go very far."

It had already gone far enough to give Rupert's trained ear one useful clue. Bluntly, in English, he said, "Where did you get it?"

"Well, as I said, it was my first good deal—when I was getting started after the war."

"In the States or in Europe?" Rupert was examining the diamond eyes with his glass again. They were real all right.

"Ah . . . in Europe."

"You know its twin, of course?"

"Twin? Fabergé made a lot of animals. I guess many of them are similar."

"No, its twin." Rupert had the knife in and wasn't taking it out till he got more information. The diamonds were clearly original, too.

The lady from St. Louis came unexpectedly to his aid.

"What do you mean by twin, Mr. Conway?" she said.

It was time for the oracle to speak.

"Hendrik Wigstrom made two of these, identical, in 1898. To the order of Prince Ivan Stirislavski." He paused to let the implications of his research sink into Schwarz's brain. "The other one is in the Winter Palace in Leningrad."

"That's amazing!" said the lady. "My goodness, you certainly have a head full of knowledge."

Rupert acknowledged the well-deserved tribute with a modest bow.

"In the third room of the North Gallery, to be precise."

Schwarz realized very well what he was up against. He still said nothing. Rupert twisted the knife just a little.

"It's all in Bainbridge's book, Mr. Schwarz. Surely you knew that?"

There was no way of avoiding that one.

"Yeah, I guess I must have," Schwarz said lamely. "It's a long time since I handled this sort of thing, though. If you really must know . . ." He seemed to have decided to try to make a joke of it. "If you must know, Mr. Conway, this was my first deal. But I didn't buy it. I won it in a poker game."

Rupert now had quite enough clues to work on. He turned on all his charm to make amends for his aggressive behaviour of the last few minutes. There were several other pieces of information he wanted to impart to his host. "You must forgive my enthusiasm, but I have a passion for Fabergé."

Schwarz said, "Really? I always understood Italian paintings were your specialty."

"That's right. But I was brought up on Fabergé. My grandfather had a fine collection."

"Lucky you."

"Alas, no. The Nazis pinched the lot. I'd dearly love to get it back; always on the look-out."

"You still looking after all these years?"

"Unlikely, I agree. But anything is possible in the art business."

"Too true," said Schwarz.

That was easier, more relaxed, more sociable. The tensions disappeared. Tommy, taking his cue from Sandra, polished Schwarz's ego with a velvet glove, assuring him he would ask Mrs. Buchanan to invite him to a reception at the embassy. Rupert could not resist one last mischievous flirtation with the ebullient lady from St. Louis. As she rose to say goodby, he bent low to assist her and stared blatantly straight ahead of him into her ample cleavage as he kissed her hand. A little flustered by such gallant manners, she blurted out, "I just love this Austrian furniture."

Unfortunately the chair was Chippendale. Rupert's Welsh integrity routed his Viennese savoir faire. The embryo affair came to an abrupt halt as he murmured, "Made in London actually, 1772."

They left.

They drove out to Schloss Loudon for a quiet dinner in sympathetic baroque surroundings. The food and wine were good; Fritz the pianist, inevitably, an old friend; and though Rupert was excited by what he had learned, he had far too much self-control to let it interfere with a thorough enjoyment of the occasion and his companions. It was not until the *Apfelstrudel mit Schlag* that they got back to the serious business of the evening. Rupert wiped his mouth heartily with his napkin and started to think out loud.

"Our friend Schwarz. Not more than fifty. You'd agree? When the States came into the war, he'd have been about . . . what . . . eighteen? So by 1945 he'd be . . . twenty-one, twenty-two. Not more. He speaks German like a Bavarian farmer; that would fit. And he claims he won it in a poker game. Hmm . . ."

"And what does all that tell the master mind?" inquired Tommy.

"I accept the compliment. The elephant must have been loot at that stage of its life. So add it all up and it tells me he was a sergeant in the United States Army Air Force who ended up the war somewhere in Bavaria."

Sandra enjoyed this. "How do you figure that out?"

"He's not a university type. At his age he was too young to be an officer. Poker games for very high stakes were famous in sergeants' messes in the U.S. Air Force—or infamous, rather. Eisenhower ordered all sorts of purges to stop them, but they went on just the same."

"Adds up," Tommy said.

"Next move's up to you, Tommy."

"What do you want me to do?" Tommy smiled in anticipation: during his four years in Vienna he had gotten used to Rupert Conway giving orders to the British and American ambassadors, the Burgomeister of Vienna, the director of the Staatsoper, and anyone else who suited his purpose. And the funny thing was he did it in such manner that they nearly always did what he asked.

"Get on to Washington first thing in the morning. It's a job for Pentagon Records. Don't know anyone there anymore. I know, ask Jimmy Rosimer at State to help; he's an old MFA&A man—won't be able to resist it. Ask them to trace a Sergeant Jacob Schwarz, born approximately 1924, Army Air Force, stationed somewhere in Bavaria in 1945 or 1946. Anything at all they know about him, then and since. They will have it all on their computers."

Tommy made an entry on his omnipresent note pad.

"And one other thing. He said he won it. So the odds are he must have won it from someone else in the same mess. Once they locate Schwarz's old outfit, ask them to trace any other noncommissioned Joes who were in it."

Sandra whistled. "You often order the American government around like this?"

Tommy laughed and answered for Rupert, who was now busy lighting a cigar. "Frequently," he said. "Why we obey him I'll never know."

Rupert puffed benignly. "Only a request, dear boy, only a request."

Three mornings later in the office, Rupert and Sandra were going over the results of her research in the firm's archives.

"I've found the catalogue of items Karl Meulheimer loaned to an exhibition of Russian art at the Belvedere in January 1938."

"Good," said Rupert. "That means it was still in his collection just before the Anschluss. The Nazis probably picked it up from the Belvedere the same time as they did Grandfather's things." He examined the catalogue; it was slightly faded, but reproduceable. He handed it to the devoted and tireless Frau Hauptmann.

"Frau Hauptmann, get this Xeroxed please—it should come out all right. Just pages eighteen and nineteen, where Mrs. Fleming has marked them."

The air was rent with a fearful crash; there was a thud and an unlikely, pained cry of, "Mein Gott von Israel!" Charlie, a high-strung animal, leaped three inches off his chair and barked. Sandra and Frau Hauptmann winced. Rupert showed no sign of surprise nor emotion of any kind.

"Ah, that will be the professor now."

The door opened, but what came through it was not the professor but a large pile of books that fell with a thump and promptly spread themselves across the floor in a neat row, like a pile of fallen dominoes.

Then came the professor. Looking his usual shaggy,

bespectacled, innocent, constantly-buffeted-by-a-malign-fate-but-quite-resigned-to-it self. From the moment Rupert had first met Max Kallendorf at the historic party in the Hofburg library in 1946, he had seldom if ever seen his partner and soulmate uncut, unbruised, or unbandaged in some part or other of his anatomy. Max's brain, like his artistic perception, was razor-edged, if somewhat overspecialized. But his eyesight was terrible, and his arms and legs just never seemed to coordinate at all in whatever it was he was intending to do.

This morning his right arm was in a sling, and there was a nasty cut across his right ear. Trying to carry a large pile of books up a dark staircase, maneuver a shifting carpet, and open the door with one hand all at the same time was just too much for a half blind arthritic getting on to his seventy-ninth year.

Still, Max's smile was just the same as ever. His imperturbable manner, as always, unruffled.

"Max, my dear fellow, what on earth have you done to yourself now?"

"Hose," Max said noncommittally.

"Hose?" replied Rupert. "What do you mean, hose?"

"Hose," repeated Max. However terse or obscure his remarks, he was one of those learned old men who always took it for granted that anyone with half an ounce of sense would automatically know exactly what he meant.

Rupert and Sandra both rose and went to help pick up the books. There were twelve of them, weighing nearly twenty pounds in all and probably worth every cent of a hundred thousand dollars. They contained some of the rarest manuscripts ever compiled on ancient Sumerian art, with translations and commentary in manuscript by Max himself. Frau Hauptmann tried to get him to sit down and leave the picking-up operation to the others; Max would have none of it. Ancient art, really ancient, was Max's work—his hobby, his love, and his life.

"Yes, hose," he said again as he finally sat down puffing heavily like a recumbent ram. "No more vicious inanimate object has ever been invented by the wit of a crazed humanity! The damn thing attacked me!" This was strong language for Max.

"The hose attacked you, Professor?" Sandra, who after three months had not begun to plumb the depths of Max's genius for self-destruction, was incredulous.

"They always do," said Max firmly. "I was working in my greenhouse on Sunday. The lilies need a lot of water at this time of year." Apparently that seemed sufficient explanation to him. Rupert's heart was full of sympathy as ever, but Max's gentle resignation to his embattled fate and the piquancy of his innumerable accidents, were always good narrative.

"Do tell us Max. The hose attacked you?"

"Of course. I told you. I was watering the lilies. Surely you know the kind of things hoses do? First the nozzle came off, and the water went all over Pauli's cactus, which made her mad. Then while I was turning the water off, I tripped over it and the water went all over Pauli—which made her madder. And then when it came on again, it squirted all over me and I fell down and hit my head on the rake. And . . . and . . . well, what does it matter.

"Rupert, I've finished rewriting the chapter on the Twenty-second Dynasty, but Leinzardt's proofs won't do. Philip Susserot checked them for me with Dürer's drawings in the Albertina. Philip entirely agreed with me. The quality would be all right for black and white, but his printing just can't get the delicacy of these faded colours."

He plonked a large pile of papers covered with pictures and hieroglyphics down on Rupert's desk. They were pictures of friezes of warriors, winged bulls, and other fabulous animals, some of them the most ancient representations of living forms known to mankind. At first sight they looked pretty realistic, even to Rupert's practised eye. He took out his jeweller's glass and switched on the blue daylight lamp kept on his desk for just such painstaking examinations. They still looked reasonably good to him. But he knew his Max. Max could spot a flaw in these photographs of primitive carvings as he could a touch-up stroke on a Fra Angelico. Nothing but perfection would do. Max saw Rupert's puzzled look.

"Here," he said. "Let me show you." Max's eyeglass looked like a telescope compared to anyone else's—since he could scarcely see to read the print in a newspaper, it had to. He carried a fine, blunt-pointed polished steel rod, like a knitting needle. "You see these lines? Simple though their arts may appear, the Sumerians early perfected a technique of differentiating emphasis with lines of infinitely small variation of width. The great eighteenth-century engravers never surpassed them in skills. Few people can do it even today. It is a vital part of their authenticity. Look at that one. Too thick. And that line next, too thin. It's a highly technical problem of the dying qualities of the ink. The paler the colour, the more difficult for the printer. These proofs lose the whole point I am trying to demonstrate. The relationship of the lines is vital to convey the correct colour value to the human eye. Here it is distorted."

"We must go to the Dutch?"

"Ach! If only we could. There are only half a dozen printers in Europe with machinery of sufficient precision. They're all busy. Our friends in Amsterdam can't touch it for months. We can't wait that long. No, the only people who can print these quickly are Altenburg's, in Dresden. The Tautz family still have that skill. And the machinery. For that finesse, even the newest presses from Japan can't touch the East Germans. Only Zeiss makes lenses to do that work, and not many people have them."

Rupert sighed regretfully. "Which means you want me to go to Dresden again."

"No other answer, Rupert."

"I only got out alive by the skin of my teeth last time," he said ruefully.

Max shrugged with cheerful indifference. "But this time, my friend, please to keep your mind on the business. We are art dealers, not politicians. And our New York publisher is already fussing about his deadline for the autumn book fair."

"All right, old friend. I'll go."

Max gathered up his papers with loving care and a sense of having accomplished a great deal this morning.

"Look, Max. There is something I must tell you."

He outlined the developments of the past few days. To Max, the artistry of such as the great Peter Karl Fabergé was very much just pretty, modern stuff—toys for pampered ladies. But he revered Rupert's grandfather, and he knew how much this meant to his senior, though younger partner.

The buzzer on the desk sounded. Rupert flicked a switch.

"Commander Thompson on the line, Herr Doktor."

"Right, put him on, Mini."

"Good morning, Rupert. The fleet's fine and I've got your information from Washington." The commander had obviously been busy.

"Jolly good, old boy. Pray proceed. Frau Hauptmann, note all this, please."

"I'll read you the telex. Reference yours . . . etc., etc. Here's the meat: Jacob Schwarz, born Wappinger Falls, New York, November 7, 1923, enlisted U.S. Army Air Force May 1942, Recruit Depot, Training Squadron, etc., etc., promoted Sergeant, England, October 1944. Posted

No. 886 Squadron, Maintenance, France, April 1945. Stationed at Air Force Base Kronach, American Zone of Germany until repatriation twenty-first March 1946."

"Fine, fine. Got all that, Frau Hauptmann?"

"Jawohl, Herr Doktor."

"Great, Tommy. What more?"

"They only have the names of five other nco's who served at Kronach same time as Schwarz. Fellow called Gemaldi, a carpenter living in San Diego; there's a Smith, a civil servant in Washington; Howard, who's a doctor in Janesville; none of them sound very likely; Jordan's a possible—you can see him any time. He's doing twenty years in Colorado State Penitentiary for strangling his wife; and Ruttgers may interest you."

"Ruttgers? I know that name. Rings a bell somewhere."

"Could be. He seems to be in your business. He was master sergeant of 886 Squadron 1944 to 1946; he returned to Europe in 1947, married a German girl, took her back to the States. They returned to Germany in 1951, and he's reported to be an art dealer in Munich."

"Of course! Karl Ruttgers. Specializes in this dreadful abstract stuff. I do know him."

"Okay, maestro. Any more orders for the United States government?"

"No, no. Tommy, really I'm very grateful. Awfully kind."

They rang off.

"Well, we've got something to build on now." He gazed at the ceiling for over a minute, lost in thought.

"And something you may have forgotten," Max said quietly.

"What's that?"

"I share your aversion to much of what passes for art these days; but turn your memory back to what Herr Ruttgers used to sell."

Rupert sat up with a start. "Of course. Of course. Max, God bless you. In the early days after the war, friend Ruttgers wasn't in pictures at all! Jewelry, especially Byzantine and Russian stuff. He was the king of the Fabergé trade in Germany."

"According to an article in *Weltkunst* last month, he is becoming so again."

There was another long, pregnant silence in the office.

Rupert mused, "How can a man who deals in such beauty waste his time on blobs and dribbles?"

Max grunted philosophically. "Ach! Simpletons pay money for it. It has nothing to do with art."

"Max, I'm so grateful. My dear friend! That must be the clue. There must be a connection here. At least it gives me something to go back and have another crack at Schwarz with. Sandra, love. We must get into that apartment again. Call up Schwarz, say we must come and see him. Tonight, if at all possible. Say I can't live without seeing him again."

"Suppose he doesn't want to see you?"

"Then tell him you can't live without seeing him again. Tell him anything you like," he said impatiently.

Sandra left to go about her delicate business with Mr. Schwarz. Max sat quite still, wearing his most cherubic smile, while Rupert continued to concentrate his thoughts on the information just received from Washington. Frau Hauptmann came back with it typed in large block capitals, well spaced—the way he always wanted notes that had to be browsed over and brooded on. At last Max caught his eye.

"Max? You were saying?"

"That you must go to see the printers in Dresden, Rupert. We must have this book correct, and quickly." After a pause for emphasis he added, "We have already spent thirty thousand dollars on it." Max was too modest to mention having spent the better part of thirty years of his life. He also knew well that the mention of hard cash usually brought Rupert back down to earth.

"Okay, Max, okay."

He looked solemn; he often had to travel into Karl Marxland. The concentration of soldiers and guns and barbed-wire fences and scowling faces always oppressed him. The ponderous bureaucracy, which made it difficult to get in, even when, as now, all you wanted to do was buy from them, infuriated him.

"You deal with the formalities, Max."

"Certainly. Frau Hauptmann knows all about visas, and I will see the cultural attaché—he is quite reasonable. Especially when I tell him we pay in American dollars."

"How long will it take?"

"About a week these days."

Sandra did her best. Like many Hungarian women she had an extra dimension to her voice that unsuspecting males found irresistible. They arrived sharply at nine, and Rupert kept the conversation inconsequential until Schwarz's curiosity got the better of him.

"Mrs. Fleming mentioned something about business, Mr. Conway. Naturally, I'd be honoured to do business with you, but . . . ah . . . I don't think we are quite in the same league."

"My dear Mr. Schwarz, you are too modest. You have some beautiful things right here. You are a dealer, after all. Perhaps you would like to see what I have to offer? Trade prices, of course."

"I'd be delighted to see what you have, Mr. Conway. But I'm damn sure you keep the best for your Chicago store. Right?"

"In some lines, of course. But we're specialists, you know. Now, that Venetian scene over there. Looks interesting. Mind if I examine it?"

"Go ahead. I just happen to like it. But I doubt if it's in your class."

Rupert had no doubt at all it wasn't in his class. Pretty, pleasant painting, but very much a "school of" picture, and the subject too hackneyed. It was all part of the usual predealing ritual, and you never knew when it might work.

It was not until midway through the second whiskey, while Sandra was getting more and more puzzled and Schwarz began to show the first glimmering of impatience, that Rupert gently worked his way round to Fabergé.

"I told you about my father's collection?"

"Yeah, you did. Damn bad luck."

"Quite. If you ever come across a likely piece in your travels, I'd be grateful if you'd let me know about it."

"Sure. Glad to."

Rupert got up and went over to admire the elephant. He was not so forward as to seize it again. He just tapped the head gently. The gold mechanism was so perfectly balanced it moved with a rhythmic smoothness that could almost hypnotize.

"Lovely thing. Lovely. You know, I remember as a boy standing tapping this head, just as I am now."

Rupert saw a flicker of surprise pass over his host's face.

"My grandfather took me on a visit with him one day. He did business with Karl Meulheimer. He had probably the finest private Fabergé collection in Austria. I think grandfather learned his interest from Karl."

Schwarz was listening carefully. He made no comment.

"I should love to do a deal with you on this, Mr. Schwarz."

"Sorry, that's right out. The elephant is not for sale."

"Oh, I don't want to buy it, Mr. Schwarz."

Schwarz, puzzled, tried a facetious approach.
"You don't expect me to give it to you?"
"To me? No, no. It's not mine."
That was a little too provocative.
"You're damn right it isn't. It's mine."
Rupert immediately switched to a soothing tone.
"Of course, my dear chap. But I would love to see it returned to its rightful owner."
That stung. "I'm its rightful owner." Schwarz's manner made it clear he knew he was on treacherous ground, but he was no softie.
"In a way, certainly. But I'm sure you must know that it was looted from the Meulheimer collection by the Nazis?"
Schwarz took a deep drag on his cigarette, not nearly as useful as a pipe in giving oneself time to think. He inhaled deeply, frowned, and said quietly, "Yes, I know that. And I know you are the man who tracked down all Hitler's private loot right after the war."
It was one of those moments for modesty.
"I was only a member of a team."
"Yeah, sure. And it was a great team. But that was a long time ago, Mr. Conway. You can't go on doing this Sir Galahad stuff forever."
"You think not, Mr. Schwarz?"
"I'm sure not. For one thing there is the statute of limitations."
"Indeed there is. Thirty years was the time laid down at the Nuremberg trials."
"I seem to remember that. Thirty years."
"And the thirty years ran out on the thirty-first of December 1975. Isn't that interesting, Mr. Schwarz?"
"Yeah. I suppose it is. But it's no concern of mine."
Rupert changed tactics before his welcome wore out. He walked back to the handsome Chippendale chair and

relit his pipe. Encouraged, Schwarz even offered them another drink, which was accepted. Sandra thought Rupert seemed a sort of shaggy version of Perry Mason. His technique was similar as well. But what, if anything, he had found out was still a mystery to her. Just like Perry. She smiled to herself.

Rupert opened up again in his suavest manner.

"Do you know anything about Karl Meulheimer, Mr. Schwarz?"

"Not much. He was a minor collector, lived somewhere in Austria, was arrested by the Nazis. Usual story."

"You know how he died?"

"No, I don't."

"In Auschwitz. In the gas chambers."

"Sorry to hear it." Pause.

"Did you know he had a sister?"

"No, I didn't."

"She still lives here in Vienna."

"I'd like to meet her one day."

"I doubt it. She was hideously scarred by the Gestapo. Since Karl's home was in the Russian Zone, she was never able to secure any compensation. All their records were destroyed. She lives in an attic room near the Sudbahnhof. Runs a little newspaper stall."

"Aw, come on, Conway. You're breaking my heart." He realized this did not make an attractive impression. "I'm sorry, very sorry. But really, the old lady's troubles are nothing to do with me. I've told you—I acquired the elephant legitimately. Nobody knows better than you that there were piles of this stuff floating about Europe at the end of the war. The D.P.'s, the refugees, plenty of soldiers on both sides—everybody—picked up anything they could lay their hands on. So some jerk brings this thing into my unit, uses it to settle a poker debt, and I end up with it. It first got me interested in the art business. I'm not parting with it to anybody."

Rupert saw the moment had arrived for a strategic withdrawal. He had no more shots to fire at present, and the door must be kept open. He got up, smiled, turned to the door and put out his hand.

"Okay, Mr. Schwarz. I understand your position." As he helped Sandra on with her coat, he turned. "But on behalf of the old lady, I'll just keep a bid in."

"You're wasting your time."

"Let's say, a hundred dollars?"

"You must be kidding."

"Well, please keep an eye open for anything that might have belonged to my family. Good night."

They got into the elevator and descended in silence. As they approached the Jensen, Charlie exploded with excitement in the back seat, barking and leaping all over the seats as though he had been missing them for years. "All right, old chap. Relax, relax. You'll get your walk. And drained for the night."

They did a double right turn into the Gürtel and then down Prinz-Eugen-Strasse to the Ring. Sandra said, "He's got a funny look, that man."

"Hmm . . . You're right. There's nothing unusual about his story. I heard it many times back in MFA&A days. But he doesn't tell it convincingly, does he?"

They drove into the traffic on the Ring before Sandra spoke again.

"I don't think even you can talk him into giving it to Frau Meulheimer."

"Perhaps not." Rupert sucked his pipe. "But I'm going to have a damn good try." He stepped on the accelerator and the high-powered car shot away from the stoplight. "And it must lead me at long last to Grandfather's property. Thirty years I've waited for this." He leaned over and kissed Sandra on the cheek.

7

RUPERT and Sandra spent the weekend at the hunting lodge at Semmering, the only part of his family's inheritance Rupert had ever been able to salvage. An old, tastefully modernized, rambling one-and-a-half story frame structure built on a slope, it stood on the edge of a pine forest halfway up the mountain, looking southwest down the Murz valley to Kapfenburg. The view was a postcard publisher's dream. They walked in the crisp early spring air, read books in front of an open log fire to the accompaniment of von Karajan's latest recordings of six Mozart symphonies, and returned to Vienna Sunday evening refreshed. Sandra felt a solid contentment she had seldom known in her life; Rupert tingled like a race horse waiting for the start.

By shortly after nine-thirty Rupert had the whole establishment of Conway Wien humming with the sort of slightly confused activity in which he felt most happy. He sat contentedly at his own desk. Files and papers were scattered all over the room—on chairs, tables, and cabinets. Those in front of him already bore a gentle film of tobacco ash. Sandra was in the archives room, searching for more clues to the mystery that was absorbing every waking moment of Rupert's time. His indefatigable Man Friday, Heinz Burgmann, moved quietly, unobtrusively checking a host of questions on fifty different matters that were thrown at him helter-skelter by his employer. The cut on the professor's ear had turned septic, so his endlessly patient and loyal wife Pauli had ordered him to bed for a few days, thus dramatically reducing the accident rate in Stephansplatz temporarily. Martita Hauptmann sat in her usual straight-backed chair making careful notes and endeavouring to make some kind of order out of the sporadic instructions and queries hurled at her between constant interruptions. "Where were we, Frau Hauptmann?"

"Your last sentence, Herr Doktor. . . ."

Down at the switchboard, Mini was doing her best to cope with the Herr Doktor's staccato inquiries and deal with foreign operators and secretaries in four different languages. Mini must have been the highest-paid switchboard operator in Vienna but she earned every schilling of it.

Buzz.

"Mini, get me Mr. Hughes in the London gallery."

"Jawohl, Herr Doktor. But, Herr Doktor, it is only eight thirty in London. The gallery won't be open yet."

"Then get him at home."

"Jawohl, Herr Doktor."

Rupert returned to dictating a letter to a dealer in Amsterdam, quoting a price on the ikon collection.

"Mr. Hughes on the line, Herr Doktor."

"Good. Put him on, Mini. David, good morning. Sorry to trouble you at home—I'm in a hurry. It's important. I want you to check on a man called Jacob Schwarz. Jacob Schwarz, got that? Right. American, aged fifty-two; a sort of commission art dealer with an office in New York, but spends most of his time in Europe. Been living in Paris, before that London. Right? Now, the point is Schwarz has recently come to live in Vienna, and he has a piece of Fabergé that interests me very much. No, he won't sell it; that interests me even more. But I want to know all I can about him—especially where he might have got it from. Look up Bainbridge's book, page one ninety-four. You'll see a chalcedony elephant there, photograph from the Winter Palace in Leningrad. Brother Schwarz has its twin. It must have been wartime loot, and its source could be very important to me. There are only four people in London worth asking. If you don't know them all, say I asked you to call. Kenneth Snowman of Wartski's, of course. Charles Rayner at the Victoria and Albert. Maria Bowater. I don't think she is dealing any more—I'm not sure. Anyway, she knows a lot about Fabergé. And old Count Bobrinskoy. I haven't seen him for years, but I think he is still around. The elephants used to belong to a relative of his."

Rupert paused so David could make notes.

"That's right. I want to know if any of them know anything about Schwarz. Or if they could have any idea where he got this elephant from. Yes, page one ninety-four.

"I've very little to go on, and I want to get his full history. No, I'm not saying he's crooked—not yet at any rate—but I'd love to know his story. This may help find the clue.

"Good. Everything else all right there? Did you get the de Heems at Sothebys on Thursday? How much? How much! You must be kidding. Daylight robbery, old man. What happened—didn't the New York boys turn up? Jolly good. Right, David. Love to Elizabeth. Don't forget to go to the gallery.

"Sorry, Frau Hauptmann, where was I?"

"You finished the letter to Vandenbergh in Amsterdam, Herr Doktor. I think you were about to consider who to phone in Paris."

"Ah. Yes, of course." Rupert always thought out loud in front of Frau Hauptmann. "It seems Schwarz spent a lot of time in Paris. Plenty of people must know him. But who? And who might know anything about his precious elephant? Fabergé specialists. Paris is full of them. No one I know well enough to really trust—they all gossip too much." He mused in silence for a minute, gazing out at the majestic roof of St. Stephan's, hoping its heaven-seeking spire might pull down an inspiration from the Almighty. Surprisingly, often it did.

He relit his pipe. Sandra came in with an armful of magazines but, seeing the look of almost transcendental meditation on his face, quietly put them down and tiptoed out again. The buzzer sounded. Frau Hauptmann picked up the receiver and after a second's pause said quietly, "Tell him to call back in an hour, Mini."

"No. We'll have to go through the police."

Sandra came in again and sat down on the edge of Charlie's chair to await the right moment.

"Paris police. Anyone at the Sureté owe us a favour at the moment, Frau Hauptmann?"

"Not that I know of, Herr Doktor."

"Armand Durand? No, nice chap—not his line of country. No one at Deuxieme Bureau—they're far too grand. Ah, got it. Just the man. Lebel. Commissaire Claude Lebel. He's semiretired but still has an office at the Brigade Criminel of Police Judiciaire. Try Hervé Bracque's secretary at the French embassy. They should have his phone number."

"Jawohl, Herr Doktor." Frau Hauptmann left to use the phone in her own office.

"Now, what can I do for you, my dear?" He smiled at Sandra.

Sandra's mind had gone off on a tangent.

"You said Lebel? The man in the famous Jackal case?"

"Indeed," replied Rupert. "And he really is the greatest detective in France. That's why they won't let the poor man retire. He's been in shocking health for the last few years."

"You know him?"

"Yes, of course I know him. It's my business to know him. We worked on the de Marignie case together. Great fellow." The pipe needed relighting, and to indicate that he was for the moment satisfied with the rate of progress, he buzzed Heinz to bring in two cups of coffee, then turned the volume switch on the tape remote control up a few notches; the cascading strings of the second movement of Mozart's Thirty-ninth Symphony rose like a gentle mist from four hidden speakers strategically and perfectly placed around the room. Sandra picked up the pile of magazines and started noting certain pages.

"I've searched copies of *Weldkunst* back to 1955. Ruttgers seems to have advertised on a monthly basis pretty regularly. Here's October '55. It's all jewelry, some small carvings, ivory, jade; six of the important pieces are marked Fabergé. January '56, March '57, and so on. Now take 1959. Nothing but abstract stuff—completely new look. But Max was right—this may be interesting. Almost nothing but abstracts and a few primitives right up to March '75. Then there were no advertisements for nine months." Rupert followed her line of thought with cursory glances at the advertisement pages as she ran through them.

"Now here's January '76. Another new look. A two-page

spread, abstracts on one side—ever so Paris and New York; the other side all Russian and Byzantine work—jewelry again, including our old friend Fabergé."

"Hmm. Interesting, very interesting. Could be pure chance, of course. The art business goes through fads and fashions like any other. But significant. Why did he decide to drop the jewelled objets d'art lines in 1958?"

"The supply ran out?" Sandra guessed.

"And has now run in again," he responded, and gazed back at the cathedral spire. "Our helpful friend—Mr. Schwarz, you remember—he reminded us . . . the statute of limitations. Under the Nuremberg rulings, the statute of limitations on looted property ran out on thirty-first December 1975! So . . ."

"So?"

"So, if you had stuff stashed away somewhere that was too easily identifiable to risk selling all those years, now you might be in the clear."

"Might be?"

"It's a long time since I read it, but as I recall, it was a pretty complicated document. There were a lot of ifs and buts. I must look it up."

He turned the music volume switch down again. "Do you know, it must be over ten years since my last abortive clue to grandfather's possessions. I wonder if someone here made a slip at last?"

"I feel happy for you."

"Chickens."

"I beg your pardon."

"I just said, 'chickens.' Don't count 'em too soon."

Frau Hauptmann rang on the through line.

"Commissaire Lebel is out, Herr Doktor, I left a message asking him to call as soon as he returns to his office."

"Thank you, Frau Hauptmann."

Rupert sat staring down at Ruttgers' recent monthly advertisements in Germany's prestigious art magazine. Over the last three months the pattern was the same. Certainly Ruttgers must have found some large and reliable new source of supply—possibly a perfectly legitimate one. The Poles had a major war on their hands against people smuggling art treasures out of their "worker's paradise," but there was no law against selling it in anybody else's country provided one obtained customs clearance. For reasons of their own, the Polish government had not asked for any arrests or extraditions—not yet, anyway. There was always a trickle coming through pretty shady sources into Greece and Turkey. The trade had been carried on in South America for years, but there were fewer and fewer good pieces and more and more fakes. Ruttgers must be pretty sure of himself to announce his refound treasures to the world on this scale. And since Ruttgers and Schwarz had been in the same unit back in the heyday of postwar looting, there just had to be some connection.

"Looks as though all roads lead to Munich."

"Do you know this Ruttgers?"

"Yes, but not well. We did some business together back in the fifties. We used to attend the same kind of auctions in those days—before he went in for that dreadful abstract business. Sandra, make a special note to check all auctions in the future where any of Fabergé's work is listed—anywhere in western Europe. We must keep a sharp lookout. Refresh your memory on the catalogue of grandfather's pictures—better keep it on your desk. I think we get all the relevant papers and magazines?"

"I'll check the list to be sure."

"In the meantime, I must get to Munich. Let's have a look at the diary. Oh damn! Tomorrow's no good. I have to lecture to the American Women's Club lunch. What's it on? Eighteenth-century German porcelain. Get Max to do it."

"Max is in bed. I doubt if Pauli will let him out."

"Blast! No, you're right. Wednesday looks clear. McIvor will be here from San Francisco to see the Machiavelli. You can keep him talking—he's not going to have it anyway." Whatever he offers? Sandra thought. He buzzed Frau Hauptmann. "Try to get Karl Ruttgers, art dealer, Munich, on the line for me. Wait a moment. Mrs. Fleming will bring the number in to you."

The Herr Doktor Ruttgers had already gone to lunch; his secretary would have him call back. Rupert turned his own mind to lunch and pondered some good excuse to tell Ruttgers why he had to be in Munich on Wednesday and why he would like to "drop in and renew acquaintance" with his "old friend." He ambled across to his club, the Rennverein—the only place in Vienna an Englishman would recognize as a club—and over lunch fell into conversation with Karl Reidinger, Vienna's brilliant police president. Karl was keen to show all his friends his new baby, the finest police headquarters in Europe, complete with helicopter pad on the roof. Rupert wondered what Emperor Franz Josef would have thought of it.

In the afternoon David Hughes phoned back to say that none of the London dealers had ever heard of Jacob Schwarz.

Claude Lebel phoned from Paris and, after a brief exchange of greetings, carefully noted Rupert's questions and promised to turn his penetrating and eternally suspicious mind to seeing what he could dig up.

That evening Rupert left Sandra behind—they both had their own lives to live, after all. And both of them were quite free. Rupert was taking a lady out to Kobenzl for dinner. They might go on to the Cercle casino afterward. Sandra had not met the lady, but all of Rupert's friends were aware of her existence. She was a nightclub singer from Bucharest who just happened to turn up in Vienna from time to time. As old Princess Stephanie zu Tauffenburg had been known to say, "It really is a pity dear Rupert never married again—the boy's taste in women gets worse and worse." Stephanie, a distant cousin, had known him since he was three, and she was no prude herself.

Wednesday, March 30th, dawned crisp and bright, a perfect early spring morning. Rupert breakfasted quickly and by eight thirty he was heading the Jensen out the west side of Vienna and onto the Salzburg-Munich Autobahn, accompanied only by Charlie. Charlie, unlike most canines, just loved travelling. Over the eight years since Rupert had imported him from his mountain kennels in Cardiganshire, he had barked and slept his way around many of the highways and byways of Europe. For Rupert he was the perfect travelling companion. Charlie never interrupted his thinking, and Rupert did much of his best thinking while at the wheel of this superb automobile. Also, Charlie was the most appreciative of audiences, and he never argued. He was also willing to eat anything and everything that a benevolent providence might put in front of him, and his sanitary habits seemed to be tuned by nature to exactly the same time cycle as Rupert's own.

The suspension and road stability of the Jensen were such that a steady hundred and twenty kilometers an hour along the Autobahn was pure pleasure and allowed even so careful a driver as Rupert leisure to drink in the spring loveliness of the Danube Valley. The road wound its way past the magnificent baroque towers of the abbey of Melk, through countless miles of grape vines and rich farm lands, on toward the factory chimneys of Linz—he never passed this pleasant but undistinguished country industrial town without thinking how fortunate it was that Hitler had failed to convert it into the Teutonic art capital of the world—and then turned southwest to climb up into the tourist paradise of mountains that surround Salzburg. His favourite stretch was the bit just west of the great cathedral city on to the German border, where every side road ascended upwards toward a thousand tiny kingdoms of innumerable dreaming lakes and streams, each more breathtaking than the last. No one with an ounce of imagination could fail to understand why the South Germans were such passionate enthusiasts for mountain views, nor why this fairy-tale scenery had inspired Ludwig II of Bavaria to build such extravagantly romantic castles, until he exhausted both the taxable capacity and the patience of his subjects.

Rupert knocked out his second pipe of the morning just as they were passing the intersection for Oberammergau and murmured to Charlie, "Beautiful, beautiful. Quite overpowering." Charlie had been overpowered by sleep for more than an hour and snored blissfully on his way. At this speed they would be in Munich comfortably by noon. He would have a quiet lunch at the Kungshof, hoping as many people as possible would recognize him, and then spend a pleasant hour in the archives room at the Bayerische Staatsmuseum, thus establishing a perfectly acceptable alibi as to why he had to be in Munich today. His casual dropping in on Karl Ruttgers was fixed for "sometime between three-thirty and four." Ruttgers had sounded very happy to hear from him again after all these years.

The Kunsthaus Karl Ruttgers was a very different setup from Conway Wien. It was a large modern, concrete-and-glass structure on one of Munich's most fashionable streets. Its huge windows were entirely given over to enormous abstract canvases. As the artists currently favoured by the proprietor seemed to specialize in massive and shapeless blobs of red, it gave Rupert the impression the whole place was running with blood. On closer inspection he was relieved to see that there was a printed poster in each window on either side of the stainless steel and glass doors informing the curious that beautiful objects from the workshops of Peter Karl Fabergé and other great craftsmen could be viewed within. The charming young man with long blond hair hanging over his slender, stooping shoulders was expecting the Herr Doktor and ushered him into the inner sanctum.

Ruttgers rose from his enormous, very Germanic desk and greeted him affably. They shook hands, exchanged the usual greetings of men on easy terms who have not met for some years, and Rupert was invited to occupy a deep white leather chair standing next to a chromium and plate glass table that carried an indescribable piece of sculpture in white marble and a very practical ashtray of the same material. With some difficulty Rupert resisted the impulse to knock out his pipe against the sculpture and used the ashtray provided.

Karl Ruttgers was a big man, about the same height as Rupert—a fraction over six feet—very broad shouldered and with the ample paunch that went with his success, his appetite, and his sixty years. He was swarthy; his dark brown hair brushed straight back from a wide forehead and beginning to thin on top. He wore a neatly trimmed goatee that suited him. His eyes were dark, deep-set, and hard as granite. He opened a large black and white onyx box on his desk, helped himself to a cigar that would have satisfied Winston Churchill or Ludwig Erhard, and offered one to Rupert, who preferred his pipe at this hour of the day.

Rupert gazed round the huge, Mussolini-esque office with the studied carelessness of a lady at a cocktail party who has just spotted another female wearing the same dress. To him the extraordinary mixture of some superb pieces of Russian jewelry—cigarette boxes, even an exquisite pale blue enamel jewelled Easter egg studded with diamonds and turquoise—all set off with the most garish examples of abstract pictures and sculptures was incongruous in the extreme. This room was a gallery by itself. Too ostentatious for Rupert's taste, but his commercial sense registered that the big spenders from Texas must just love it. He pictured some latter-day William Randolph Hearst striding in and shouting, "I'll take the lot!"

"It's too long since we did any business together, Rupert." Though they were both perfectly fluent in German, it seemed natural to converse in their mutual native language. "You should come to Munich more often."

"I don't have much cause to these days," Rupert replied casually. "I go to Rome and London a lot. Most of the things in my line seem to find their way to Vienna now. I'm very traditional by your standards."

"Someone had to fill Duveen's place."

"You flatter me. I find Chicago and Los Angeles better markets for Renaissance paintings than New York."

"Exactly what Duveen would do if he were still alive. You opened a gallery in Chicago, I think I heard."

"That's right. Nice little business." That was a form of expression Ruttgers would never use. The white telephone on the desk gave a deep resonant hum and a little yellow light flashed. Ruttgers murmured, "Excuse me," and answered it. While he was talking Rupert took the opportunity to wander round this extraordinary room and examine his surroundings more closely. The Easter egg was certainly genuine, though probably not from the late czarina's personal collection—many of the Russian aristocracy had copied their czar's amiable custom. He moved on to closer inspection of one of the abstracts. There were still moments, increasingly rare, when he thought that just possibly there was something here he had failed to appreciate. Ruttgers finished his call.

"What do you think of that?" he inquired with a laugh.

"Tremendous, just tremendous," Rupert commented. "What is it?"

"It's a Dallotzi," Ruttgers spoke with obvious pride. Well, thought Rupert, he owns it, I suppose.

"I'm not surprised. What's that?" He refused to say *who.*

"Who is Dallotzi?" Ruttgers said pointedly, almost indignant. "Why, one of the most famous of the new Italian red school."

Rupert couldn't resist showing his irreverence.

"Ah, it's a painting then. What's it supposed to represent?"

"It's not supposed to represent anything. Modern paintings don't attempt to represent. They *are.* The results of a talented artist's innermost thoughts. One doesn't have to understand them—in intellectual terms, that is. One *feels* them."

"Oh, I see. I haven't felt like that since my leg got shot up at Cassino."

Ruttgers refused to be roused.

"You don't move with the times, my friend."

"No, perhaps not." Rupert moved back to the case containing the Easter egg. "Now this," he said, "this is real beauty. Interesting to see you are coming back into the Fabergé market after all these years."

"It's business, Rupert, business. I thought it was time to bring about a change of fashion." Ruttgers spoke with complete self-assurance, as though changing a fashion in the modern world's taste in art was something comfortably within his competence. Perhaps he even believed it?

Rupert decided it was time to move a little closer to his real target. "I'm surprised that after so much time you can still find sufficient resources to specialize again. After all, Fabergé has been dead for nearly sixty years."

Ruttgers also had a suspicious mind. It was a characteristic of the trade.

"I've sold more Fabergé in my time than anyone else in Europe. If I certify an object you can take it as final." There was silence for a moment. Ruttgers clearly had no intention of volunteering information about any new source of supply.

"Of course, of course. No offence meant." After the inevitable pause to relight his pipe, he said quietly, "As a matter of fact, I've recently come across a piece that might interest you."

"I'm always interested. What is it?"

"Very rare. Very rare indeed."

"They never made anything so rare I don't know about it."

Rupert was encouraged. He wondered when Ruttgers' impulsive urge to boast would open an unexpected door somewhere.

"Good. Good. You'll be pleased then. How would you like to buy one of the Stirislavski elephants?"

Ruttgers did look startled. He was just about to speak when the phone rang again. He grabbed it roughly and snarled into it in German. Had his mood and manner completely changed gear, or was he just annoyed at being interrupted at that particular moment? Rupert went wandering again, keeping carefully in a position where he could see Ruttgers' eyes in the mirror on the opposite wall. No doubt about it, he decided. The man was watching him like a hawk. The phone went down with a bang.

"What do you mean, the Stirislavski elephant? Have you stolen it from Leningrad?"

Rupert, totally at ease, chuckled as he dropped himself back into the big white chair.

"No, no. The twin. The missing one," he said smiling.

"There's no such thing. It was destroyed during the war. Everyone knows that." This time his manner was positively aggressive.

Rupert said very softly, "You think so?"

"I know so. If it had been around, I'd have found it years ago." Maybe you did, Rupert thought. This boasting habit was going to be very helpful. The thought clearly crossed Ruttgers' mind at the same moment, and he lapsed into his former, more genial style. It was his turn to relight his cigar, take a moment to think.

Rupert decided to take the next, obvious step.

"Forgive me for disagreeing with you. But I've seen it. The man obviously doesn't want to sell at present, but I think he might be persuaded—if the price is right."

"The man? What man?"

"Fellow called Schwarz," Rupert said casually, his eyes doing the hawk act this time. Ruttgers seemed to be ready for that one. He didn't bat an eyelid.

"Never heard of him. You stick to your Italian painters, and leave Fabergé to me." The door opened and a stunning woman came in. She was middle aged, perhaps forty-five, immaculately turned out and made up, every hair and stroke of the cosmetic brush calculated for maximum effect in enhancing the allure of her unquestionably handsome face and well-rounded body. She was just a little too hard, a little too dominating, to be called sexy, but there was no doubt about the overall effect. Her hair was shiny black and fell in a smooth natural wave almost to her shoulders, giving the only touch of gentleness to a face that, though attractive, was just a bit too formidable for Rupert's taste. He liked women to be completely feminine. She wore a close-fitting plain black dress and black shoes, gold jewelry, and carried a striking bright red crocodile handbag. There could be no doubt about who she was.

Ruttgers rose from his desk and said, "I don't think you have met my wife?"

Reasonably certain the lady was German, Rupert bowed low over her hand and brushed his lips gently across the exquisitely manicured finger tips. He didn't quite click his heels. Gallant, yes, but never overdo it. He had also early in life discovered that if you examine a lady's hands up close they sometimes tell you things you might not otherwise find out—faces can be disguised, not hands.

"Delighted to meet you, Herr Conway. I do hope I'm not interrupting?" Her pronunciation of English words indicated that Rupert was right about her birth. The Pentagon's computer seemed to be entirely accurate.

"Not at all, Frau Ruttgers. We were just reminiscing."

The phone hummed again, and Ruttgers went back to his desk to take the call. Rupert turned aside to knock out his pipe ash while Frau Ruttgers lowered herself gracefully into another large white leather chair. It was almost too studied, Rupert thought. She moved like a well-trained actress rather than a born lady. She opened her crocodile bag, took out a compact, touched up her lipstick, and gave her hair a conventional pat. Just as Rupert looked up smiling, she returned the compact and took out her cigarette case. Rupert, perfect gentleman that he was, immediately rose and moved across to light her cigarette for her. She selected a king size and put it to her lips, Rupert's lighter flashed, and she murmured *"Danke schoen, mein Herr."* He could not help admiring the case —green and white enamel on gold with some kind of floral design that looked like a monogram, mainly set out in emeralds. There wasn't time to examine it more closely. As her eyes met his, she hastily put it back in the handbag. Keeps some of the best in the family, was the thought which triggered Rupert's mind, and his computer-like memory surged into action.

Ruttgers had finished his call. Rupert was quite ready to go. He looked at his watch and said, "Nearly four-thirty. If I leave now, I can just beat the traffic rush getting out of town." The goodbys were polite, even friendly, but Rupert would not have been surprised had he been able to return to that room a minute later and overhear the conversation.

When the door shut on Rupert's well-shaped back, Ruttgers walked slowly back to his desk and stood there looking intently at his wife, clasping and unclasping his hands. When he was sure Rupert had had time to be clear of the building, he pounded the desk with a powerful right fist and spat out, "The damned fool! The stupid, vain, bloody fool!"

Totally unmoved and with her usual glacial self-control, Gerda Ruttgers simply said, "What fool?"

With heavy sarcasm her husband said, "Your lover, my dear. Your damn, stupid lover! Can't you keep him from behaving like a lunatic?"

A secretary came in and the quite unruffled Frau Ruttgers gave her cigarette a lady-like puff, smiled to the girl, and said, "We can discuss it in the car going home."

Rupert walked without haste back to the underground car park some two blocks away, to receive the usual wildly enthusiastic greeting from Charlie. As though they hadn't seen each other for years. "All right, old chap, all right. Keep calm. I know a nice stretch of green grass just before we reach the Autobahn." He drove off in silence and deep thought. Traffic through Munich was heavy, and they did not reach the little park at Unterbiburg until after five-thirty. There was a parking space right opposite the wrought-iron gates. Charlie was thoroughly road trained and well disciplined, but the moment he got inside those gates he went delirious, running round and round the little plot of greenery as though chased by devils, stopping every few yards to express his relief and exuberance. He never missed a tree. Rupert sometimes thought there must be a little camel blood in Charlie's family—he seemed to be able to store it up for weeks! The evening was just beginning to get chilly. Rupert lit his pipe and had a brisk walk to stretch his muscles before the three-hundred-mile drive home. He also came to a very important conclusion.

As they settled down in the car and turned to climb up onto the Autobahn, he said, "Do you know what we're going to do now, Charlie boy? We're going to stop off at Schloss Fuschl for dinner, and you and I are going to share the finest, juiciest piece of sirloin that Gerhard Pischl has served up for years. Well done, with Béarnaise sauce. Pity you don't like claret." He swung into the line of traffic heading south, and the Jensen accelerated up to a hundred and thirty kilometers with an almost silky smoothness.

"It's been thirty years, Charlie boy. Thirty years. But today I've seen oil. Real genuine high grade crude."

Some two hours later, as Rupert was surreptitiously slipping small chunks of sirloin steak into a plastic bag in his pocket—the sumptuous Schloss Fuschl did *not* provide doggy bags—Gerda Ruttgers made a telephone call to Vienna. "Karl is very angry, Jacob. I can't talk on the phone. You must come. We are going down to the farm at Weilheim tonight. No, you can't come down there. I'll drive over to Neuschwanstein. Can you make Friday morning? I'll meet you in the courtyard at eleven o'clock. And put that damned elephant away in your safe." For a lover, her tone was decidedly authoritative.

8

AT the same time that Rupert was driving happily past Mondsee—the Jensen's wheels seemed barely to touch the surface of the Autobahn—and enjoying the translucent village lights splashed across the rippling surface of the lake, Karl Ruttgers was driving his cream-coloured Mercedes off the Starnburg intersection and heading into the *gemütlich* picture-book villages along that lake shore where successful Muncheners relax in a high degree of sophistication.

The only similarity in the atmosphere pervading the two diverging vehicles was the response of the listeners to two very different monologues. Gerda Ruttgers sat calmly listening to her irate husband's harangue, weighing and measuring every word while displaying as much emotion as a hard-boiled egg. Rupert's intermittent commentary on what was passing through his mind simply lulled Charlie into peaceful sleep.

"You've got to pump Schwarz," Karl concluded. "We

can't decide anything until we know exactly how much Conway does know. What did Schwarz tell him?"

"There is no use guessing. At the moment we can only be sure of two things. One, he knows Jacob has a valuable work of art that must have been wartime loot. For some reason we don't know, it interests him enough to take a lot of trouble. Right?" This woman had a way of saying even "Right?" in a tone that sounded more like a command than a question. "Two, we also know that sooner or later he is bound to find out you lied to him about not knowing Jacob." She paused long enough to let that sink in. Ruttgers knew his formidable wife well enough to be certain there was no escape. From the beginning their relationship had been a strange mixture of physical love and happiness and admiration for each other's remarkable ruthlessness. He took the cigar out of his mouth and tapped its ash out the window as they pulled up at the stoplight at Hindenburgstrasse.

"I know. I know. That was a mistake."

He hoped she would let it go at that. No such luck.

"A very dangerous mistake, with a man like Conway. You can't believe it was just a coincidence he came to tell you about it." She highlighted the word *you* as though with a knife. "He must have known something more or he wouldn't have come in the first place."

"I'll talk my way out of it. Tell him I forgot. Thirty years, long time . . ." His voice trailed off. He was conscious he would have to think of something better. "Anyway, Schwarz isn't vital to our operations. He's expendable."

"You think of killing him?" No glimmer of human feeling of any kind in her voice.

"Not me, no. If we get really pushed, it's a job for one of Rolf Heinrich's boys. They're professionals."

"I shouldn't tell Heinrich about this, if I were you. He won't be pleased."

Ruttgers was silent for a moment. He couldn't think constructively with Gerda jumping on his back every moment. Try changing the tack.

He said, "Conway may be even more dangerous than you think. He has a long memory."

"Meaning what?"

"You remember when you delivered Seligman's gold coin collection to Rio in 1948?"

"Very clearly. Conway wasn't there."

"No, he wasn't. But if his plane had not been seven hours late, and the Brazilian customs officer had been any more difficult to bribe, he would have been."

"You never told me that," she said accusingly.

"No. Well, we were young and romantic in those days. The point is, you don't know how close you came to spending the next ten years in a French jail."

He meant it to intimidate; but it came back faster than a boomerang.

"Why only me?"

The implication was unmistakable—and menacing.

"I mean us, of course." For good measure, "All of us."

"Conway was one of those Allied military art detectives, wasn't he?"

"That's right. Monuments, Fine Arts and Archives."

"That means he probably has access to a lot of military police material dating from those days."

"Undoubtedly, I should think."

Gerda sat quiet and stared at the road ahead for a minute.

Then she said, "In that case, if there is any killing to be done, the first name on the list is Herr Conway."

Ruttgers smiled. He had always admired her brain. She had the great faculty of always being able to put her finger right on the key issue.

"Heinrich's office is just across the river from Conway's

place," he said lightheartedly.

"No, no. Whatever needs to be done, not in Vienna. Conway is too well known there—too many friends."

"True. What would you suggest?"

As matter of factly as if they were discussing what to have for dinner, Gerda said, "An accident somewhere." She lit another cigarette from the enamel and emerald case, inhaled deeply, and then said, "Leipensche."

"Leipensche? Where the hell is Leipensche?"

"A village on the East German–Polish border."

"And why Leipensche, of all godforsaken places?"

"Border accidents are easier to arrange. The Poles and our friends could argue for months about who was responsible. Neither Vienna nor London would even expect to get any satisfaction."

Karl turned right at the crossroads in Weilheim and out onto the road for Peisenburg. Another five minutes in thoughtful silence and they turned up the driveway to their farm, a handsome black and white half-timbered Bavarian house whose every window box would soon be sprouting geraniums. It sat in two hundred hectares of land, of which most was farmed with the same determined efficiency the Ruttgers brought to everything they did. As the car neared the house, Karl pressed the electronic beam switch; the wide garage doors opened and all the outside lights came on. The car stopped in a large garage-cum-workshop, he turned the ignition off, and asked, "And how do we get Mr. Conway to oblige us by going to Leipensche?"

Gerda picked up a small overnight case and the red crocodile handbag. "I don't know—at the moment."

Over a leisurely breakfast at 5B Stephansplatz on Thursday morning, Rupert was going through yesterday's mail and a series of memos from Frau Hauptmann. Pauli had rung to say that, if he didn't fall down getting out of bed, Max should be back in the office on Friday. Sandra looked up from the pages of *Die Presse* and decided it was time for a little light communication.

"I see your old favourite Julia Homburg is opening at the Akademie in a new revival of *Who is Sylvia?* She's going to play Caroline."

"She'll be superb, as always."

"I remember seeing Athene Seyler in the part in London, years ago."

Rupert had always had a special liking for Terence Rattigan's plays—"Terry writes about people, not Yahoos," was his seal of approval.

"Do get tickets, we must see it. When is the first night?"

"April twentieth."

"Sounds all right. Make sure we are free."

"La Homburg must be seventy if she's a day."

"Don't be catty. Julia Homburg is ageless and as beautiful as she was thirty years ago. Who's producing?"

"Fritzi Keppel."

"Oh, good. Phone him up and tell him if we're not invited to the first-night party I'll tell his wife about that weekend in Kitzbuhl last winter. More coffee?"

"Yes, please."

Sandra put the paper down. She said, "McIvor offered three hundred and eighty thousand dollars for the Machiavelli."

"Ridiculous!"

"I told him you would say that." It was obvious to her that Rupert was in his enigmatic mood. It amused her, when he did not overdo it; then it began to irritate. Sometimes he showed the irresistible symptoms of a man who had lived alone too long. His attitude to this great picture was quite out of his usual character; it puzzled her. The fact he never talked about it was even more out-of-character.

"I don't understand your attitude. You always pride yourself on being so businesslike, but this is the third offer —good offer—for the Machiavelli you have turned down out of hand."

"True. You know I want four hundred thousand plus."

"Naturally, but in this oriental bazaar business called art, I always understood that an offer like three hundred and eighty thousand was a sure buying signal at four hundred."

Rupert sipped more coffee, smiled, and said, "That's right."

She put down her paper with just a sufficient hint of impatience. Sufficient to ensure Rupert registered it. He wiped his mouth with the table napkin, looked up at her, and smiled again.

"I'm sorry my dear. Mind preoccupied. I know what you think. Actually I want closer to five hundred thousand, and there is only one collector of these rare, minor Italian painters who will pay it."

"Why don't you sell it to him then?" It seemed pretty obvious.

With sudden, unexpected vehemence Rupert said, "Because he has not yet come to me direct. And I won't deal through his channel."

"What's wrong with his channel?"

"A dealer who made a fortune at the expense of his fellow Jews and their families. He spent the whole of World War Two in the safety of New York directing his Paris business in preying off all the great Jewish art collectors in Europe. Their pictures ended up in the hands of Hitler and Goering, most of the owners were slaughtered by the Gestapo, and the dealer became a millionaire."

"What a ghastly story!" Sandra, who for her quarter Jewish blood had suffered her share of physical and mental torture at the hands of the Nazis needed no more explanation of Rupert's feelings. "But, surely he is long since dead?"

"Huh," Rupert snorted. After all these years the contempt and loathing he felt for the man and a few others like him had not even begun to mellow. There were few fellow mortals he despised, but when he did, it was forever.

They both rose from the dining room table and headed for work. As Rupert stood aside at the door for Sandra, he said, "Frau Kroner's scrambled eggs are a bit off this morning."

"She's upset."

"Good Lord, why?"

Sandra laughed. "You came in late last night—and left the refrigerator door open—all night. Charlie got hold of a pound of sausages and the kitchen was a wreck when she arrived this morning."

"God bless my soul! Little devil! He had steak for dinner, too. I am sorry. Better go and apologize to her. Where's Charlie?"

"You guess."

Rupert went to his office via the kitchen, where a few carefully chosen words of humility were quite enough to pacify the easy-going Frau Kroner.

"Charlie, get off that chair!"

As he came through the door, Rupert did not even look up from the sheaf of papers he was reading. Since he had left his office door open, too, it followed that Charlie would have gone in on his own, and his favourite pastime after breakfast and a brief walk with Heinz Burgmann was to fall asleep on the tapestried Gainsborough chair until forcibly removed to his own scruffy old leather one. Rupert had too much on his mind to talk about sausages. Anyway, it was his own fault for leaving the door open. As this was a morning for some quiet thinking, he picked up the first six long-playing records that came to his hand under the label "Haydn" and slid them into place on the turntable. He sat down in his big velvet-covered chair, selected his first pipe of the morning, and gazed wistfully for a few moments at the silver-framed likeness of the beautiful girl who had shared his life for such a tragically short time. That was a daily ritual, too. He was soon lost in thought.

The buzzer went.

"Yes, Mini?"

"A Monsieur Lebel from Paris on the line for you, Herr Doktor."

"Ah, good. Put him on please, Mini."

"Morning, Claude. Thanks for calling."

It was raining in Paris. The headquarters of Police Judiciare on the Quai des Orfevres was low on the priority list of the Department des Établissements, the wind was howling down the Seine making the windows rattle, and drafts like small gales chased each other along the gloomy corridors. The ailing and asthmatic Claude Lebel felt worse than usual.

"Not much to tell you, I fear, mon ami. One of my old sergeants, very trustworthy fellow, checked your Schwarz's apartments—landlady, neighbours, and so on. We traced half a dozen dealers he had done business with. Had an account with the Chase Manhattan Bank here; well known at American Express. All negative. No entry in police files at all. Sorry." Poor old Claude sounded as though he might collapse at any moment. Besides his health he had a passionate hatred of negative reports.

"That's all right, Claude. Most grateful for your trouble."

"Any other leads you would like me to follow?"
"Well, I had an interesting experience in Munich yesterday. Another art dealer—fellow called Ruttgers, connected in some way with this Schwarz, but lied about it."
An asthmatic cough, followed by a small spark of interest came over the phone from Paris.
"What name did you say?"
"Ruttgers, Karl Ruttgers."
"Of Munich?"
"Yes."
"Rupert . . . yes, that does strike a chord. Don't suppose you have a scrambler on your line, have you?"
"No, sorry, I haven't."
"Hmm. That makes it difficult."
"You know something about Ruttgers?"
"The name you mentioned, yes. *Know* isn't quite the right word. And I can't talk to you about it on an open line. Can you . . ."
"Yes, of course, Claude. I understand. Are you in your office all morning?"
"I've nowhere else to go." He sounded so gloomy again.
"Right. I've got a few things to do here in the office, then I'll go over to see Josef Liebmann at the police headquarters and call you on his phone."
"Jo Liebmann? Mais oui. Good man, I remember him well. Department I, isn't he?"
"That's right. Call you within the hour."
Oberpolizeirat—literally translated Higher Police Councillor—Josef Liebmann was at that time third ranking officer in Department I of the Vienna Police Presidency. Department I dealt with internal security in all its aspects—political surveillance of extremist elements, control of foreign nationals, counter-espionage. Although Austria normally had no quarrel with anyone anywhere, the invasion of terrorists—Palestinians, Croatians, Japa-

nese, and free-lance professionals financed by the Libyan dictator Qadaffi, like the gentleman known as Carlos—in recent years had caused its men to become highly skilled in counter-terror operations. They worked smoothly with their colleagues in Department II, Criminal Investigation, under Vienna's able police president, Dr. Karl Reidinger. It had been Reidinger's sharp eye which had spotted the Libyan ambassador leaving the OPEC meeting for Prague only an hour before Carlos and his gang arrived to give all the others a forced free ride over the Mediterranean. Neither the ambassador, Al Ghadansi, nor his boss, seemed to give a damn that Carlos's girl friend shot one of their own men for no particular reason while they were about it. Like so many other people in responsible positions in Vienna, Jo Liebmann was accustomed to having Rupert Conway ask him to do things that no private citizen, let alone a foreigner, had any right to ask. But, as Rupert so often reminded him and others, "I do pay my taxes in Vienna, you know, old boy." They were good friends.

Liebmann's office was on the third floor of the impressive modern Polizei Praesidium on the Schottenring. The whole place had the proper air of careful planning and astringent efficiency—no concessions to art or fashion here. Its communications system was among the most sophisticated in the world. The call was in hand, the tape switched into the telephone instrument, and the police councillor's secretary instructed he was not to be bothered. A light flashed on the white phone with the scrambler button on it. Liebmann picked it up.

"Yes, he's here. Put Commissaire Lebel on the line, please."

He handed the receiver across the desk to Rupert, activated the tape, and pressed the scrambler down.

"Claude, you've no objection to our taping this?"

"Of course not. I'm doing the same."

"All set then."

"The information I have is most delicate. You understand? I would like to hear from you first, so I can judge just where there may be a fit."

"Oh, righto. Well, then. I'll try to put it in a nutshell."

"Don't leave out any material fact, that is the important thing." Claude Lebel's fame for painstaking thoroughness was well earned.

Rupert outlined what he knew, while Liebmann listened intently, and Lebel coughed his lungs out at the Paris end of the line.

"Jacob Schwarz, American, you already know about. Possesses a chalcedony elephant made by Fabergé in 1898. Looted by the Nazis in 1939 from a private collection in Austria. Hidden, somewhere in the East German–Polish border area, I think; looted again in 1945–46; and passed into Schwarz's hands in an Air Force mess near Kronach. Most important to me, because there were several such collections stolen from Austrian Jewish families and none of them have ever turned up. I know Schwarz and Ruttgers served together in the same unit in 1946. Ruttgers denies he ever heard of Schwarz. Ruttgers returned to Germany in 1947, married a German girl, and became an art dealer. He used to specialize in Fabergé and objects of that kind. Last year he suddenly started to do so again. Seems unlikely he had the stuff hidden around Munich all this time. Is there some new racket opening up here, like the recent stories from Poland about church pictures being smuggled out? The connection between Ruttgers and Schwarz with his elephant may be purely coincidence, but I do know that some of the stuff I saw in Ruttgers' office was loot. I've traced several pieces in my old MFA&A files."

Lebel coughed, spluttered, and gave a grunt of satisfaction.

"Oui. Oui. That is good. Good, Rupert. We here in Paris know little of all this, but there is some kind of a pattern. It's confusing, but there is a pattern. First, you know there is an organized ring working from West Berlin smuggling refugees out of East Germany. Recently they have started operating farther south, especially in Bavaria. We know there have been at least two successful operations from Czechoslovakia recently. One of the men who got out of Prague in the car of an Arab diplomat is here in Paris. He asked for political asylum and voluntarily handed over a valuable painting that the Louvre says belonged to the Radziwill family and had been hidden in a monastery near Cracow since 1939. Four pictures of similar origin have turned up in auctions here in the last six months. Also in Rome and London. We are working on all the cases, but the web of art smuggling, refugee smuggling, spying and counter-spying operations is a very tangled one. Maybe they are all part of one organization, or maybe just coincidence. I don't know. Now, our people are cooperating closely with the German police, of course—there is a total exchange of information and records. Since they have nothing better for me to do these days than solve puzzles, I sit here all day and brood on them. I can tell you only that a G. Ruttgers, female, driving a car with a Munich license registration, crosses the border at Hof into East Germany with extraordinary frequency."

Rupert took his pipe out of his mouth for the first time. "That fits. Karl Ruttgers' wife's name is Gerda. Who's in charge of the investigations in Munich, Claude?"

"Staatspolizei, Captain Wolfgang Gottfried. First-class man."

"May I use your name?"

"Certainly. I'll call him and tell him of your interest. This whole picture is such a muddle, one cannot guess. You might have the thread we are all looking for."

"What's your own theory, Claude?"

"Haven't got one, cher ami. The whole picture is too confused these days. With the OAS one at least knew who one was looking for. Ten years ago, even with the Communists, the same. Now the Russians, East Germans, Poles, Irish, Chinese, Trotskyists, Arabs, Palestinians—they've all gone mad! The only ray of happiness in the whole ugly business is that they all hate each other more than they hate the West. But the key to this puzzle lies in East Germany, of that I am certain."

The embassy of East Germany, which officially, and with no sense of humour at all, calls itself the German Democratic Republic, was at 8 Frimbergerstrasse, but like most Communist embassies, it was difficult to get inside. Next door, at number 6, was the "Commercial Representation," and in Brandstatte, not a hundred yards from St. Stephan's, was the "Travel Bureau." One could get in there all right, but you had better speak German—neither the usual array of coloured pamphlets, nor the two formidable middle-aged ladies in charge had a word of any foreign language between them. The Commercial Representation office was a little more forthcoming. The Commercial Representation was a perfectly sincere operation where visitors were greeted politely and regaled with catalogues and price lists of automated machine tools, mining equipment, and highly sophisticated optical lenses. There were even two or three coloured brochures proclaiming the delights of a summer holiday on the Baltic coast managed by the Workers' Rest and Holiday Organization, and the inevitable posters announcing the annual Leipzig Trade Fair.

Whether the friendly gentlemen in number 6 Frimbergerstrasse knew anything about what went on in the political department of the Kommandatura next door was a matter for speculation. In March 1976, even the Austrian security authorities did not know that the Kommandatura had a kind of annex, a small group of very discreet East Germans whose headquarters were in a dingy apartment block on the interminable Brunnerstrasse, across the Danube in the very unfashionable Twenty-second Bezirk.

Rupert Conway and Jo Liebmann were reviewing their tape and notes of the conversation with Claude Lebel. The police councillor was keeping the discussion strictly to the question of possible subversive activity that might affect Austria. He wanted no part of East-West refugee tangles or any kind of international political skulduggery. This suited Rupert fine.

Over in the apartment on Brunnerstrasse, East German intelligence man Rolf Heinrich and two of his agents were studying more or less the same set of facts, but the niceties of Austria's official neutrality did not come within their purview at all. Early that morning the contact man who regularly delivered the milk to the service entrance of the GDR embassy had returned with a message. Having spent the last two hours decoding it, they were now giving it most careful consideration. It came from a reliable source in Bavaria via the very efficient recently established network that carried signals played off high speed distorted tapes from agents in West Germany to East Berlin, thence to an ultra-high-frequency transmitter on a communications tower in Leipzig railway yards, and down to the embassy in Vienna. It had covered the course in just under six hours.

The gist of the signal was that a series of operations that had been working very effectively for a number of years might now be endangered by the meddling of an English art dealer in Vienna called Conway, who had a passion for playing private detective games. Heinrich knew a great deal about these operations. His henchmen knew only what he chose to tell them, and Heinrich lived in a world where one never told anybody anything if it could possibly be avoided. His instructions from East Berlin were to find out all he could about the unwelcome intruder and to meet the agent in five days' time at the usual rendezvous near Freiburg. There were four towns of that name in the two Germanies; this one was in East Saxony, near Dresden. He was informed of the tenuous connection with an American named Jacob Schwarz but ordered on no account to approach him.

His first move was to find out all he could about the interfering Conway. The following morning the man who delivered the milk returned with another missive from Heinrich's official colleague in the Kommandatura at Frimbergerstrasse. As he had anticipated, they had been able to secure a full dossier on the Britisher from the Russian Kommandatura on Jaurèsgasse, just round the corner from the British, German, Italian, and Chinese embassies. The only fact that offered a glimmer of hope to Heinrich was that his quarry and the female who lived with him were both part Jewish. A job for some of his Palestinian friends, possibly. That was easy to arrange. The only problem dealing with them was to get it clear that what you wanted was information, not corpses. Not at this stage, anyway. Berlin was quite definite about that.

In the meantime Rupert had had little difficulty in persuading Jo Liebmann that it was within his duty as a policeman and a neutral Austrian to contact Captain Wolfgang Gottfried in Munich. Gottfried was a little annoyed that this was the first he had heard of the Ruttgers association with his problem.

"I suppose it hadn't occurred to anyone to ask Lebel," suggested Rupert innocently. Asking Paris was certainly not the first instinctive reaction of a Munich police officer, Gottfried admitted with good grace. In due course he agreed to Rupert's request that they get a full record of Gerda Ruttgers' frequent crossings into East Germany, and to warn the border guards to keep a sharp lookout for her and report.

On Friday morning Rupert was in the workroom, glued to the large microscope. His full concentration was riveted on a glass slide that looked as though someone had dropped ink on it. Actually the bluish stain was the result of an alcohol rubbing he had made on a picture he had been asked to authenticate for a Swiss chemical manufacturer. After fifteen minutes of study and five changes of light angle, he was quite sure of his conclusions. And the chemical tycoon wasn't going to like it. The picture was certainly handsome, well painted; but when you got the light at just the right angle to use the spectroscope, those tiny green traces were unquestionably copper. The blues mixed in Umbria in the sixteenth century were lapis lazuli, so the picture was certainly not what its owner thought it was. At that moment Jo Liebmann dropped in unexpectedly.

"Just thought you'd like to know," he said. "Gottfried called this morning. Bavarian frontier police records show that your friend Frau Ruttgers visits the GDR nearly every month—to visit her mother, a Frau Wolfburg, at a place called Frauenstein. Must be just a village—it's not on any of our maps."

"She doesn't look the type, does she?" said Rupert.

That wasn't Liebmann's business.

9

ON Monday, three cars set out for East Saxony. Heinrich to meet his agent near Freiburg, Conway to see a fine art printer in Dresden, and Gerda Ruttgers to pay her respects to her aged mother in Frauenstein. Three cars, each carrying a very different kind of person on a highly personal mission; all heading for East Saxony from three different directions; all with very different thoughts and very different reactions to the constantly changing scenery, the western foothills of the Transylvanian Alps where they descend into the broad basin of the northward flowing Elbe. Now bleak, and then suddenly breathtakingly beautiful. Here luxuriant pine forest reflecting a veritable rainbow of shades of green, yellow, and blue, as the first blushes of early spring growth burst the withered winter skin of a thousand varieties of tree and bush to greet the morning sunshine. There, as quickly as the heavy clouds blotted out the gold and the warmth, turning to barren waste and the unkempt outcrops of long abandoned mine workings of coal, iron, and potash whose tailings had blighted whole areas centuries before the word conservation was thought of. Many miles of mountainous beauty where the rushing cataracts of spring flood and the stark ruins of still snow-capped medieval castles outlined against the skyline made it inescapable that a romantic part-Celt part-Jew like Rupert Conway would daydream of the Ruritania of Victorian novels.

Just as instinctively, and with a deep foreboding that penetrated even his determinedly optimistic nature, he found himself oppressed by the inescapable evidence of drab, inhuman tyranny which had marked central Europe for thirty years. Crossroads that in the West would not merit the attention of one policeman, here bristled with gun-slinging soldiers; gaunt concrete watch towers with searchlights manned by armed soldiers twenty-four hours a day; barbed-wire fences and the interminable, often inexplicable, menacing signs blaring "Achtung" and "Verboten." "Kamera Verboten" was a recurring favourite, frequently causing any observer from a free country to look frantically round to discover what on earth might be the terrible secret he was not supposed to photograph. Frequently it was nothing more imposing than a railway siding or a storage tank.

Rupert had the longest journey. Unlike Rolf Heinrich he could not go straight north from Vienna, through Prague. He had been very much *persona non grata* with the Czech border guards ever since an unhappy little incident in 1971, as a result of which an unfortunate young Czech officer, unbeknownst to Rupert, was still languishing in prison for having let a "dangerous Western spy" slip through his fingers. It had been Jo Liebmann, allowing the bonds of friendship to override the rigours of official neutrality, who had warned him that the Czech embassy in Vienna had been instructed to be sure to let

Conway have a visa next time he asked for one—they would like to "detain him for questioning." Rupert was too busy to afford the time for such unwelcome activity.

He always enjoyed the drive up the mountain-hedged Danube valley in the springtime. He crossed into West Germany near Passau, the border crossing a mere formality, and took the secondary road through the Oberpfalzer Wald, joining the Nuremberg-to-Berlin Autobahn at Bayreuth. On any other occasion he would have enjoyed a night in that lovely old city, just to visit its world-famous opera dedicated to the worship of Richard Wagner, but he had too much on his mind. Anyway, it was Monday night—no opera. The Adler Hotel would be less crowded; he always liked spending a night there. Next morning it was only half an hour to the border crossing near Hof, and provided the East German frontier guards were no more than usually surly, officious, and time wasting, he could be in Dresden comfortably by noon to keep his appointment at Altenburg's. He had a very good reason for going there, one that pleased the authorities of that schizophrenic country—he was going to do business that would be paid for in American dollars. He was accustomed to the strange phenomenon that always shocks the American tourists who venture into Marxland, the Communists' remarkable covetousness to acquire dollars. What his other reason for going might be was nobody's business but his own, and he knew Tautz in Dresden would not betray his confidence.

Before Rupert reached Bayreuth, Rolf Heinrich was already relaxing at the security police barracks in Heidenau, just outside Dresden—insofar as Rolf Heinrich ever relaxed. Life had not been easy for him. Schooled as a boy in the frenetic turmoil of the Hitler years, orphaned and set adrift by the fearful tide of the revenging Red Army, his world in ruins, he was left to live by his wits at the age of twenty-two. Like many other central Europeans of his generation and half-education, he had made the transition from the Hitler Youth into the S.S. and then into the ranks of the Communists without even noticing the change. One had to eat, one craved security, and the ambition for advancement in life was only natural. One swam with the tide and obeyed whatever rules the caprice of authority laid down. What politicians and intellectuals chose to endlessly debate in the name of ideology was simply necessity to men and women of his kind and generation. Their life plan was to survive, and whatever the ruling dictatorship called itself made little difference. In 1946 he had joined the party, with total commitment but no glimmering of enthusiasm, and had drifted from one minor realm of officialdom to another. He had just that precise mixture of dour, dogged obedience, complete lack of scruple or morality of any kind, and the animal cunning of the eternal peasant, which drew him inexorably and unprotesting into the ranks of the security police. At eighteen the S.S. had taught him to kill human beings with no more qualms than killing rats or chickens. It had been a useful training. And like most of his kind it was equally natural to be pleasant to his friends and family, kind to children and old people—one carried out orders, that was all.

But even the toughest of Germanic peasant stock cannot live on nerves forever. He had been afraid of taking this present assignment in Austria—not physically afraid, but afraid for the effect it would have on his mind. He knew instinctively he was not equipped mentally to deal with the strains imposed by living in a completely different world. Not at fifty. He would rather have been pensioned off to go and grow potatoes on a little farm in the valleys of the upper Elbe. It was not just the habit of obedience to authority, but a genuine fear of disapproval from his superiors that kept him at his duty these days.

The actual effect of exposure to the free world had been even worse than he had anticipated. For the first time in his life he had experienced the spectacle of countless people going about their everyday business without any scrutiny by the state, with no directives how they should think or what they should do, with no visible evidence of gun-carrying authority to keep them cowed. How does one know what to do, what to think, if there is no leadership to direct? He was disturbed by the huge car parks outside every factory where the Austrian workers parked their own cars. He had no experience from which to rationalize the free and cozy air of the streets swarming with foreign visitors, the lighted signs, the quality of the clothes people wore, the entertainment brought into homes by television, and the fact that his landlady's son and daughter drove their own car to Italy for their holidays. It made no kind of sense to him. It seemed to have no connection with his life or that of his friends and colleagues. He did not envy these people. It did not shake his intellectual theories about human behaviour, because he never had any. He just found it unsettling. It made him nervous. In his profession that was a dangerous weakness, and he was all too aware of its possible consequences.

In his own peculiar way he was happy to be back in the barracks near Heidenau. Over many years it had been the closest thing to a home he had ever known. It gave him the feeling of security which he, like millions of others all over the world, always craved. Even as he took comfort from the familiarity of his surroundings, his mind was clouded by the remembrance that right in the cellars of this very building there were cells and an execution chamber and a crematorium. In his time, in the ordinary course of his duties, he had received orders to arrest men and women right in this building, to take them below and hand them over to the officer in charge, knowing that within minutes living flesh and blood would be nothing but a small pile of ashes. And nobody, nowhere, would ever be told why. He had never hesitated to obey those orders. The discovery that the Communists behaved exactly as the Nazis had never struck him as strange—that was the only kind of government his generation had ever known.

He unpacked his small suitcase in the bedroom assigned to him and went downstairs to the officers' mess. There were a few old friends there; the warmth of an open log fire and strong draughts of schnapps with good German beer soon restored his spirits. Politics were taboo here; they talked about their families, duck and deer hunting, the prospects for the spring fishing season as soon as all the roads to the mountain lakes were free from snow. The discussion could have taken place almost anywhere in North America.

Heinrich was confident as to his briefing of the Palestinians, but pointed out that even the huge Russian intelligence machine had on one notorious occasion recently lost control of their unpredictable Arab proteges. With his superiors he discussed his plans for the morning. They confirmed that his meeting with the Munich agent had been arranged for the usual place and in the usual way. Heinrich looked forward to those meetings with special pleasure, for very personal reasons that his superiors were fully aware of and indeed even seemed to approve. It was not his business to find out why.

Gerda Ruttgers had the easiest journey of the three travellers. She drove her own high-powered bright red Porsche, and as with everything she did, even driving a car, she did it like a pro. In less than two hours from leaving the apartment in Munich she pulled up to the

West German customs post along the Autobahn west of Hof for the usual cursory examination of papers Western style. She lowered the window of the car door and handed her passport to the official in the box. The normal procedure was a quick glance at recent entries, a note of the East German visa number for the records, and a casual wave of the hand as the green light flashed "Go ahead." The officer this morning seemed to have mislaid his glasses. As he fumbled about on the desk in front of him, a uniformed policeman and a truck driver ambled out of the customs office and stopped to admire the Porsche. The policeman said he had once been a racing driver for Willi Porsche; the truck driver wandered slowly around this lovely piece of automotive machinery, eyeing every curve of its svelte lines with beaming admiration. Coldblooded though she was, Gerda was not unappreciative that both men blatantly admired her well-formed lines, too. Strict health discipline, a brilliant couturier, and painstaking skill with makeup knocked a good ten years off her age. She worked hard at it. The man in the box handed back her passport and she drove on.

The no man's land dividing West from East which caused Conway such depressing ruminations, had no effect on Gerda Ruttgers whatever. What Conway, like all but the most star-struck Westerners, found menacing and sinister left Gerda Ruttgers indifferent. There were another car and two huge Mercedes trucks in front of her, completely shutting off the view ahead. She waited patiently. She knew the form. This, the first obstacle to entering the brave new world of peace and brotherly love for all except imperialists, capitalists, and fascist hyenas, was just a preliminary check. The real detailed work of examination and possible harassment came fifty meters farther on, where the wheat was separated from the chaff —where the privileged were waved on their way with *demokratische* salutes and bows and greetings, while ordinary mortals were roughly ordered to get out and stand in line surrounded by armed guards while experienced mechanics combed their vehicles looking for the slightest trace of any evidence that might forbode danger to the peace-loving people of the world's most heavily armed group of nations. Rupert never crossed any of these borders without thinking what a shame that most Western visitors flew across this cultural abyss with no knowledge of its stark brutality, of what it was really like. Travelling by air told one little—all airports are pretty inhuman places. Gerda never suffered from such thoughts. She knew her place in this Orwellian monstrosity.

She unconcernedly smoked a cigarette while she waited the ten minutes until the trucks had passed through and the car ahead of her was signalled into the high fenced compound to await examination as and when the officer concerned felt like it. Ordinary travellers sometimes sat there for two or three hours, trucks or buses frequently longer, while nothing appeared to be happening at all except that the glowering faces of the guards and the itchiness of their trigger fingers got more menacing all the time. Babies could howl, old ladies faint with either the heat or the cold, bladders could burst, the guns never wavered—stay in your seat and don't move until you are ordered to. To Rupert it seemed a strange way to convince the world what a wonderful system communism was supposed to be. Gerda knew what was good for her.

She restarted the deep rumbling engine. The barrier immediately ahead of her swung up as the one only ten meters farther on clanged down. The moment the vehicle was inside, the first one came down again with a thud of doom. One was in a cage of high tensile steel ten meters long and five meters wide. The moment the trap was shut, a frontier police officer brandishing a revolver, three armed soldiers, and two uniformed females leading guard dogs surrounded the car. "Show your papers!" Gerda very calmly opened her passport and held it to the window. In her case the result was magical! In an instant the gun muzzles were lowered, the officer shifted his revolver to the left hand and saluted, *"Guten Tag, gnädige Frau. Guten Tag. Willkommen."* The next two barriers went up one after another with electronic precision, and she was swept through with smiles and salutes. Frau Ruttgers was an old friend. Very special orders related to her. She was always welcome to come back and visit her dear old mother at Frauenstein. After all, she carried the special pass reserved for high officials of the party.

Gerda swept up the Autobahn, nearly deserted on this side of the border except for the occasional convoy of Russian army vehicles, and that strangest of sights, a thin but constant stream of BMW's, Mercedeses, and other symbols of capitalist decadence whisking prosperous West Berliners back and forth on their legitimate business.

Gerda savoured every minute as she unleashed the power of Willi Porsche's superbly designed engine until the speedometer touched two hundred kilometers. This was what appealed to her about the system—the sweet rewards were reserved for those who served the party, and she had it made both ways. She loved the speed, she thrilled to the exotic feel of this racing animal responding to her slightest whim. And the road was not cluttered up with fat bourgeoise getting in her way. She would not have sacrificed the luxuries of living in the West for anything, but the feeling of importance, of power, which people like her could only find in a totalitarian regime, was the breath of life to her.

Half an hour's drive from the border brought Rupert to the turnoff where he would head east. The road signs with their historic names momentarily diverted his thinking. He would have liked to turn west, just for a few miles to explore the countryside around Jena and Erfurt, scenes of two of Napoleon's greatest battles. "Probably just another modern collection of concrete boxes," he muttered to Charlie as he turned right at the sign marked "Karl-Marx-Stadt." The contrast was too great to pass unnoticed. He always thought of himself as a rather easygoing progressive sort of chap; had he had a vote in Vienna he might easily have voted for the Social Democrats. Well, at least once in a while anyway.

As the Autobahn scythed its way through the industrial heartland of East Germany, there were few oases of joy to distract his thinking processes. The villages looked attractive enough. In some ways the absence of modern buildings, gas stations, hotels, and brightly coloured signs was pleasant to look at. The country people, in particular, looked contented enough—perhaps because they really did not know how much lower their living standard was than that of their cousins west of those damned watch towers. The sun shone, the fields were reassuring.

He turned off the tap of humanitarian speculation and thought about business. Max had briefed him with his usual meticulous, professorial care on the technicalities and aesthetic problems of printing plates for the book on Sumerian art. It was to be the most scholarly and authoritative treatment of the subject attempted this century, presenting to the world the research to which Max had devoted a large part of his life. It was the sort of book on which both the publishers and Conway Wien would probably lose money, but the prestige would be immense and it would establish them as the principal authorities on the subject. While Rupert's fascination with ancient artistic techniques by no means approached that of Max, he agreed with his elderly partner that as the world became more and more sated with books covering the entire post-Roman and Greek world, scholars struggling to probe the enigma of man's ceaseless and erratic search for truth and beauty would delve further and further into the past. There was no evidence as yet that even the Chinese or the Indians were likely to get any further back than the mysterious Sumerian civilization. No reputable university or reference library in the world could afford to be without a volume. That was a pleasant thought. Maybe they would make a profit on it after all. At any rate, he had ample resources to pay Wilhelm Tautz on delivery for the delicate and precise job he would make of printing the photographs and sketches for Max's *magnum opus.*

His immediate problem was going to be how to find the right opportunity to ask Tautz about the other matters on his mind. Did he think it possible there were any caches of wartime art loot still lying hidden in old mine workings or obscure country houses in southeast Germany? Would it be possible, with or without official approval, to get a look at them? Could he help to establish whether there was or was not any connection between Ruttgers' new-found source of supply of Russian objets d'art and Gerda Ruttgers' mother in the obscure little country town of Frauenstein? Munich police research had discovered that the formidable Gerda had been born in Dresden, that her family name was Wolfburg, that the destination and purpose of visit she entered on her East German visa was always Frauenstein to visit her mother; and that she had worked at Weesenstein under Hans Reger on the compilation of Hitler's endless catalogues that were to be the basis of the fantastic project for the Führer Museum at Linz. That that experience must have formed the link between her and Karl seemed fairly obvious. In the early days of the war, before Dresden was blasted off the face of the earth by the American and British air forces, it was even possible, indeed likely, that Altenburg's had actually printed some of those famous documents that had formed a large part of the prosecutors' cases at the Nuremberg trials. Perhaps Tautz knew somebody in Frauenstein, somebody who might even know old Frau Wolfburg, who might provide some clues as to Gerda's unusual relationship with the East German authorities which gave her privileges here normally denied to foreigners. But would it be somebody to whom one could entrust such questions?

Rupert had the questions he wanted to ask Tautz clearly formulated in his mind. The initial problem would be seeking the chance to ask them. Would he be allowed to talk to Tautz alone? It always seemed to depend on the current state of ideological alertness being enforced by the East German government. In the half dozen visits he had made to the Dresden printer over the last twenty years, there had been times when everything seemed comparatively free and easy—and other times when police surveillance was so close that intimate conversation had been impossible. One thing he knew from experience, the first approach must be absolutely discreet. A wrong move on his part that might compromise Tautz's own safety would make any further inquiries impossible.

Gerda turned off the Autobahn at Karl-Marx-Stadt, wound her way through the drab colourless streets of the city, out on to the familiar, featureless secondary road that leads to Freiburg and through the flat fields and woods to the village of Frauenstein. As she neared her destination, her mind also concentrated on immediate problems. Naturally she had given much thought to what she would tell

Heinrich, but her mind was still far from clear. She had not solved her puzzle either. She knew that the special bond between the two of them was strong enough to protect her even from his icy sense of duty to "higher authority," but she valued his respect for her ability and her shrewdness even more than she valued his affection. If anything, she was the more assured, the more determined of the two. Where Heinrich accepted orders because they were orders, her more guileful, scheming brain pondered what was behind them, what else she should be thinking of, what else it might be useful to know. Only rarely would she admit to herself the sense of dependence on him that crept over her as the years went by. Even more disturbing was the thought that he knew it.

The routine reports she had to give were easy; whatever they had to tell her she would deal with in her usual competent, matter-of-fact way. What worried her was her present inability to analyze to her own satisfaction the real message, if any, of what she had gleaned from Jacob Schwarz.

They had met, as they did from time to time, wandering like innocent tourists on the mountain paths that surrounded Ludwig II's dream castle of Neuschwanstein—now and again alone to talk seriously together, easily melding into any passing group of trippers so that they were never conspicuous. Jacob always brought that ridiculous camera, which he never used, draped around his neck, and tried to make himself look like any other American tourist. "Why not? That's what I am," he always said. It was beginning to irritate her.

There was no doubt Jacob really was still in love with her after all these years, and like most frustrated middle-aged Lotharios who have had two unsuccessful marriages, he seized every moment when no one was uncomfortably close to try to embrace her. His eagerness was flattering, but her mind was usually on other things. At every possible opportunity he would take her arm and try to fiddle about with her sleeve until he could touch her skin—the feel of her flesh, anywhere at all, seemed to give him an erotic thrill. There were times when she thought, I'm glad I have Karl to keep me from getting that hungry. Their conversation was becoming more and more punctuated with her remonstrances, "Not here, Jacob"; "Please, you'll smear my lipstick, Jacob"; "Later, Jacob." Last Saturday he had greeted her like an excited teenager with the news that he had taken a room at a nearby hotel in Füssen, where they could have lunch and spend an hour or two in bed together afterward. She knew Karl had deliberately asked friends to lunch at the farm in order to prevent just such an encounter, which made digging information out of Jacob that much more difficult. Naturally he had sulked, as she knew he would.

Jacob himself had no fears about Conway at all. Just an art dealer who can't forget his youthful adventures in the army. The Nazis stole a lot of his grandfather's stuff, and he wants it back again. Who wouldn't? How was I to know the damned elephant would remind him of his grandfather? So his grandfather knew the guy who owned it? For God's sake, so what? Hasn't that lousy husband of yours caused me enough trouble? Come on, Gerda. When are you going to come clean. I'm not getting any younger. Come back to the States with me. Now. Yeah, he had put the elephant away like she asked, so as not to risk more comment. There was no mystery in Conway's knowing about its origins—he was an expert in that sort of thing. No, he had never heard of Conway's grandfather before, but once he did it was no surprise that the man had been a friend of the Meulheimers—it was natural that wealthy Austrian Jews should know each other. What the hell was

Karl getting all steamed up about anyway? Are you sure the real trouble isn't that Karl has found out about us and is jealous? Gerda couldn't answer that one.

But Gerda was far from satisfied. Why had Conway within a week of visiting Jacob's apartment unexpectedly turned up in Munich and talked as he had to Karl? They had not seen each other for years; they had never been close friends. Why, why, why? Jacob had all sorts of innocent explanations. The more he tried, the less he convinced her. Despite all his assurances, they parted unhappily. Fortunately he seemed completely unaware that her state of anxiety and dissatisfaction arose from entirely different causes than his. There was no enthusiasm to her side of their farewell kiss.

Now as she approached the meeting with Heinrich, her normally unemotional, analytical brain was more and more assailed with doubts concerning what she did not know about the Britisher. Was Conway's interest in the elephant just coincidence, as Jacob believed? Even if it was, was it likely to lead him blundering into their whole operation? What, if anything, did Conway know about her and Karl? She had never been totally happy with Karl's ideas about the statute of limitations business giving them such freedom. Maybe he was right that what they were doing was now perfectly legal, but if anyone pried into their sources of supply, there were bound to be other questions, and questions lead to more questions. Karl had been certain there was no one interested enough to ask questions, but they had not reckoned on Conway getting into the act. Had they made a serious error blinded by the enormous value of the objects whose secret they had guarded for so many years? After so long and successful a career founded on their ability to exploit the East–West German situation, was Karl getting overconfident and careless? Or was she getting weary and losing her nerve?

She went round and round with the same questions as the Porsche passed a column of parked Russian army vehicles, bristling with guns, just outside the high barbed-wire fence that surrounded the ancient abbey of Frauenstein. Distasteful though it was, her only course was to tell Heinrich all her facts and all her fears; he would decide, as he always did.

In Dresden Rupert followed the route laid down in his *laissez-passer* from the East German visa office in Vienna, through the shabby, featureless boxlike streets of what had for centuries been one of the loveliest cities in Europe. Well, its destruction had been almost totally carried out by the British and American air forces, there was no getting around that.

Of the buildings, only the famous landmarks, the great Dresden Museum and the art gallery had been restored —and well restored. The rest were comparatively new, had never been designed as anything but functional concrete boxes; a few years of smoke, rain, and snow plus a stubborn refusal to take any interest in maintenance aged them prematurely, just as it did the people who lived and worked within them. East Germany was a joyless place, however hard they tried. Rupert crossed the Elbe and drove through the city to its eastern suburbs, finally stopping in front of a large concrete pile bearing the legend "Druckswerke Volks Eigener Betrieb"—"The People's Own Managed Printing Works." Underneath in smaller letters, and solely for the benefit of foreign buyers like Rupert who came to place work with the skilled craftsmen of the Tautz family, it said "Altenburg." Only a handful of world-famous names, like Zeiss and Altenburg, which contributed to the state's vital foreign exchange earnings, were grudgingly allowed to keep some small token of their identity. It was good for foreign advertising, but made no difference whatever to actual operations—

the firms were owned and managed just the same by the *Volks.*

Rupert picked up the carefully packed briefcase and the tissue-wrapped, ribbon-bound picture folder from the back seat, wound down both front windows just two inches to ensure Charlie's health and comfort, chucked the dog's right ear, which was their mutually understood assurance he would be back in due course, locked both doors, and climbed the three steps into the bare, unwelcoming reception hall. He knew, of course, that typical German thoroughness would have ensured anyone and everyone remotely concerned with his visit being fully informed—they would have a full description of himself and his business. Fortunately for his peace of mind, he was unaware how well informed. Nevertheless, it came as no surprise when he was accosted by a young man who showed no glimmering of recognition, insisted on examining all his compulsory papers, and promptly disappeared with them behind a door that he immediately and loudly locked. Oh, so it's like that is it, Rupert thought; talking seriously to old Tautz isn't going to be easy. He lit a pipe and waited patiently.

After some minutes another young man, a little more forthcoming than the first, appeared and said in English, "This way, please."

Rupert remained quite still, and looking his escort squarely in the eye, said firmly but politely in German, "My papers, please." The German looked disconcerted. Rupert knew this routine from experience. If you didn't get those precious papers back before you started, they were likely to keep you hanging around for hours or even days afterward before you could leave. Nothing more was said. Rupert made no effort to move.

After a moment of embarrassment the young man disappeared again, relocking the door. More minutes passed.

He returned with the papers and handed them over without a word. Rupert carefully checked every document before returning them to the inside panel of his briefcase and locking it. Then he looked back at the young man, favouring him with his most engaging smile, and said, "Now."

The inside of a printing works is pretty much the same in any country, and this one was first class by any standards. To Rupert, the inside of a factory was the only possible place to apply the rigid, puritanical, utterly joyless methods and standards that the East German bosses applied to everything in life. The whole place had an air of clinical efficiency and dedication to work, the lighting was superb, the temperature control precise, the floors spotless, and the walls unsullied by pin-ups or graffiti of any kind. One did not have to know anything about printing to see at a glance that the plant layout was a production engineer's dream of perfection. The whole air of smooth efficiency was highlighted by the use of a different colour scheme demarking every department. The whole shop was open plan, but the colour chart showed you instantly where everything was—Supplies Inward was yellow, Block Making was red, Colour Photography green, the newest numerically programmed computer operated presses were clean stainless steel, and all foremen's and section heads' desks shining white. Every worker wore an overall the colour of his department. It certainly made for efficiency; it also made it much easier for the resident political officer to keep track of everybody.

At the far end of the model plant, Rupert and his guide mounted the open metal staircase to a balcony above, where the draftsmen, artists, and next senior layer of management worked in the privacy and quiet of glassed-in boxes, from which they could still scrutinize every movement on the floor below. Behind these beehive structures were the citadel of higher management and conference rooms for dealing with customers. It was simple and austere—but efficient. They finally stopped outside a door labelled "Herr Direktor." The young man knocked and they entered.

There were three men in the room—old Wilhelm Tautz; his son and chief engineer, Johannes; and someone Rupert had not met before. As an experienced visitor to Communist countries, Rupert knew never to make the opening move. He paused just inside the door. Tautz, with a blank, expressionless face and level voice, said in German, "Welcome, Herr Doktor, we are glad to do business with you again." Rupert got the message. On the rare occasions when one of the Tautz family was allowed to go to Vienna, it had long been "My dear Rupert." Such familiarity was obviously out of place in front of the third man. That meant he was the political officer, what Rupert called "the nark."

He advanced to the table, cooling his usual welcoming smile several degrees, laid down his briefcase and the folder, and then extended his hand politely but formally to Tautz. "And I with you, Herr Direktor."

For a moment the old man's back was to the nark, and Rupert felt a firm squeeze of recognition and caught just the glimpse of a smile in the lined, bespectacled old face. He exchanged a similar greeting with Johannes, then was introduced to the cold fishy handshake of Herr Kamerad Greitz, "our planning director." I'll bet he is, Rupert almost said out loud.

The four of them—and the young man who had escorted him in—sat down around the table and Rupert opened up his briefcase. As soon as they got to the work in hand, both Tautz father and son came to life—became animated, bursting with comment and ideas. They could relax now they were really in their own field, making no effort to conceal their delight at the intricate technical problems that confronted them, problems only their skills could solve in a hurry. The Herr Kamerad Planning Direktor made two early interventions in an attempt to maintain his prestige but was out of his depth from the beginning. Johannes said nothing and stared at the ceiling. Old Tautz affected to ignore the intrusions, on both occasions quietly continuing his own line of thought, indirectly making it clear why he considered the nark's observation unlikely to be feasible. For no apparent reason and without a word the young man left.

Having set the problems and in full confidence that the Tautzes knew their business, Rupert lit his inevitable pipe and sat back to study and enjoy this strange conference. Wilhelm Tautz was a pipe smoker, too, and Johannes lit up a relay of small, strong-smelling black cigars of Turkish and Greek tobacco. Kamerad Greitz became noticeably less sociable; he was an openly aggressive non-smoker. Rupert was quite sure he'd received a clear signal from Tautz, which he read as, "The only way to get rid of this pest is to smoke him out!" The three of them could almost hear poor Greitz wrestling with his conscience, his personal comfort increasingly clashing head on with his sacred duty to prevent the Tautzes being alone with this foreigner for a single moment. Fortunately for Rupert's enjoyment of this little charade, he, like the Tautzes, was unaware that Kamerad Greitz had been fully briefed three days ago by the security police that the Westerner was expected and a detailed report was required of his every word and movement.

After more than an hour of technical discussion, much of which Rupert did not understand, they seemed to have agreed on the processes and mechanical details, and he felt it was time to bring up the problem of delivery. How quickly could they do the job? Time was vital.

Old Tautz gave him a quizzical look and said, "I think you said your publisher was American, ja?"

"Ja. I did."

Tautz shrugged, smiled, and looked at his son.

"That means you want it yesterday. Any fool can print quickly. The quality you require takes time. Johannes?"

The younger man examined some doodles on his note pad and said, "If I take Hans Wlaka and his crew off the Polish work and put young Krebs to help him, we could have the first prints ready in, say, four days. After that, if you approve them, we could deliver at about five sheets every week."

Rupert said, "Ready, but how long would they take to reach Vienna?"

Johannes was about to speak when his father cut in. "Ah. Delivery is a matter for Kamerad Direktor Greitz." They all looked earnestly at the uncomfortable political officer.

"The people's state transport service to Vienna is excellent. There is no problem," he said curtly.

No problem and no commitment either, Rupert noted.

It was now half past one, and Rupert's stomach thought his throat had been cut. Twice he made broad hints that they should adjourn for lunch, but each time one or other of the Tautzes suddenly got a new burst of enthusiasm for the work in hand and started yet another long detailed technical discussion about the chemical basis of some high-speed ink or colour pigment they were considering using for some part of the work. They went over and over the same ground, always in different patterns and with different conclusions. Rupert's digestive system was by now in open revolt, and Greitz had settled into sullen, smoke-shrouded silence. Rupert was sure he heard a faint click; suddenly Greitz jumped to his feet, mumbled in obvious embarrassment to Tautz senior, and rushed out of the room.

The moment the door shut both Tautzes broke into broad grins, but old Wilhelm instantly put his finger to his lips commanding silence. He leaned over and whispered in English in Rupert's ear, "His tape recorder only runs for two hours!" Rupert grasped the old man's hand and said, "Can I talk to you alone? Some time, any time. I want your help."

Wilhelm Tautz exchanged glances with his son. Their eyes betrayed the anxiety under which they were forced to live—also their inescapable resignation to it. He smiled wanly and said, "Yes, I will show you when."

Greitz came bustling back in, making no attempt to hide his annoyance. Both Tautzes immediately resumed their formal, ideologically correct attitude toward their visitor. Wilhelm looked at his watch and expressed feigned surprise. He changed back to German again.

"Herr Doktor, how rude of us! Please accept my apologies. I had no idea it was so late. You must have some food. We can conclude this interesting business after lunch." He turned to Johannes and said, "Please have my car brought to the front door. You take Kamerad Greitz with you, and I will drive our visitor to the guest villa."

Greitz began to protest these arrangements, but clearly it was a matter which fell within the discretion of the old man, the titular head of the firm.

The group divided on the workshop floor. Johannes and Greitz, the latter exuding disapproval from every pore, turned right to the courtyard, which was reserved for the cars of the Herr Direktors and senior management. It adjoined the bicycle park for the workers. By the time Wilhelm and Rupert reached the street door, a Polish Fiat, status symbol of the first rung up the ladder of importance, was parked behind Rupert's Jensen, and a man handed the Herr Direktor his keys with a servile bow. The man disappeared.

They got in, and once again old Tautz silently held a finger against his lips. Rupert watched closely, saying nothing. The old man bent forward and fumbled with the keys. He dropped them to the floor. Rupert instinctively leaned down to pick them up, but Tautz silently gripped his arm to prevent him. Then as the old German bent over to reach them, his glasses fell off. He moved his right foot from the accelerator pedal and deliberately stamped his heel on them. "Ach! My spectacles! I become so clumsy in my old age. I cannot drive without them. Kamerad Greitz has left already. We must use your car."

With an agility that did not entirely suit his old age, he was out of the Fiat, signalled Rupert to move, and they got in the Jensen.

"Quickly," Tautz said, clearly enjoying both the game and the chance to practice his English. "I will show you where to go." He looked at his watch. "We have just seven minutes to talk."

Rupert took all this calmly, but it was not a relaxing atmosphere.

"They bug your car, too?" he enquired.

"Of course," Tautz replied. "Our last planning director became too complaisant for the liking of the party. He is now running a small post office at Pirna. Greitz takes no chances." Then he added, "Neither do I."

Rupert turned left at the bottom of the street as instructed, and said, "Okay?"

The old man smiled. "Okay."

They headed south along the east bank of the Elbe.

Rupert went through his carefully rehearsed list of questions. Tautz thought it most unlikely there were any private or secret stores of wartime loot still around. During 1946–47 the Russians had removed everything they could lay their hands on. In the early fifties, once the gentlemen in the Kremlin were satisfied with the subservience of Ulbricht's regime, the Russians meticulously restored and returned everything classified as "state property"; Dresden's famous public galleries were once again as fine and full of beautiful works as before the war. They were the Communists' great showcase, living proof of the goodwill and friendship of Moscow. Still, it was just possible. There were always rumours. He knew of a case two years ago when a prominent official defected to the West; it was said he took many valuable objects with him.

Discuss this frankly with the government? Three or four years ago, when Willi Brandt's overtures demanded some response, it might have been possible. One day again, perhaps. At present, out of the question.

There were only three minutes left when they reached the edge of town where the villas allotted to party officials and leading companies like Altenburg's were located. Rupert was not feeling very encouraged so far.

He asked, "Do you know anyone in Frauenstein?"

Tautz sat up as though stung.

"Do I know—what?"

Rupert was surprised by this reaction.

"The village of Frauenstein. Do you know anyone who lives there?"

"Ah, the village of Frauenstein," Tautz spoke slowly in querulous tones.

"What's special about Frauenstein?" Rupert asked.

"You do not know what is Frauenstein?"

"Just a small country village, as far as I know."

Even in the privacy of the car Tautz had suddenly become nervous. "Turn right here," he said and looked carefully along the deserted road.

"There are no ordinary people left in Frauenstein—they were all removed years ago. The abbey is the headquarters of the security police for the southern district. It is also headquarters of their Russian masters, their training school, and their experimental prison." His emphasis on the word *experimental* spoke volumes. "In Frauenstein, the only thing that has changed since Hitler's time is the uniforms. I strongly urge you not to try to go there, my friend."

Rupert was down to his last shot. Any chance of getting information about a Frau Wolfburg—she must be over seventy, her daughter lived in Munich, and it was was believed that she lived—or had lived—in Frauenstein?

"It is possible." He thought a moment. "This gate." The car pulled into the driveway of a riverside villa that had once housed some wealthy Dresden family. Possibly even the Tautzes. Old Wilhelm said, "The prints I send you must go through the office of the commercial representative in Vienna. Examine them carefully."

The slightly nervous Johannes and the indignant Kamerad Greitz were already standing on the marble steps; Wilhelm Tautz stumbled out of the Jensen bemoaning the loss of his glasses and during an uncomfortable lunch managed to spill his wine all over the table.

Gerda Ruttgers thoroughly enjoyed her lunch in the wing of Frauenstein Abbey that was kept especially for privileged visitors on missions like hers. Although the case officer she reported to first was new to his job, he had been courteous and had obviously studied her file carefully. He knew—and showed he knew—that she was no rank-and-file agent to be bullied and scolded just to demonstrate who was in charge of operations. She handed over the usual metal cases of microfilm with which she had been entrusted. The case officer was visibly impressed by the code sign on each tiny package proclaiming they were only to be opened by someone much senior to him. She answered his routine questions with the complete confidence that came from her knowledge that she knew far more about her work than he did. They parted with his assurance that he looked forward with pleasure to working with her. He sounded as sincere as anyone trained in his profession can sound. Gerda had no qualms or worries in this department.

Her visit to the technical supervisor had been equally satisfactory. He demonstrated two minor improvements in equipment that had become available since her last visit. It was interesting, but she was not overly impressed. Over the years she had come to rely more and more on her own wits and photographic memory than on the gadgetry that fascinated the writers of spy thrillers.

To crown her pleasure, she and Heinrich had been given the privilege of discussing this new problem of theirs over lunch in a private room, instead of having to sit facing each other across a bare table in a gloomy monk's cell turned interview room. Both of them were sure they served the regime well; the evidence that their superiors thought so, too, was gratifying. She told Heinrich everything about Conway, about Schwarz, about Karl's anxieties. She admitted her own uncertainty as to how serious a threat Conway might be.

Heinrich had, of course, known for many years exactly the past history of her association with Ruttgers and Schwarz—it was all part of her job. Although the Fabergé elephant had not figured in their discussions for over twenty years, he understood its significance for Gerda and Karl. He had never been entirely happy about this private arrangement of hers relating to what was still officially always referred to as "enemy property," but it was not his business, and whoever was involved clearly had sufficient authority that no one else ever interfered with her. It was a little embarrassing to have to admit that he, too, had been unable to discover any positive intelligence about this troublesome Conway, but all he had learned reassured him. Conway was the sort of man their Russian friends had always kept a pretty full record of—you never knew when it might prove useful—but neither they nor the Palestinians had turned up anything sinister. The Russians knew, of course, about the escapade at the Czech border five years ago, but it appeared to them no more than indiscreet. The Czechs were angry at the time, but no harm had been done. Heinrich would continue close surveillance; he knew he could rely on Gerda to report any developments from her end; in the meantime any positive action on their part might only stir up trouble. He made no mention of the uncomfortableness of his present post, but Gerda's acute mind and feminine intuition sensed that something disturbed him. As they said goodby, he talked openly about the prospect of retirement, of his somber weariness. She had never heard him speak like this before—he was, after all, only fifty.

It was nearly five o'clock by the time Rupert finished his business with the Tautz family; the sky had clouded over and it started to rain. He had not asked for permission to stay overnight in Dresden, as it was always an uncomfortable and disquieting experience, so his visa required him to report back through the Hof frontier post before midnight. As he travelled slowly through the city, carefully studying the confusing mass of road signs, he pondered everything that Wilhelm Tautz had told him. Thank heaven the business of Max's book had gone so well—he seemed to have little else to show for his day's work. He stopped to study the map. He looked at his watch. Though the daylight was starting to fade, he had enough time to reach Bayreuth for a late dinner. But too late for the opera tonight. He lit a pipe, patted Charlie till his tail wagged, and whispered, "Sorry, old man, you'll just have to hold it for a few hours yet." He had total confidence in Charlie's prowess in these important matters, and Charlie had had a good session in the guest villa's garden, much to Kamerad Greitz's disgust. Old Tautz had enjoyed that.

He pulled away from the curb and headed for the bridge over the Elbe. There were several huge Skoda lorries in the street, a handful of midget cars, Trebants and Wartburgs, the only cars produced in the "people's" factories, and swarms of bicycles carrying Dresden's weary workers on their homeward journeys. It always seemed the case in large cities divided by broad rivers that everyone worked on the opposite side from where they lived. He had to stop at a traffic light before crossing over onto the bridge that a massive plaque identified as the Comrade Brezhnev Bridge.

As he approached the main intersection in downtown Dresden, Rupert studied the bewildering array of signs with the utmost care. It was necessary not only to find one's directions, but there were always important notices announcing what was *verboten.* He noted it was the second fork to the right for the westbound Autobahn and deliberately took the next one on the left heading to a place called Dippeldiswalde. He pondered Tautz's warning to steer clear of Frauenstein, but the map showed him there was a turn-off from this road that would just miss it, and the temptation to have a quick look was overpowering. Sure enough, four miles beyond Dippeldiswalde there was a lane turning northwest, which would eventually lead him back toward the Autobahn. He travelled along a reasonably straight track flanked by farmers' fields and a small lake on his right. Three miles to the west there was a slight rise upon which, silhouetted against the setting sun, rose the baroque onion-domed spires of what had once been Frauenstein Abbey. The light was still just sufficient for him to pick out the mass of military-style barracks surrounding it, the huge barbed-wire fences, and the familiar concrete watch towers at intervals of about every two hundred meters. As if to reassure himself, he said to Charlie, "I think we're just far enough away not to interest those gentlemen." Charlie clearly couldn't have cared less.

As Rupert travelled slowly northward—but not so slow as to attract undue attention—he came level with the outer perimeter of the police complex and could clearly make out what there was of the village outside those menacing entanglements. Tautz is probably right, he thought. Those cottages would mostly be occupied by civilian workers, clerks, cleaners, artisans, and so on. Still, there must be an inn or some kind of social meeting place, even in this grim atmosphere. He wondered why Frau Wolfburg fascinated him so? She must be quite a character to inspire such devotion in a daughter who doesn't look like the devoted home-loving type. The old lady couldn't possibly work in that place? In charge of the officers' recreation department maybe? But the solution of the mystery must lie here. Why must it? The only answer he could think of was the somewhat illogical one that his life-long reading of thrillers suggested: there was always a woman at the center of every spider web; all the best detectives solved their problems by *cherchez*ing *la femme.* Was it the old lady or Gerda? Or perhaps he had lived alone too long.

He came to the crossroads where the country lane came to a tee junction with the road leading north from Frauenstein up to Freiburg and back on to the Autobahn. He was still undecided which way to turn. The slow gait of a horse-drawn farm wagon coming toward him caused a momentary delay. There was a car coming up the road behind the cart. It had its headlights on—the dusk made visibility poor. Rupert took the time afforded to relight his pipe. The car slowed down behind the farmer's wagon, then, as he looked up from the glowing tobacco and blew out the match, it accelerated and disappeared to pass the wagon on the opposite side. The warm, familiar glow of Mr. Lewis's contentment-inducing smoking mixture, reminding him of pleasanter surroundings, persuaded him it was wiser to go home. Fifty-seven and with a game leg, he was in no fit condition to try playing James Bond games again. He turned north. As he passed the trundling wagon, he noticed the other car had pulled into a farm yard; its lights were switched off.

Gerda sat there in silence for a few moments while the Jensen, an unmistakably English car, with the unmistakable profile of its pipe-smoking owner, disappeared in the direction of the Autobahn. She switched the engine on again, backed out onto the now-deserted road, and turned south to retrace her way back to the abbey. That couldn't be coincidence, she said to herself. Heinrich and I were wrong.

10

HEINRICH reached the Czech frontier, feeling more relaxed and easier in his mind than he had expected. There seemed to be no unpleasant tasks immediately facing him. He would stop for a quiet meal at a nice little restaurant he knew in Prague and be safely back in the apartment on Brennergasse by eleven o'clock. He reckoned without Gerda. When his car pulled up to the frontier point at Bad Schandau he got the first shock. The frontier policeman on duty asked his full name and destination, checked a piece of paper in his hand, then saluted and said woodenly the Herr Hauptmann was wanted in the control office. Heinrich cursed mildly under his breath, pulled into the car park, and walked over to the office apprehensively. At half past seven he found himself back in Frauenstein, was ordered to report to General Zweiboden's headquarters on the second floor, and cooled his heels there for half an hour before being summoned to the great man's presence. All this was ominous

—and felt worse on an empty stomach.

He felt better, though surprised, when the first person to greet him in the general's room was Gerda. One did not expect intimacy or affection in this atmosphere, but she at least was smiling at him. The general was coldly polite, as always. There was no welcome in the eyes of the other two officers in the room. He did not recognize either of them, but when he caught sight of their insignia he knew one never expected any show of warm-hearted friendship from these quarters. One of them was German, the other Russian; they were the local heads of the department known simply as Thirteen. Their specialty was violence. It was a long time since Heinrich had had the misfortune to have to work with these gentlemen, and the sight of them only added to his feeling of unease, his increasing tendency to think about retirement and a more peaceful life. He was introduced curtly but politely and was relieved when the general told him to sit next to Gerda at the table. He was not on trial for treasonable thought—not yet, anyway. He still had no idea why he had been recalled.

The general explained to him what had happened to alter the situation since he had left only four hours ago. Gerda had had no trouble in convincing them there could be no shadow of a doubt it was Conway she had seen here in Frauenstein. They knew all about his activities in Dresden and quickly decided it was a cover. A typist and two intelligence analysts would work all night trying to find the clues hidden in Greitz's tape. This was the third time the enigmatic Englishman had blundered into Gerda's life in the last two weeks. It could not mean anything but danger, for herself and for all the vital work in which she was involved for the party and the state. She insisted that positive action must be taken to liquidate Conway, and quickly; the next two weeks were critical to a particular operation of the greatest importance. She did not explain what the operation was, but the general's look at them made it clear he agreed, and there was no need for anyone to ask further questions. Heinrich just listened. He regarded himself merely as an observer in the discussion and wanly hoped they did as well.

Having set the scene, the general put down the silver pencil with which he had been continuously tapping the table and scratched his outsized hawk's-beak nose. The wide-spaced deep gray eyes were as bleak as the Prussian marshes where he had been bred. With no more emotion than he would exhibit in sending for his car, he pronounced sentence on Rupert Conway.

"Right. The question to be considered then is how."

There was a pregnant silence in the room. Heinrich lit a cigarette and tried to keep his eyes down on the table. He couldn't for long. He could feel Zweiboden's piercing stare going right through him. Heinrich remembered that as a young man he had once heard someone talk about Himmler's ruthless silences. He wondered if that was who Zweiboden had learned the trick from. He put his cigarette down and spoke very slowly.

"I understand the position, Herr General. Of course, if you wish my section to undertake the task, your orders will be obeyed." Better start with the declaration of loyalty and then try to work back. He looked encouragingly at Gerda, and what he saw in her ivory mask of a face assured him that their long-standing partnership was intact. "I would like to ask you to consider a very interesting suggestion that Frau Ruttgers put forward earlier today. There are . . . ah . . . very real political risks in taking action in Austria now." He knew Gerda would understand his position, even be flattered. The general shifted his glacial stare to Gerda, but not another muscle of his leathery face even flickered.

"As you have seen from the dossier, Herr General, Conway is well known in Vienna. He has good friends in the Polizei Praesidium. A watertight cover would be difficult. Since he has provided himself with reasons to come to Dresden," she paused only a second. "An accident?" she concluded.

"An accident?" Zweiboden repeated. "Yes, it could be arranged. We still need a cover, however. The man is a British citizen, I think?" He leafed over some of the papers in front of him. "Yes, he is. Now that we have diplomatic relations with the British, we must be a little more discreet. One can tell their politicians almost anything. The—what is it called?—the Helsinki agreement seems to have them hypnotized. But the ambassador in Berlin is no fool. . . ."

Gerda said, "But if the accident were to take place somewhere along the Polish border, General . . . The whole thing could become very complicated."

The idea appealed to Zweiboden. For the first time he actually smiled. He looked round at her with obvious approval. "Indeed. Very complicated. Very complicated." The two Department Thirteen men showed no appreciable interest. Such an exercise would be just routine for either of them. The general spoke again. "An accident. A motor car accident. Somewhere in the border area, east of Dresden. But I think, gentlemen, not a fatal accident."

The German colonel looked up from his notes.

"Not fatal, Herr General?" he said.

"Not at first, at any rate. We have decided that this man Conway should be . . . ah . . . disposed of. Frau Ruttgers has suggested a suitable method. I am sure Hauptmann Heinrich can devise a way of ensuring the compliance of the intended victim. The great problem is we still do not really know why."

He beat out another tattoo on the table with the silver

pencil. His eyes riveted Heinrich bolt upright in his chair. "Why, Hauptmann Heinrich? Why? Ridding Frau Ruttgers from the interference of this man in her important work is simply a matter of routine. The interests of the state seem to require it, so it shall be done. But we know so little about him." The pitch of the general's voice lowered; he spoke like an inquisitor, with exquisite, slow clarity. "Is he just some kind of officious busybody? Is he a romantic who has blundered into our path in his search for lost wartime art treasures? Or is he in fact an agent of one of the Western powers?"

Heinrich chose his words with more than usual care.

"There was no mention of any such possibility in the dossier sent me by the Soviet Kommandatura, Herr General."

The Russian colonel glared across the table at him, but the remark brought a look of positive pleasure to General Zweiboden's face, and some uncomradely thought died unborn in the Russian's throat. The days had passed when Russian colonels spoke to generals of satellite countries as though they were corporals.

For the first time Gerda looked nervous.

"How you dispose of him is not my business, Herr General. But I must stress again the importance of moving quickly. Our lack of knowledge about him only adds to the danger; we cannot guess where he is going to turn up next."

Rolf Heinrich thought to himself for the first time in years that Gerda was showing some sign of nervous tension. Her tone was impatient, and she failed to hide it.

"Of course, Frau Ruttgers." The general sounded almost gracious when he addressed her. "Hauptmann Heinrich, I am sure you understand Frau Ruttgers' point. You will continue to be in operational charge, under my direct control through Oberst Steinhoff. Your priorities are as follows." He gave a quick glance at his notes, ticking priorities off as he spoke. "One, you will take *all* measures possible to secure information about Conway and his activities—what is he really up to and why? Have him kept under constant surveillance; get listening devices into his home and his office; get into his files, his safe."

Heinrich's heart sank. There was no point in arguing. Zweiboden was like all the senior officers in the service who had spent their lives working in a dictatorship where they could do as they liked—if they wanted to search someone's house, they walked in and searched it. They had little experience of working in other people's countries and less patience with the difficulties. Like all the East German leaders, they were suffering the inevitable effects of nearly three decades of isolation. Their Russian masters attempted to train them, but as admission of Russian failures was unthinkable, there were great gaps left that only experience could fill. Officers of his generation were the guinea pigs—expendable.

"In particular," the general continued, "find out about this Hungarian woman who lives with him. Oberst Steinhoff will instruct our own Kommandatura to provide you with every facility you need." Cold comfort. He turned his flinty smile on the Russian. "I'm sure Oberst Koniev can arrange the same cooperation from his colleagues in Vienna?" He paused only long enough to register the Russian's unenthusiastic agreement by a note on the pad in front of him.

"Two, you will work with Oberst Steinhoff to plan the border accident operation; bear in mind, both of you, not a fatal accident until I personally order it.

"Three, you will also devise a contingency plan to dispose of Conway instantly in Austria, should any urgent reason require it. I am sure your charming Palestinian friends will oblige you."

Heinrich in all his career had never felt a more unwilling hero. "Jawohl, Herr General." He tried to make it sound convincing. "Just one further matter, sir. As you know, Palestinians don't work for love."

"You can call on Steinhoff for all the money you need."

"It isn't actually money they usually want, Herr General. More guns and bombs are their favourite currency."

The general indicated that would present no problem.

Instead of a pleasant dinner in Prague, Heinrich had had to content himself with a large cup of coffee and some cold bratwurst to fortify him for the drive back to Vienna. It rained nearly all the way. He reached the flat in the Brennerstrasse just as the sun was struggling up from the sodden Hungarian plain and had two hours' sleep before going out to the third-nearest phone box, where he learned with disgust that the terrorist leader, Javed al Husseini, had gone to Yugoslavia—his two henchmen did not know when he would return and would not commit themselves to anything in his absence.

The whole of Wednesday Heinrich spent in a series of frustrating phone calls, all from different phone boxes in different parts of town. Husseini would be back some time Thursday night. Heinrich's own embassy and the Russians had a mass of electronic gadgets to offer and the technicians to install them, but there seemed to be a shortage of skilled housebreakers. That was more in the terrorists' line. He put his own two men on immediate surveillance of 5B Stephansplatz and even managed to get them into Conway's car in the underground car park. They attached a radio listening device, but all they found of any interest were some dried-up bones stuffed down the sides of the back seat.

Neither Conway nor the woman left the building all Wednesday and Thursday. Nothing had been learned of any value by Friday morning, when Husseini finally returned and came to the flat in Brennerstrasse. They were still deep in argument when Heinrich's own men reported that Conway and the woman had gone away for the weekend.

Dealing with all these "liberation" organizations was never easy. Most of them genuinely wanted to please the Communist countries. Since some of their more recent blatantly pointless killings and increasing failures had turned the richer Arab leaders against them in disgust, the Soviet empire was their most reliable source of much needed supplies. Libya was more generous, both with arms and money, but the semi-crazed religious fanatic Colonel Qaddafi was totally unreliable. The Arabs also suffered from an incurable passion for feuding among themselves; you could not be certain from week to week just who was cooperating with whom. Husseini was a highly trained and completely ruthless killer of men, women, or children, but he was an uncomfortable accomplice. Whatever it was he had been discussing in Belgrade seemed to have made him more than usually nervous and difficult to deal with. The Warsaw Pact countries were now acting on the general assumption that, since Tito had become increasingly friendly with President Sadat of Egypt, and since Sadat and Qaddafi of Libya were once again calling each other fascist hyenas and blood-crazed murderers, the Palestinians were drawing closer to the Croatian nationalists, who wanted to oust Tito. That may have suited Moscow fine, but it made things vastly more complicated and hazardous for Heinrich in Vienna.

He spent four hours in his dull, cheerless little flat contending with the highly neurotic Husseini. He stressed the urgency of his problem, the need to get some really hard information as fast as possible about the English Jewish art dealer and what he was up to. Heinrich's careful training in interrogation techniques soon convinced him that he was wasting his time in stressing Conway's Jewishness—like all the P.L.O.'s gunmen, and women, Husseini's hatred for his fellow humans was completely indiscriminate. Good Communists were trained to kill when it was necessary for the good of the state. It was as impersonal as the autos-da-fé of the sixteenth-century Inquisition. This new race of terrorists, so carefully trained in the refugee camps of Lebanon and Gaza for twenty-five years under the nose of the United Nations, had been first taught to hate with an intensity that repelled even so worldly a professional as Heinrich. It took great patience to keep the terrorist leader concentrating on details. Conway's flat and gallery must be meticulously reconnoitered; a means of getting a technician into his office must be discovered, and private papers must be photographed; details of the burglar alarm system must be investigated in order to deactivate it. As the inmates of number 5B had obligingly removed themselves for the weekend, it was decided no time must be lost in commencing detailed examination of the property.

After agreeing on a price that horrified his own modest standards in these matters—but which he judged would meet with General Zweiboden's approval—and agreeing to supply more arms and ammunition for Husseini's own purposes, they made a deal. The three Palestinians would devote their weekend to the problem in hand, starting now.

Two days away from the office in the busy period just before Easter was quite enough to cause a work accumulation that made Rupert's office look like a senate committee room at the end of a particularly juicy vice investigation. There was not a level surface in the room uncluttered with paper. The gallery itself was full of potential customers talking in seven different languages. The wife of an obscure Middle Eastern delegate to OPEC had made an offer for the five items of the ikon collection which were on display; she was quite happy to pay the full amount across the counter in American Express travellers checks, but Max's aesthetic soul rebelled at the thought of letting these beautiful treasures, created and preserved for centuries to the greater glory of his God, fall into the hands of such an infidel.

He kept grumbling about tents and camels and sand—*"Zelte und Kamele und Sand"*—and made it sound like a litany of doom. Furthermore, he knew Rupert wanted to sell the collection as a whole. He refused to authorize the deal and left the matter on Rupert's desk. The total sum involved was eighty thousand dollars. David Hughes' London customer—Rupert never could get David to say client—had backed out of the deal for the de Heems, and David wanted instructions. The City of Chicago tax department had written to say that their computer had made a mistake in calculating the tax rate for the new gallery on Michigan Avenue and they were now demanding more than double what had been budgeted for. What else was new?

Sandra and Max were both on the gallery floor from morning until night; Frau Hauptmann was down with the flu. Even Heinz Burgmann's Tyrolean stoicism was showing the strain as he vainly tried to placate the invasion of elderly ladies with rebellious husbands, Americans, Germans, Italians, and Arabs who wanted to see someone who could sell them something—and had then changed their minds by the time Sandra or Max could get round to dealing with them. Rupert's desk was piled high with letters and valuations. Seven important auction catalogues remained unopened, and Mini was quietly getting hysterical at the phone exchange, talking French to Germans, German to Italians, and trying to understand the English of an irate gentleman calling from Belgrade about something of enormous importance to him but totally unintelligible to her.

There was nothing they could do about Max's book now but patiently await the summons from the East German commercial representative's office to come and collect the first batch of prints—after, no doubt, that gentleman had spent two or three days examining them himself to be quite sure they contained no vital state secrets—as if he could tell! It was a big risk going straight to a finished print without studying proof copy first, but they were hard pressed for time. If they missed the deadline with the English binder, who had no great reputation for meeting delivery dates himself, the whole project might be delayed a year. Max was an old man, and Rupert was prepared to run a lot of risks not to disappoint him. They had good reason to trust the Tautzes. He just had to take the chance. There was no news of Schwarz or Ruttgers, nothing from Captain Gottfried in Munich. For the moment the pink elephant saga seemed to have come to a dead end. Late Friday afternoon Rupert and Sandra, with great sighs of relief, sped away for a quiet weekend at Semmering.

The gallery and the apartment in Stephansplatz were exclusively Rupert's own creation. From the day he first leased nine barren, war-battered rooms from the church, only a week before Alexie died in childbirth in a still war-damaged Vienna hospital, he alone had been responsible for turning them into what was now one of the most sophisticated and elegant bachelor's establishments in town. But like all those with a strong background of British blood and education, his sense of achievement was grounded in a broader, insatiable longing for historical association, for visible reminders of family continuity, especially with those he had known and loved. As a boy it was at Semmering, at the hunting lodge, that he had spent many of his happiest hours. His elder brother had gone off to boarding school in England six years before he did. They had always been intimate friends and confidants; Rupert had wept openly in front of his own troops when he received the news that George had been killed while serving with the British 8th Army in North Africa. Being Welshmen, they understood. The effect of those formative years, however, had settled the pattern of his life. As their solemn, conscientious father progressed in rank from one British embassy to another, always preoccupied with an unending series of insoluble crises, immersed in the minutiae of despatches, conferences, and hush-hush negotiations, Rupert's inborn love of beauty developed under the tutelage of his gifted Austrian mother. Through the five European capitals and Washington where the Conways were successively stationed, mother and son combed art galleries, museums, dealers, and libraries to discover their most profound secrets. From these early years sprang his encyclopedic knowledge and impeccable taste. Discovered in museums and art galleries, it was nurtured during every moment they could escape from the diplomatic treadmill to stay with his beloved grandparents in the blissful peace and volume-rich library at Semmering.

Rupert's passion at the hunting lodge had been not creation, but restoration. It had taken seven years to prove his title to the property and gain possession of it from the Restitution authorities. Its previous owner had suffered the fate of all prominent Austrian Jews who fell into the hands of the Gestapo; the place was in poor shape when Rupert started on it. Now its every room and aspect spoke to him of those who had created him;

he had too much humility ever to be smug, he was always grateful. Sandra had never known either their grandparents or this house, but as her relationship to them was a shared one, Rupert also shared the lodge with her, in a way that felt quite different to both of them from the relationship they shared at 5B Stephansplatz. The house was not big, but rambling, comfortable, old-fashioned, surrounded by pine trees and roses. It was from here that Rupert's rich, middle-class, brilliant Jewish grandfather had been carried off by the Nazis, never to be heard from again. And it was from here that his beautiful, aristocratic Hungarian grandmother had finally escaped over the Kamniske Alps soon to die from exhaustion and exposure as Hitler's armies drove the partisans higher and higher into the frozen mountains. There were many houses like this in Lower Austria and Steiermark. This was the only one with both a mezuzah and a crucifix at the front door.

They had a guest for the weekend. Her name was Susie Carlson, from Des Moines. Neither of them had ever actually met Susie, but her eldest sister had been Sandra's roommate at college; and Susie, now a stewardess on Pan American, had telegraphed from New York that she was due for a two-day stopover in Vienna and would just love to visit them. A friend from Pan Am delivered her to the hunting lodge soon after Sandra and Rupert arrived, and as Susie, suffering from jet lag, was as exhausted as they were, they all ate a quick snack in the kitchen, washed it down with a bottle of Kremser Schmidt, and went straight to bed. Even having been up for seventeen hours with a five-hour time change, Susie bubbled like a soda siphon, overflowing with bonhommie and zest for a great big beautiful world occupied apparently exclusively by beautiful people doing beautiful things. Sandra liked her but thought she was bound to prove a bit tiring over a two-day stretch. Rupert noted that she was pert and pretty in the best American college-girl style and, without being obnoxiously women's-libbish, did not suffer from any noticeable inhibitions. He decided that a rest from intellectual pursuits would be just what any sensible doctor would order for a man in his condition, and determined to enjoy himself.

Over a rustic lunch the next day, Rupert suggested that they should arrange some entertainment for their visitor to enliven the weekend a bit. There was an accomplished jazz quartet in residence every Saturday night at a nearby hostelry called the Kaiserhof. The food was agreeable, the wine good, and Susie volunteered that she just loved dancing. Sandra thought it would be more fun for Susie if they could find some attractive, younger man to be her escort, but neither Rupert nor Susie showed any enthusiasm for the idea. After lunch he phoned his friends and neighbours, Manfred and Liësl Foglar, who said they had no commitments that evening and would love to join them for dinner at the Kaiserhof. Manfred was a sub-editor on *Die Presse,* Liësl one of Vienna's top dress designers, and they were both amusing company.

The evening went with a gentle swing. Susie was entranced by Rupert's gray alpen coat with green velvet collar and cuffs. When the *Schmankerlcremebomb* was succeeded by coffee, Rupert succumbed, without noticeable resistance, to an invitation to sit in with the band, all of whom were old friends. Ten years ago a girl of Susie's years might have regarded his Fats Waller style at the piano as hopelessly dated, but taste among the young for music as opposed to sheer noise was once again becoming fashionable. Fastidious in the visual arts, Rupert was an "all-brow" in music. His great expertise and delight was in Mozart, but after that he was happily at home and blissfully amateurish with everyone from Wagner to Dizzy Gillespie. His keyboard technique might not have passed examination at the Royal School or at Juilliard, but then his object was not the concert hall but having fun. It was fine by the management and the musicians at the Kaiserhof. Susie was impressed; she told Liësl Foglar, "he's really sexy."

After coffee everyone settled down to soft smoochy dance music. Twenty-four hours of solid relaxation had restored a lot of energies; Rupert's cares were in another world. The *gemütlich* romance of the Styrian mountains and rather more than her usual intake of delicious wine combined to induce in Susie's eager young heart a mood which she informed Rupert made her "really relate" to him. The boys in the quartet knew exactly what the atmosphere required; they played nostalgic numbers like "Lara's Theme" from *Dr. Zhivago,* "J'attendrai," "Sorrento," and "Stardust." Rupert was delighted to find that Susie preferred the old-fashioned style of dancing he had been brought up on—none of this "you go that way and I'll go this way" nonsense. She cuddled right in close and planted her peach blossom cheek firmly against his. They danced for fifteen minutes like this in a tender little dream world of their own, joyously oblivious to everything around them. By the time Susie was firmly deposited on Cloud Nine, and Rupert's bad leg gave him his first reminder that he was old enough to be her father, a waiter interrupted them. The Herr Doktor was wanted urgently on the telephone. Susie could have shot him.

When he came back to their table, the band had switched to a livelier pace. They sat sipping brandy and soda, the conversation started to become a little sleepy; when Rupert suggested it might be time to go home, Susie was enthusiastic.

They all left the Kaiserhof happy with themselves and

the world in general. Susie admired with a tingling expectancy the worldly yet affectionate way that Rupert kissed Liësl Foglar good night. She made sure she got in the front seat beside him before Sandra could reach the door. Even the high-powered English sports car was a new experience for her.

When they got back to the hunting lodge, she purred as she watched Rupert throw more logs on the glowing embers in the big stone fireplace. He switched on two large china-and-ormolu table lamps, which gave the lounge exactly the right degree of sympathetic illumination. Susie langourously draped herself in a big brown leather armchair while Rupert selected an album of private recordings by his good friend Kurt Meyer playing the dreamiest of Strauss waltzes. He suggested a nightcap. Susie happily accepted another brandy and soda. She glowed when Sandra, yawning, said she was tired, refused the proffered drink and announced she would go straight upstairs to bed. Politeness required Rupert to demur just a little, but Susie was sure his heart wasn't in it. Sandra said good night, climbed the broad open staircase to the balcony that led to the bedroom wing, and Susie's romantic imagination was already running well ahead of events. Rupert helped himself to a whiskey and soda, toyed with a pipe, and changed his mind. He stood for a moment silhouetted by the glowing log fire, looking very masculine and dominating. Susie gazed at him with expectant ecstasy and started to consider the delicate problem of whether he was coming to her or expected her to go to him. Before she could reach a decision, the doorbell rang.

Momentarily embarrassed, Rupert put down his glass, mumbled an apology, looked at his watch. He couldn't admit he had been expecting a visitor—there was nothing he could do but go to the door. He went out into the wood-panelled, stone-floored hall, which bristled with examples of the fine marksmanship of his grandfather. Through her idyllic haze, Susie heard another man's voice, the exchange of muffled greetings. Rupert came back and introduced the Herr Oberstpolizeirat Liebmann, who had called at this unexpectedly late hour on some private but apparently urgent mission. Josef Liebmann was full of apologies, but he accepted a whiskey soda without hesitation. Rupert somewhat stumblingly explained Susie's presence to the new guest and reluctantly, so she thought, sought her understanding and forgiveness while he and his visitor retired to the library—just for a few minutes—to deal with the purpose of this intrusion. He topped up her glass a trifle heavily and left her smiling encouragingly by the fire with the promise of his quick return.

The two men went into the massive book-lined room and closed the door. Susie picked up a copy of *The New Yorker*, savoured her third brandy, and settled down contentedly to wait.

"My dear Rupert," Liebmann protested. "I am sorry. I had no idea you were . . . ah . . . engaged. What a charming girl."

"Friend of Sandra's," Rupert murmured.

"Of course, my dear fellow . . . but . . . I would have waited until the morning, only you were so positive on the telephone, and . . . ah . . . it is urgent."

Rupert just smiled and indicated a comfortable chair. The police councillor lowered his enormous bulk into it with care.

Jo Liebmann, too, was a devout pipe smoker, and, like all of the genuine breed, a man of deliberate if not ponderous action. He specialized in meerschaums, which required extra care. He got the tobacco burning to his satisfaction, sipped his whiskey soda, and then said, "You have heard no news this evening, Rupert?"

"No. I try to avoid it on weekends if at all possible, Jo. The day has been complete bliss—until you arrived." He said it with a grimace, making clear the remark was facetious and not personal. Jo understood and smiled knowingly.

"You are not aware then that there has been a nasty shooting incident in Vienna this evening?"

If Rupert felt any emotion, he did not show it. He just dropped a quiet "No," into his smoke clouds.

"One of our men was killed. There appear to have been three criminals involved. We are still searching for two of them. One was wounded and captured. It was my weekend off, but Karl Reidinger ordered an alert just after noon. Werner kindly said he would call if he needed me. I was dining with friends near here when he phoned." Werner was Jo's boss.

Rupert often thought that Jo Liebmann must have written the most precise, accurate reports any policeman ever turned in. Every sentence was staccato and terse, as neatly trimmed as his graying military moustache.

"It was one of two men on the ground they caught. He was an Arab. The officer who seized him first was shot by a high-powered rifle fired from the roof."

"A well-aimed shot," Rupert remarked.

"A very well-aimed shot, as you say." He paused, then said, "It was fired from your roof."

"Was it? By George!"

"It would appear they were reconnoitering the rooftops and courtyard at the back of your flat. As you are well aware, no one else lives in the building; nor would one expect thieves to be interested in the minor clerical departments of the cardinal's staff—especially Arab thieves."

For once Rupert's well-practiced calm deserted him. He was shaken and didn't try to hide it.

"I find it difficult to fault your logic, my friend." He was glad he had a stiff scotch in his hand. He needed it, as the impact of this news began to sink in. He had proved he knew how to handle danger, that he was a brave man and a tough one. But that was all a long time ago. At age fifty-seven, even so enterprising an art dealer as he was had grown unaccustomed to having people shot from his own roof. He addressed Liebmann again:

"Arabs, my God! Have you any idea who they were?"

"At the moment, none. However, the area was rapidly surrounded; with luck they should get at least the man on the roof. Two officers saw him fire the shot, and they believe they wounded him. We will have the ballistics report by morning, for what it may be worth. What, if anything, the prisoner will tell us remains to be seen."

"You seem to have had a lot of policemen around town tonight."

"Everyone available. There was a good reason." He made no attempt to explain further.

Rupert said, "Had they tried to break in?"

"We don't know yet. You have burglar alarms, I remember?"

"Yes, indeed. The alarm did not go off?"

"No. It seems likely that they were interrupted before they had time to attempt an entry."

"There is plenty of valuable property in my gallery," Rupert said almost hopefully. His hopes were immediately dashed.

"Of course. Just the kind of things to attract our local petty criminals. But there are no gangs operating in Vienna at present. The prisoner is an Arab and was carrying a Schmauser with a silencer. One of his confederates killed a man with one shot at forty meters. These men are professionals; they would have known your valuable pictures were well guarded. They are concerned with something more important to them than stealing pictures, of that you may be sure."

"Like what, for instance?"

Instead of answering the question directly Liebmann asked, "Why should Arab terrorists be interested in you, Rupert?"

Calmly but seriously he replied, "I'm partly Jewish, as you know."

"So are half the people in Vienna. Palestinian terrorists have tried attacking prominent Jews in Paris and London, but, ah . . ."

"Of course. I'm pretty small beer compared to Teddie Sieff and Gui de Rothschild. You think they were after me?"

"It is certainly a possibility we must consider. We could judge its value better if we could guess why such a thing should happen."

Rupert was thoughtful, frankly worried. He liked excitement, but he had not been shot at since Monte Cassino and had no desire to be a target again. He pondered the problem for a moment and said, "I really can't think how I could be involved with Arabs—except as clients, of course. We get quite a number these days, but that is all straightforward business." He got up and paced the room for a minute. "Just one thought crosses my mind. . . ."

"That is?"

"You remember when we were talking to Claud Lebel on the phone the other day. He mentioned something about Arab diplomats and refugees from East Germany being connected with pictures. They interest me very much. For your very private ear, I did make some inquiries along those lines in Dresden last Tuesday." There was a pause while he slowly crossed the room and back to face Liebmann. "It seems a long shot, Jo."

Liebmann said, "So was that of the man on the roof. I

should not tell you, but cooperation between some Communist countries and Middle East terrorists is not unknown to my department."

Rupert considered for a moment. "What do you suggest I do?"

"Can you not stay here for a few days?"

"Quite impossible. This is one of our busiest seasons. I can't take days off to play hide-and-seek now, of all times."

"No, I see. Well, please stay here until Monday morning, at any rate. We'll have the house watched. My colleagues in Vienna think you are in some real danger. I'll radio my report and return to town first thing in the morning. Give us a little time, Rupert. We can put your apartment under twenty-four-hour surveillance. The captured one may tell us something. With luck we may catch the murderer. I'll phone you tomorrow as soon as I have anything to tell you. But please, stay here until Monday morning at least." He emptied his glass and stood up.

Rupert suddenly remembered the amorous Susie in the next room. He lowered his voice to a whisper, said "Just one moment," and silently opened the door a few inches.

Susie was just where he had left her—fast asleep.

The two men tiptoed quietly across the lounge into the hall and Liebmann disappeared into the night. Rupert locked the big front door without even a click sounding, and stood there for a full minute listening to the police car wind its way carefully down the steep sloping driveway in the pitch darkness. With the soft streak of light shining through the open lounge door, the array of heads on the wall cast eerie shadows across the black pine panelling—the deer, elk, and wolves' heads looked like savage medieval gargoyles. The trophies of a skilled hunter, he thought to himself. Like the man on the roof? Who was he?

He moved silently across the thick Afghan carpet. Susie slumbered peacefully on, *The New Yorker* fallen to the floor, her slightly pouting, smiling pretty face reflecting what were clearly happy dreams. He carefully switched off the lamp nearest to her. The only sign of consciousness was a gentle, contented sigh. Her silky blonde hair was tousled, her skirt slightly askew, revealing a charming patch of well-shaped thigh.

Rupert sighed, and took the stairs, slowly; his right leg ached a little. At the top he turned to survey the enticing and unaccustomed picture of his favourite fireside chair. He went quietly back down the stair again, picked up a camel hair rug, laid it with a fatherly gentleness over the sleeping beauty, and went upstairs to bed.

11

ALTHOUGH Sunday dawned warm and sunny and the Prater was full of pretty girls airing their new season's outfits, Rolf Heinrich spent a miserable day. He had slept fitfully with an ear always alert for a phone call that he hoped would report some progress from Husseini so they could proceed with entering 5B Stephansplatz. The phone call he did receive at just after seven summoning him to an emergency meeting at the embassy Kommandatura was a disaster signal. At the meeting he discovered that the whole of the Palestinians' operation had gone wrong—and why it went wrong. He had had no knowledge, and though the Russian officer present refused to admit it, it was clear neither had he, that the whole Austrian police service had been put on the alert early Saturday afternoon. The guards on all foreign embassies, ministries, the president, and the chancellor were heavily reinforced; all the Vienna police and Department I's best marksmen were patrolling the central area of the city.

It was now known that sometime Saturday morning Interpol had informed Police President Reidinger that the notorious Carlos might be arriving any moment in the Austrian capital, and Minister of the Interior Dr. Rosch had ordered the whole state security machine into high gear at once. Before the 21st of December last, the Russians and the Palestinians would have had advance notice of any such movement, but since the notorious OPEC fiasco, this hired killer's Libyan paymasters had been ostracized by the other Arab countries. By a strange chance, it had been the Vienna police who first spotted the odd fact that the Libyan ambassador, Ali Mohammed Al Ghadansi, was the only OPEC member who had managed to avoid the kidnapping of the oil country ministers. He had left the meeting and flown to Prague on unexpected and unexplained private business just one hour before Carlos and his hired thugs had entered the conference room firing in all directions, killing two men, an Iraqi and, oddly enough, a Libyan.

Now Heinrich learned that the fully alerted Vienna police had disturbed his Palestinian hirelings in their reconnaissance of Conway's apartment, as a result of which one of them had been captured, one was on the run somewhere, and Husseini was lying badly wounded in the attic hideaway of a Czech agent while every street was being heavily patrolled. None of them as yet knew how much Husseini had told his henchmen, nor whether the man captured was likely to talk or not. One thing was quite clear to the men around the table: now any chance of getting at Conway and his secrets here in Vienna was nil. They could only inform General Zweiboden accordingly. Whether that great man would accept their judgment no one could guess.

Heinrich left the meeting knowing he would be blamed for the failure. His colleague in charge at the Kommandatura had smilingly repeated his assurance of full cooperation, but never missed a chance to emphasize that he was in no way involved in the responsibility. Heinrich had not wanted to stay at the embassy one minute longer than necessary, and he certainly did not want to go back and brood in the gloomy loneliness of his dreary little flat in Brennerstrasse. He took a tram across the Danube Canal and walked. It tired him in the end and did nothing to calm his thoughts. Neither he nor his superiors had much experience in dealing with this kind of situation. From the earliest days of the German Democratic Republic the Volkspolizei had been almost entirely an internal service—external intelligence and espionage had been left to the Russians. His service was well trained in strong-arm methods, but these could seldom be used when operating in other people's countries where such practices were frowned on.

Heinrich's brooding eyes were blind to the enticement of two pretty girls obviously looking for business outside the Praterstern; he boarded the suburban train, got off at Am Spitz and walked back to the uncomfortable and lonely austerity of his apartment in Brennerstrasse. He was a worried man.

Rupert had taken a Soneril and slept through mass, which he had not intended to do. Officially an Anglican and a supporter of the Evangelische Kirche on Dorotheergasse, he was a dedicated ecumenical. If there had been a synagogue near Semmering he would have gone to it.

He had decided not to say anything that might alarm Sandra—her childhood memories of terror were too vivid, and he was determined not to allow anything to revive them if he could help it. He was able to fob her off with a reasonable explanation of Jo Liebmann's unexpected visit, and the exuberant Susie, giving no hint of having suffered grievous disappointment, was a big help. She kept up a running fire of repartee and questions until her friend from Pan Am came to pick her up after lunch. Rupert's farewell kiss had nothing fatherly about it and her parting words as the car drove off were, "Gee, what I missed!"

Sandra fell happily in with his suggestion that they stay overnight and motor back to work after an early breakfast Monday morning, and by good luck Liebmann's call came through while she was out walking Charlie, so he did not have to explain that at all. Not that the police councillor had much to tell. The captured Arab spoke little German, and the official Arabic interpreter had been able to get nothing of any value out of him beyond the not very helpful fact that he had recently arrived from Lebanon by way of Cyprus. It might take days to wear him down, and the Austrian police did not go in for rough stuff. The search was still going on. The whole area was closely guarded, but neither of the other two fugitives had been caught in the net yet. The rifle, a new Czech model with a telescopic sight, had been found lying abandoned in some old guttering behind a blocked-up chimney, three houses down Schulerstrasse. It was covered with fingerprints and blood, which confirmed that its owner had been hit; all the data was being fed into the Interpol computer in Paris. An Israeli agent in Damascus had informed Tel Aviv, who told Paris, that Carlos had arrived there. All in all, everything seemed to have calmed down in Vienna, but they would maintain full surveillance of number 5B and would Rupert please keep them informed of all proposed movements. He assured Jo he would be glad to.

Monday morning was reasonably quiet in the office. The most difficult immediate problem confronting Rupert was deciding how to deal with the now irate Middle Eastern lady, who was offering cash for the five ikons he had chosen to exhibit. Fortunately this time she brought her husband, who spoke passable French. Rupert had not given her a moment's thought since last Thursday, but he was in no mood for offending any Arab. His keen commercial instinct combined with professional charm to produce a ready explanation: he was terribly sorry there seemed to be some misunderstanding between madame and his elderly colleague, caused very naturally by the language barrier. Of course madame was very welcome to buy the ikons, but, ah, there had been a small misunderstanding about the price as well. There followed a somewhat violent scene between the diplomat and his wife, which caused quite a stir throughout the gallery. Nobody else present could understand a word of the altercation, but Rupert's stolid, smiling patience at length paid off. The irate lady quieted down. Her husband had apparently surrendered to her ultimatum, the effect of which turned out to be that she wanted the ikons and didn't care how many damn oil wells it took to pay for them. Rupert asked the man to tell madame that in his opinion they would look beautiful in her palace. That sealed it, and the Arab started signing American Express checks in ten-thousand-dollar denominations.

Another good deal, another satisfied customer. Palace or tent, it was no business of Rupert's. No one but he knew exactly how many there had been in the collection originally, and he had been amply remunerated for any drop in overall value by the subtraction of these five. He was also relieved that no one but he appeared to notice any unusual activity in front of the shop—the Arab's terrified Austrian chauffeur was almost submerged in a group of large, hatless men in brown raincoats, all with their hands bulging ominously from their coat pockets. They disappeared into the walls, the concrete, and the cathedral as Rupert ceremoniously escorted his clients to the door and wished them a smiling goodby. He walked quickly back to his office and said to Charlie, "Comforting, that." He lit a pipe with a sigh of satisfaction and turned to ponder the thorny problem of taxes in Chicago. The art business was getting too complicated. Oh, for the simple days! No, he could not convince himself he wasn't enjoying every minute of it.

It was just after lunch that Police Captain Gottfried called from Munich. They exchanged the usual greetings, then Gottfried said, "Sorry I couldn't get through before, Herr Conway. We did a careful check on the Ruttgers woman. Not so positive as we had hoped."

"Anything useful?" Rupert asked.

"What little we have confirms her alibi. We put a bug on her car when she crossed the frontier. Clever little gadget—you can get an electronic reading off a copper wire that gives you the distance travelled and changes in direction. It worked perfectly for the first three hundred and twenty kilometers, which gives us an exact trace of a journey to Karl-Marx-Stadt and a turnoff to the north. After that, the distance reading indicates she stopped somewhere west of Dresden—can't guess where. Depends on how far north she drove. Then she came straight back again. The distance proves that. Must have gone over a bad bump shortly after leaving the Autobahn and dislodged one of the activators in the directional circuit."

"West of Dresden, eh? Funny. When was this?"

"She crossed on Tuesday. Came back Wednesday night."

"That's a coincidence. I was in Dresden last Tuesday."

"Did the Ruttgers know you were going?"

"No. At least I don't think so. I've certainly had no more contact with them since the last time we talked."

"She certainly did not go to Dresden. The distance reading is conclusive of that. She stopped somewhere this side of it—presumably northwest—and came back again. Do you plan to return to Dresden soon?"

"I hope not, but I may have to. We have an important printing job being done there by Altenburg's."

"I would suggest you let us know if you do go again. There are a lot of funny things going on across the border just now."

"Any trouble with Arabs?"

Gottfried made a sound somewhere between a cough and a laugh.

"Jo Liebmann told you about the alert on Saturday?"

"He did indeed," Rupert said with feeling.

"Ja. I know. We had it, too. Our net got two crazy Irishmen, a Polish nun, and a protest from the Yugoslav consul."

"Getting back to Frau Ruttgers. Did she bring anything back with her?"

"No. We had her under observation all the way from the frontier until she got out of her car in a downtown car park. It was thoroughly searched. Nothing at all," Gottfried paused, then added "—this time."

"Ah. I think I understand you."

"Sorry I can't say more on an open line. But we are grateful to you for bringing your local friend's name to our attention."

"Interesting. Any light on my problem?"

"No. The matters which have come to our attention go entirely in a different direction. The gentleman has strange business in Tangier."

"How we get around!"

"One of my men has to go to Vienna tomorrow—Heinzmann. I'll have him drop in on you. It's time we compared notes again."

Rupert went to the compartment in the mahogany bookcase where he kept maps and dug out Kummery and Frey's one-to-a-million-scale map of central Europe. He had much larger-scale maps of most countries in the world, but that was the only one the Communist countries would allow out. It gave a reasonable picture over a large area but told you little about small villages and country roads. North of Karl-Marx-Stadt and west of Dresden? Where the hell was she going? That was quite the wrong direction for Frauenstein. It was fifty miles south of this area. He frowned at the names: Rosswein, Waldheim, Hainichen, Hartha, Leisnig. Meissen, maybe? China was not in the Ruttgers' range. He spotted a town called Dobeln. Maybe she was meeting Irish art smugglers there. Silly idea. So near and yet so far. He was still bewitched with the problem of Gerda's mother, who had now taken shape in his mind as a little white-haired old lady, satins and lace, running a brothel for senior officers of the Volkspolizei.

That supposition was promptly exploded by a communication that arrived first thing Tuesday morning in the shape of a phone call from the East German commercial representative. The parcel from Altenburg's had arrived and could be picked up at 6 Frimbergerstrasse any time convenient to the Herr Doktor. Rupert sent Heinz round in the office Rabbit at once. Pity Max was out all day—he had had to drive Pauli to Graz to visit her sister who was in the terminal stages of cancer and had had a bad relapse over the weekend. Thank heaven Martita Hauptmann's flu was better so that she could help Sandra out on the gallery floor. This was Easter week and Vienna was packed with tourists, mainly West Germans and Americans; there were plenty of big spenders among them. Rupert was never one to complain about being too busy. The sight of all that lovely money rolling in gave him great pleasure, why not be frank about it?

Heinz got back at half past ten with the elaborately wrapped parcel, and Rupert locked himself into the office, giving his harassed colleagues the unwelcome order that he could not be disturbed for any reason at all for at least half an hour. That specifically included Mini at the phone exchange.

He carefully cleared his desk, switched on the blue daylight lamp, and drew the curtains, partly to be sure to get an even degree of light on the precious sheets. It required nearly five minutes to unfold carefully the successive layers of wrapping—first thin sheets of plywood, then heavy brown paper, then a carefully sealed film of moisture-proof polyethylene, more brown paper, and finally nearly a dozen folds of fine white tissue paper. There were more layers of the tissue paper between every sheet. Rupert lifted the first one out with something amounting to reverence. These were the eternal monuments to Max's life's work he was handling.

What he found himself looking at lived up to all his hopes. The sheet was forty-five centimeters long and nearly thirty high. The quality of the paper was, if possible, finer than the sample he had approved. It had been made in Lithuania and was at least as good as anything made in the West. Johannes's confidence in the excellent properties of its surface, the definition of his inks, and the skill of old Hans Wlaka had been thoroughly justified. The gamble on timing had paid off. By going straight to prints, they had probably saved three vital weeks. It had been worth the anxiety.

Rupert was sure even Max would be pleased with these. The delicate, almost pastel shades of red and ochre and brown in their fine sweeping strokes were perfectly delineated. Not only was every hair of the emperor's beard—or whoever he was—distinct and realistic, but the printed work seemed to show up the grain in the basalt itself even more clearly than the original photographs over which Max had expended months of painstaking care and anxiety. Yes, the old boy would be pleased.

With just a touch of dread Rupert moved his eyes to the printing underneath. Not a single mistake! He phoned the commercial representative immediately and asked him to signal Altenburg's to please proceed with the rest of the work with all possible speed. Then he sent Heinz round with the same message in writing, to make doubly sure.

Rupert felt he had done his duty now and skimmed through the remaining sheets with a speed that would have horrified Max. Each sheet looked at first glance as good as the top one, and right now he was prepared to gamble they all were. He got to the bottom layer and looked at the emptiness he found there with disappointment. He removed two more sheets of the thin white tissue paper and found it—a long, very formal and stilted letter from Wilhelm Tautz, typed on a very old-fashioned German typewriter, that was hard to read. It was fulsomely courteous and went into great technical detail about the difficulties of the work and Tautz's "respectful anxieties" that they would find no evidence that perfect accuracy had been sacrificed in the quest for much speed. There was a lengthy paragraph about the skill of the workers of the German Democratic Republic, and an even longer one about the great achievements of Herr Kamerad Greitz in ensuring rapid delivery. Wrote that with tongue in cheek, Rupert was quite sure. It ended with a brief expression of esteem, respect, and very formal personal hopes for the success of the book with which Altenburg's was proud to have associated the peace-loving peoples of the GDR. "Johannes sends his respects, too, as so does my wife. My wife is deeply regretful to say that the friend you inquired after died many years ago."

So Gerda had no mother—at Frauenstein or anywhere else. Another lead that ran slap into a brick wall. Or had it? It proved beyond all doubt that she was an accomplished liar. So what? Let's analyze this very carefully, step by step—use the standard formula for such a process. Rupert methodically cleared the desk, turned the daylight lamp off, and drew the curtains back. Selecting a tried and trusty old pipe, he seated himself in the big brown, velvet-covered chair and turned it to his favourite angle for contemplating St. Stephan's towering spire.

Now to think this thing through. Gerda crosses into East Germany approximately once every month. To do that she must have a visa from the GDR government. Visas are issued by the Foreign Department, only after careful vetting by the police. For "many years" she has been giving them a false reason for these visits. It is inconceivable that they don't know it is a false reason. Since they must know it and still continue to issue the visas—well, they don't do it by mistake, that's for sure. So, whatever "it" is, someone in authority in the GDR is in on the deal. Must be someone with quite a lot of authority. What deal? What was it Gottfried had said—the Bavarian police were on to something they clearly found suspicious, and that trail led to Tangier. Why Tangier? Convenient staging post for anywhere in South America? That could add up. They are smuggling works of art out of the Communist countries, somehow getting them to Tangier, and then selling them in South America at fantastic profits, of which some high German official gets a cut? Yes? Possibly, but not quite enough. What about the new-found jewelry and Byzantine stuff? What about Fabergé? Perhaps that is just coincidence, a temporary diversion from their main trade. Possible? Of course, but not very convincing.

12

RUPERT had reached this rather unsatisfactory checkpoint in sifting the permutations when the buzzer went. He glanced at the ormolu clock on the mantelpiece. His half hour was more than up.

"Yes, Mini?"

"Gentleman here to see you, Herr Doktor. Says he is sure you want to see him, but would rather not give his name."

Rupert thought for a moment. That would be Captain Gottfried's colleague from Munich, he guessed. What name did he say? Heinzmann.

"Please have Heinz show him in, Mini. Oh, and, Mini, no more calls please until I tell you."

"Jawohl, Herr Doktor."

A minute later Heinz showed the visitor in; they exchanged formal greetings and Rupert asked him to sit down. The man said nothing beyond "Gruss Gott" until after Heinz had left and shut the door. He looked around the room a little nervously. Rupert offered a cigarette, which he took and acknowledged with a slight bow of the head. As he lit it, Rupert examined the stranger carefully —about fifty, neatly but rather poorly dressed in a nondescript gray suit, red and white striped shirt, and a somewhat threadbare tie. He had sharp features and restless eyes. He looked like a policeman, detective fairly junior grade, probably. He said, "Thank you for seeing me, Herr Conway. My name is Karl Henesch."

Rupert was sure Gottfried had said Heinzmann.

"Would you spell it, please?"

"H-e-n-e-s-c-h," the man said quite distinctly, though he clearly found English difficult, and said his *e*'s like *a*'s. "Forgive me, I do not speak very much English."

"No problem," Rupert replied. "Let's talk in German then."

The man relaxed a little. They continued in German.

"You will probably think my visit very strange."

"There are plenty of strange people in the art business," Rupert reassured him, and the visitor smiled. "What can I do for you?"

"I had better explain first—who I am and why I come."

"Please do."

"You may find what I am going to say somewhat surprising. But I can prove everything to you."

This was intriguing. Probably had a stolen picture he wanted to sell—discreetly. It happened to any well-known dealer from time to time. Nevertheless, Rupert was being more than usually cautious after the weekend's excitement. The man certainly was not an Arab, thank heaven. There was no obvious threatening bulge showing anywhere. But just to be on the safe side, he fingered the alarm button under the center drawer of his desk and said, "Excuse me one moment." With his right hand he buzzed for Mini, and the man showed no sign of reaction.

With his left he activated a tape.

"Just tell Heinz to stand by," he said in English. "I may want him." If the man understood that, neither his eyes nor the lines of his mouth showed any apprehension. Mini was puzzled but did as she was instructed.

"Do you mind if I write that down?" He repeated out loud "Karl Henesch" and wrote it with a ball point on a sheet of paper firmly enough so that the outline was clearly readable on his blotting pad.

"Not at all," the looks-like-a-policeman replied quietly.

The man puffed his cigarette appreciatively. "Long time since I tasted one of those," he said, then launched into his unexpected story.

"I am a refugee. I was born and brought up in Bautzen, East Germany. I am an electronics engineer by profession. I need not tell you that life for people like me has not been easy in the, ah, Democratic Republic." He said the words rather like Rupert did, with irony that nearly cracked the teeth. Rupert counted a small point in the stranger's favour.

"Two years ago my wife died, and since we had no children, I started to make plans to escape. It was not simple—there is no point in professional people asking for permission to leave. It is not allowed. To ask only creates trouble. Six weeks ago the government communications department, where I work, sent me to Hungary to adjust some equipment that we had recently sold to the Hungarian state railways. It was a new signalling system—nothing very special about it, but containing some delicate rheostatic controls that were not working to specification. That could be dangerous, you understand."

Rupert nodded agreement.

"I will not bore you with the details. You know how these things are in the East European countries. My papers were all in order. I could move about freely. In the second week my duties took me to Sopron, which is the main western terminal of the Hungarian railways—the signal station that controls the whole sector near the Austrian border. There is a camp there, outside the town, right along the railway tracks. I watched everything very carefully and found there was a group of Russian Jews in it. They are processed there—that is the term the Communists use—before being allowed to come to Vienna. On their way to Israel. Every few months they allow some of them to leave. The guards became used to seeing me around the freight yards—working on the equipment, you see. When the chance came, I had no trouble in slipping on a train and crossed the border with the Jews. I got off at Wiener Neustadt without being noticed and made my way to Vienna."

Rupert sympathetically proffered another English cigarette.

The man murmured, "Thank you."

"And when did you arrive?" Rupert said.

"I got here three weeks ago. I knew an old man from Bautzen who has lived here for many years. He runs a little radio and television repair business across the Danube, in a poor district where people like him live—and like me. He gave me work. I found a one-room flat nearby where I sleep."

"Very interesting," Rupert said. "I congratulate you on your escape. But why tell me all this?"

"I hope this part of my story may interest you. It is my ambition to get to Canada."

"A lot of people want to do that."

"Yes, they do. But I need two things: a visa and money."

"A lot of people want those, too."

"Naturally. With money and my technical ability I would be welcome in Canada. I have a cousin there. I could start a new life and live decently."

"Well, why don't you go to the Canadian embassy and ask for political asylum?"

"Not so easy, and not so sure. I am not important. I have no secrets to offer them in exchange for my safety. The Canadians don't like this sort of problem. I think they prefer the Americans to be stuck with embarrassing entanglements. They would keep me hanging about for days, even weeks.

"I have studied these matters for a long time. The Austrians are very jealous of their neutrality—they don't like refugees from the east hanging around. And Austria is still uncomfortably close to the Communist countries. Unpleasant accidents have happened to men like me. My disappearance will by now be well known in Bautzen. They will be looking for me. It cannot be much longer before they think to start looking here. My friend in the radio shop is already nervous. He has been here a long time. But he is an old man. They leave him alone. He does not want any trouble, you understand. Every day I stay with him his danger increases. If I went to the Canadian embassy, other people would soon know."

He stood up and walked round the room. Rupert watched in silence. "Of course, I must go there sooner or later; I must have a visa." He paused to snuff out the cigarette and looked Rupert straight in the eye.

"When I go there, Herr Conway, I want to go straight from there to the airport—straight on to a plane to Canada. Everything *must* be arranged for me in advance."

The implicit threat was obvious enough, but no hint of what lay behind it. Rupert's first thought was the Palestinians, but there had been no mention or hint of them so far in his visitor's story.

"Sensible, I'm sure. But you have still not answered my question. Why come to me?"

Henesch sighed as though the strain of recent weeks

had been too much for him. He shivered visibly and sat down again.

"I am sorry to take so long, Herr Conway." Then very slowly and deliberately he said, "I have a secret I think you would like to know."

It had seemed likely for some minutes that this was the direction the conversation was heading in, but Rupert was still completely in the dark. Henesch sat quiet for a full minute, fumbling with his tie, as though selecting his next words with great care.

"Herr Conway, I think there is something in East Germany you would like to know."

Rupert chose his words carefully. "Herr Henesch, that might be so. That might be so."

Henesch showed no emotion of any kind. From the beginning his monologue had been delivered in a flat, even voice, which gave every appearance of long since having been drained of human feeling. Gray, Rupert thought, just like everything else in Marxland. The man's next remark made Rupert feel for the first time that this, the gray phase in their relationship, was about to change course.

"Does the name . . . Jacob Schwarz . . . mean anything to you, Herr Conway?"

Rupert looked lost in thought, then said, "I . . . ah . . . seem to recall having heard it. . . ."

"I feel sure you have, Herr Conway. And you are aware what he does, ja?"

No point in looking too dumb, Rupert thought.

"I believe . . . I have heard it said . . . He is an art dealer, I think."

"A very special kind of art dealer, Herr Conway."

"In what way?"

"Jacob Schwarz specializes in stolen art."

"Really? You seem well informed on such matters."

"It has been a hobby of mine for many years." Henesch reverted to the now familiar toneless, gray style.

Rupert decided to introduce a change of style of his own, just to see what effect it might have.

"Interesting. I . . . ah . . . was not aware that Bautzen was one of the world's leading art centers."

For the first time the enigmatic, gray Herr Henesch scored a point in Rupert's league. He put his head back and laughed. It sounded as though he had almost forgotten how to do it—the noise did not seem to emanate from the front of his mouth as with most people. Instead, there was a strange gurgling sound from way back in his throat somewhere, but the movement of the facial muscles and the extraordinary transformation of the inert gray eyes made it clear he was laughing.

"Bautzen?" He said, exhibiting undisguised enjoyment.

"Bautzen? No, no, Herr Conway. You are quite right. Quite right." The two of them looked into each other's eyes for the first time. Henesch spoke again in a new tone, not noticeably animated, but as though some barrier in his mind had been surmounted. He leaned across the desk, still showing his attempt at a smile.

"Give me another of your excellent English cigarettes, please." Rupert pushed the silver box across the desk to him and said softly, "Please help yourself."

There had certainly been some major change in their attitudes toward each other. It was too early to try to define it. When he had pulled his chair closer to the desk and lit his cigarette, Henesch began again.

"Herr Conway, I like you for that remark. You are a shrewd man. No, no. Bautzen is no world art center. Not of stolen art, nor of any other kind. No. My training in art was not in Bautzen. What little I know I learned in Frauenstein."

As the English would say, bowled center stump. Rupert

made no attempt to hide his surprise this time. This man must be on a totally different wave length after all.

"Frauenstein!" he said with no affected horror. "You call that art?"

Henesch, too, showed surprise, and he, too, made no effort to hide it.

"I am not following you," he said.

"I thought Frauenstein was the headquarters of the East German security police—their 'experimental' prison and all that."

Henesch's eyes flickered. It was as though Rupert's remark had caused some unwelcome and vaguely distressing memory to cross his mind. Maybe it had.

"Ah. That one. Perhaps you are not aware, my dear Herr Conway, that there is more than one place in both Germanies called Frauenstein?"

Rupert subsided visibly. "No," he said. "I did not know that."

"It is quite a common name for small villages, medieval villages. You understand German well, ja? There are several Frauenbergs also—for the same reason: when a very poor nobleman wished to give his wife a present, he would give her a few peasant households. The hamlet would then be called Frauenberg—or Frauenstein. It was a nice gesture but under the Salic law it still belonged to him."

Anyone could see the point of that little tale. They were both relaxed again.

"And at which Frauenstein was it that you learned about art, Herr Henesch?"

"Why, the one near Bautzen, of course. A little village near the Polish border. There is a house there—locally we call it the *Schloss.* It is not a proper castle, you understand —more a kind of manorial farmhouse. But it is the grandest house in those parts—or was. Like everything else now, it is owned by the state, but . . . ah . . . for generations before that, it belonged to my family. Since 1965 I have been allowed to live in part of it as a kind of country cottage. The farmers who work my family's land prefer to live in the collective cottages provided for them; I have it more or less to myself." Then he added, "Most of the time."

"Nice for you," was all Rupert felt like saying.

"Nice, as you say. But from time to time, over many years, there are visitors. One of them is a woman. I do not know her name; she seems to have great authority. I have seen her often with one or two men, going into the barns and old farm buildings which are there. The men vary, the woman always comes. She dresses like a Western woman, very smart. And she drives a fancy Western car."

Rupert was not in the dark anymore. If anything, he thought, the light was getting a bit too blinding. How could this man have put this package together? He had been thinking hard ever since recovering from the Frauenstein surprise and decided to go on the offensive for a while.

"And one of these men—one of the men who come to the farm with this woman—is Jacob Schwarz. Is that what you are telling me?"

"Ja. He is one of the men. Once or twice each year he comes to the *Schloss.*"

"Well, well. Small world, isn't it?"

Henesch appeared to take no offence. He said, "So often true, is it not, Herr Conway?"

"And what makes you think I might know this . . . ah . . . Schwarz?"

"The world must be even smaller than you think. It was Herr Schwarz who told me about you."

That hadn't been the road Rupert meant to take, but it was interesting nevertheless.

"That would seem an odd thing to do."

Henesch gave a smile—it almost came alive this time—and helped himself to another of Rupert's cigarettes.

"Come, Herr Conway. We take up too much of each other's time. There is no need to play games together. I told you frankly, I want money and a visa to Canada. I have seen this Schwarz at the farm near Frauenstein off and on for many years. I know what they have hidden there. How they get away with it or how they operate I do not know. I never wanted to know. It is not my business. But I have watched the people. I have a good memory for faces.

"Only a few days after I arrived in Vienna, I was sitting in a window seat at Europa, drinking coffee, watching the people walk up and down Kärntnerstrasse. I see this man, Schwarz. He sits right near me. I was not sure at first—I think he has been ill. He used to seem bigger, a broader man. Now he is quite thin and his hair is going gray. But I see him reading the *Herald Tribune*, and I hear him order some pastry. I know he is American—or pretends to be. He is the same man, all right. I follow him to his apartment. He does not know me. It presents no difficulties. I see his name on the door. I ring the bell. We talk."

"And he obligingly tells you about me?"

Henesch smiled again. "I do not think he intended to, Herr Conway, not quite like that. I threatened him, certainly. Not nice, but I am a refugee and in a dangerous situation. I tried to blackmail him, if you like. I have never done anything like that before. Probably I did not do it very well. I just said, 'I know you; I have seen you taking boxes from the farm at Schloss Frauenstein; I know you are dealing in stolen things; if you don't give me money, I shall tell the police.' Not very clever, not very nice, I admit. It was my first attempt at such a thing. It taught me a lot."

"You learn fast, Herr Henesch."

"I try to," he acknowledged frankly. "But after talking with Schwarz for a while I realized I was wrong—my approach was too crude. It wasn't going to work. For one thing, he said he had little money at present. I had a feeling he was telling the truth. Then he pointed out that all he had to do was get on an airplane and leave Austria. He used a phrase that caught my imagination: he said my threat did not worry him because, whatever he had done, he had no hostages to fortune."

Rupert did not need much time to figure that one out. "And you think I have?"

"You certainly cannot get up and disappear from Vienna without terrible loss. Your life's work, ja? Look, Herr Conway, I said before, no more guessing games. I met Schwarz, and during our argument he mentioned you. From him I learn that you are interested in recovering certain property, stolen from your grandfather by the Nazis, ja? From him I learn that what is at Frauenstein came from Vienna—from what Schwarz called the 'minor collections.' He tells me your grandfather was one of those men, and that you spent many years trying to find his property. Ja? Schwarz says some, maybe all of that property is among the things still hidden at Frauenstein. It seems possible. I don't know. But only I can show you where they are. Schwarz won't tell you. If you ask him, he will deny every word I have said. He must."

He waited for Rupert to consider that.

"I am not asking you for any money." That struck Rupert as a pleasant surprise, and his smile showed it. "In your case, I do not need to. I am not trying to blackmail you. I want to be your partner."

That was an unforeseen twist. The sheer audacity of it caught Rupert's imagination. Partner? Meaning what?

"You take everything you want from Frauenstein. The

woman only comes every three or four months, so it will not be difficult. You have to get it across the border, of course, but you can find a way—it happens every day. All I ask of you are two things."

"They are?"

"I have thought this out much more carefully than when I accosted Schwarz. You said I learn fast. I have tried to; I need to. I have not much time. I suggest to you an honourable deal. It is this. First: you take from Frauenstein everything you want, everything you think you can get across the border. Whatever you want. That is not my business. Then just bring one more piece—any piece—worth, let us say a hundred thousand schillings. You know these values far better than I. Bring one piece for me. You give me a fair price for my piece; you can then sell it at a profit. Fair deal for you, ja? Then the second thing: you are well known here and respected; you can talk to the Canadian embassy and the local police—arrange to get my visa for me. I go off to Canada and you never see me again. But you fulfil your life's ambition. Ja?"

Well, well, well. Small world indeed, Rupert thought. Goes round and round in circles, too. What a fascinating story. At first blush it all looked so perfect, so plausible. Was that because it was a carefully planned plot? With what object?

"Herr Henesch, you realize, of course, that I can check many of the things you have told me."

"Of course. You would be a fool not to."

"I have many good friends in the Austrian police."

"It would be odd if you had not."

No chink in his armour here.

"Will you come and see me again tomorrow?"

"No. That I won't do. I don't think I am being followed yet, but it must happen soon. One does not want to establish a pattern that could become predictable to others."

"You sound like a policeman."

"You have not lived in a Communist country," he replied.

"Touché," Rupert said, thinking, That's his round again.

Henesch got up to leave, and Rupert walked toward the door.

"But time is vital to me, Herr Conway. If you turn me over to the Austrian police, I can ask for political asylum. But that means they have to arrest me. In due course I shall be released. Then I should have no money. It would take me a long time to earn enough to get to Canada. I can't earn money in an internment camp, and by the time they let me out to earn it, I should be in danger—danger of my life."

"Are they really as bad as that, Herr Henesch?"

"Yes, they are. Every day I linger here, the danger to my life increases. Why should they go to the trouble of killing me? I'm not important. It is the principle, the system, that binds them. I don't want to leave Germany—it is my homeland. But it is their system that I and so many others hate, and they can't acknowledge that. They cannot admit it, to themselves or to anyone else. The thought drives them to a frenzy. So they will pursue me here, as they have pursued others just as unimportant. In Canada I'm too far away. Here in Austria, they will catch me in time. I can only give you a week—ten days at the most."

"And then?"

"Then? You will hear from me no more. I shall leave Vienna and find some other way. But you will lose your last chance to see your family's possessions."

"Not necessarily."

"Oh yes, Herr Conway. Very necessarily. I shall get to

Canada, be sure of that. From wherever I am, it will be easy to drop a note somewhere, in the right place. I know a few policemen myself. I can ensure the police keep a careful guard on Schloss Frauenstein in future. I shall phone you tomorrow morning for your answer. Good-by."

13

IT was just coming up to one o'clock. For the first time Rupert realized he was hungry. It had been a very remarkable morning. "My last chance," he said. "Very necessarily!" Henesch seemed very sure of himself. I wonder if I can be? After lunch he called Jo Liebmann and asked if he could come round for a talk. Jo was just going into a meeting with Rudolph Steinkellner, Police President Reidinger's number two man, but said he would be free by four o'clock. Would Rupert come round and have some tea? Rupert had over two hours to think about his situation, but he was not much further ahead when he sat down in the Polizei Praesidium at four o'clock.

The first thing he did was to play Liebmann the tape. They sat in silence for half an hour and played the whole thing right through. Then Liebmann said, "Fascinating. Now, let's take it piece by piece. You really have a problem here, Rupert."

He did not like the way Jo emphasized the word *you*,

but was pleased to notice he had made a copy of the tape. Other than a technicality of illegal entry into the country, a charge that could be withdrawn if a case for political asylum were established, there was nothing in Henesch's story which concerned the Austrian police. Rupert began to get a kind of lonely feeling. He switched the tape back and started again, keeping one hand on the control panel. Jo Liebmann sat with a pencil and paper to make a note or two when he felt like it and gazed at the ceiling.

They got as far as Henesch's crossing of the border when Liebmann held up his hand. "Let's stop there for a first check." He looked down at his notes and said, "Question one: he says he was in Sopron four to five weeks ago repairing the signal system on the Hungarian railways. If it was a job of any size, our people in Eisenstadt would know about it. Transit camp by Sopron marshalling yards, that's true—everyone knows that. A crossing of Russian Jews, three to four weeks ago; let's see."

He consulted the calendar on his desk. "That would have been, say, between March fourteenth and twenty-fourth." He wrote it down. "Question two: was there a train of Russian Jews across from Sopron to Eisenstadt between March fourteenth and twenty-fourth?"

He pressed the tiny intercommunication panel on his desk while flipping through a small pad of numbers attached to it. Rupert watched with interest; nine digits and about four seconds later, Liebmann was talking to the officer in charge of the police office at Eisenstadt railway headquarters. Impressive. Rupert could never quite believe all these new gadgets really worked.

Jo Liebmann tossed his two questions at the voice on the other end of the wire. The answer to question one came straight back—yes, the Hungarians had notified them of the operation; from his office he had been able to see men working on the control antennae. They'd finished about three weeks ago. Question two—a pause while he consulted some records. Yes again. A refugee train of two passenger cars and some freight had crossed on March 18th. Liebmann repeated the information to Rupert and added: "Either your friend was there or he certainly seems to be well informed about it." He thanked the inspector in Eisenstadt and rang off.

"Would it be possible to find out if anyone working on the signal system had defected?" Rupert asked.

Liebmann shook his head. "If I were to set up a courier operation, brief a reliable man, and endanger his life by instructing him to ask questions about such matters, it would be possible. But, to the Communists, information about defections is regarded as top secret, most damaging to the state. Anyway, it would take a week to do." He shrugged his huge shoulders. That was out, Rupert agreed reluctantly.

"Okay," said Jo. "Let's continue. Next spasm."

Rupert started the tape again. They both wrote down "Radio and television repair business across the Danube" without stopping the tape. Rupert noticed Liebmann write "Schwarz" and then passed over the Frauenstein bit without a note. Liebmann even let out a small chuckle at Henesch's comment about the Salic law. He wrote down "Western woman . . . fancy Western car."

"Let's stop there," he said. "There is one of Captain Gottfried's men about the building somewhere—I saw him at lunch." He buzzed his secretary to put out a signal for the officer from Munich. "Didn't get his name," Liebmann said.

"It's Heinzmann," Rupert interrupted.

Liebmann said, "And we assume, for the moment, that the well-dressed lady with the fancy Western car is your friend, Frau Ruttgers."

Rupert wished he would stop saying "your" all the time.

"Our" would indicate a little more feeling of participation than Liebmann obviously felt up to now. Or was it just his police training?

There was no possible doubt about the quality of Josef Liebmann's police training. He transferred his gaze from the ceiling, put down one of his treasured meerschaums carefully in a pipe holder on his desk, and tapped out four numbers on the intercom. The desk speaker spoke: "Friedmann, Herr Oberst."

"Freddie—a radio and television repair shop in the twenty-first, -second or -third Bezirk, run by a man over sixty. Comes from East Germany; been in Austria many years. Feed that into your computer and send me up a write-out of what you get."

"Jawohl, Herr Oberst."

Rupert was impressed. Jo said, "Wait till we see the results. It's early days yet. In two to three years time we'll have every single man, woman, and child in Austria cross-indexed on that box of tricks. It will make life miserable for every thief and hit-and-run driver in the country, but it's not nearly complete yet."

Detective Sergeant Heinzmann from Munich came on the line. In answer to the question whether he knew what kind of car Frau Karl Ruttgers drove, he replied promptly, "A very fancy, super-charged, bright red Porsche." Yes, Captain Gottfried had instructed him to contact the Herr Doktor Conway. Liebmann told him to come up in an hour and instructed his secretary to phone Frau Liebmann and say he would be late for dinner.

They both thought for a moment, Rupert deliberately waiting it out. What he wanted was not just official interest in his strange problem, but some show of real commitment. Jo obliged only to the extent of speaking first.

"So, up to now, your mysterious friend Henesch seems to have all his facts right. Let's play a little more."

Rupert switched the tape on again. They listened for another fifteen minutes in silence, then stopped at Schwarz, and Liebmann made a lengthy note.

"Know anything about him, Rupert?"

"Little more than you do. Remember, Claud Lebel's report from Paris on him was completely negative. They have no record of his dealing in stolen art works."

"I'll ask Department II to put one of their art specialists on his trail, but there is no knowing how long it may take to turn something up." A few more minutes of puzzled listening then the intercom buzzed. It was Friedmann from the computer room.

"Not much luck, I'm afraid, Herr Oberst. There are twenty-two radio and television repair shops in those districts—nine of them run by men over sixty. But our data is not complete enough yet to show anything more."

"Okay, Freddie. Send up what you have." Liebmann made another pencil note and said, "Another little chore for Department II. Kornek won't like this—he's up to his ears and short-handed already."

They finished the tape in silence.

Jo relit his precious meerschaum and then said, "Rupert, my dear friend, I really shall never know why we turn this department upside down just to please you. The only possible charge we can have against this character Henesch is one of illegal entry. I can order him tracked down; we can lock him up alright, pending investigation. But as he said himself, that isn't going to help solve your problem."

As always, Jo Liebmann had everything logically summed up in the simplest of words. It didn't help Rupert one bit.

"I'm afraid you will just have to go to East Germany and find out for yourself." A deep puff of soul-satisfying tobacco softened the policeman's official façade for a moment. "But for God's sake, my dear fellow, be careful. If you step afoul of the authorities there, there is nothing we can do to help you."

It was not Rupert's way to give up that easily. He said, "Henesch is due to phone me tomorrow morning. How about having my phone tapped and a tracer made?"

Liebmann smiled and made a note. "Certainly. We can do that. But I'll lay you ten to one he'll call from a phone box somewhere the other side of town."

He did.

Rupert spent most of the following morning in the darkened lab, studying two pieces of what were supposed to be eighteenth-century porcelain under the ultra-violet light of a mercury vapour tube. One he knew to be a very fine specimen of an early Nymphenburg fruit bowl. The tests would prove if the other was genuine or not, depending on whether the fluorescense given off under the ultra-violet beam was or was not identical in every detail with the control piece. And the result of that would mean anything up to three or four thousand dollars difference in its value.

He was just finishing up his notes when the phone rang. No name was given, but the voice was unmistakably that of Henesch. Rupert tried vainly to keep the conversation going long enough for the officers doing the tracing operation to reach the source, but Herr Henesch was in a hurry. All he would say was, "I have just one minute, Herr Conway. Is your answer yes or no?"

Rupert had to say "Yes."

The reply came back, "Be ready to go to Germany by next Tuesday. I will write to you." The line went dead. Two minutes later, when two detectives entered the main lobby of the Westbahnhof, the telephone booths were all empty and there were over a hundred people milling about going to and from the trains.

The Easter holiday weekend came and went uneventfully at Semmering. Rupert's only problem was to hide his anxiety and impatience from Sandra. He could not even tell her about the phone call from the Polizei Praesidium on Saturday morning, informing him that the body of the Palestinian gunman had been found in a stolen car, abandoned in the Prater late Friday night. Since the postmortem showed the man had bled to death and there were no blood stains in the car, it followed that he had died elsewhere and the body had been left in the park several hours later. The bullet removed from his abdomen was the one fired by the police officer the previous Saturday night in the courtyard behind Stephansplatz; the fingerprints matched those on the murder weapon. But the gunman's secret had died with him. Although repeatedly interrogated, his accomplice would not—or quite probably could not—tell them anything they did not already know.

Something Rolf Heinrich and his colleagues did not know was worrying them, too: had the terrorists said anything to the Vienna police which would lead back to the flat in the Brennerstrasse? Eventually, of course, the stolen car would be traced, but taking it from a crowded, darkened car park on a holiday evening and ensuring it carried no telltale fingerprints had presented no difficulties. Three things Heinrich did know that unhappy weekend worried him far more than the things he did not: General Zweiboden was furious, Oberst Gruppenführer Steinhoff was threatening, and Gerda was increasingly impatient.

Back in the office on Tuesday morning, the first instruction Rupert gave Frau Hauptmann was to deliver all the morning mail to him personally, unopened. Sandra had been puzzled at his insistence that she should devote her morning to escorting a not very important American client around the Kunsthistorisches Museum, but it was a chore she enjoyed. At ten–twenty-seven Frau Hauptmann put eighteen letters on his desk and quietly closed the door as she went out. All the ones from obvious sources Rupert put aside without hesitation. That was sixteen of them. The seventeenth, a rather grubby envelope posted from a suburb on the north side of town and addressed in hand-written block capitals, was the one he had expected. The eighteenth, from the East German commercial representative, was a surprise. He put the others in his "out" tray, for Frau Hauptmann to deal with in the usual way, and picked up the critical two, one in each hand.

For a moment he debated which to open first. He held them both to the light and felt them carefully until he was satisfied they both contained nothing but one or possibly two sheets of ordinary paper. No tell-tale lumps or bits of wire that might indicate a letter bomb. Not that he was expecting one, but there had been too many unpleasant surprises these last few days. He carefully slit open the grubby, hand-written envelope, and turned immediately to the signature. It was "Karl Henesch."

The letter read:

> Schloss Frauenstein lies four kilometers north of Ludendorff on the route to Rothenburg-am-der-Neisse between the road and the river. There are no other buildings within two kilometers of its gate, which has white and yellow stucco posts. Drive straight up to the house and turn under a gabled archway into a courtyard on your right leading to the old stables.

You must arrive between five and six o'clock, when all the farm labourers will have left but before it is too dark. There is no electricity, so you will need a torch. The only person living there is an old Polish retainer who has been with my family for many years. Say to him, Anton, Karlie is safe. I have come for his mother's ring. He will understand and help you. You will know how to arrange everything better than I. I will telephone you next Sunday to arrange delivery of the money and my visa. I trust you as an English gentleman, but remember, if you cheat me everyone will know you have stolen state property.

This was pretty much what he had been expecting. Henesch had to back himself both ways. Rupert had been able to think of little else over the weekend and had virtually made up his mind to go—after taking all suitable precautions, of course. After all, what were the odds? Henesch's story hung together; every fact they could check had fitted. It all tied in with the theories he had himself entertained for the better part of thirty years. And what was the worst that could happen if things went wrong? If he was stopped driving around where he had no authority to be—well, it was all close enough to Dresden to say he had taken the wrong turn, gotten lost, or some yokel had given him wrong directions—it was all a misunderstanding. He could spin any number of plausible variations on that theme. All he needed was another excuse to go back to Dresden; that shouldn't be too difficult.

He might, of course, get caught crossing the border with a car full of objets d'art that he considered his own property, though there would be little hope of converting the East German authorities to that point of view. He had spent quite a lot of time considering that possibility on Sunday afternoon, and while Sandra was giving Charlie his usual country ramble, he had spent a fascinating hour in the garage trying to figure out all the most obscure and unlikely places in the Jensen's entrails where items of any value might be hidden. The scope was severely limited: certainly no pictures of any appreciable size were possible, but two or three smaller canvases sans frames might be rolled up, wrapped in polyethylene and taped up under the chassis frame in various spots. The toolbox and under the seats were too obvious, but there was a protected niche between the battery and the fuel injection pump that presented some possibilities. What if Czarina Maria Feodorovna's 1903 Easter egg was there? The very thought of such a possibility set Rupert's adrenalin running like a mountain stream. That had been the crowning achievement of his grandfather's collecting—he had paid a king's ransom for it in 1919. Better be prepared, he thought, but don't let your hopes run too high. He came to only two positive conclusions: first, the quantity he dared to take out was definitely limited, but just finding them would be worth a great deal of risk; and, second, the plastic bags he always carried in the car for carrying food surreptitiously lifted from restaurant dinner tables to a place convenient for Charlie were going to come in handy.

Even as he sat alone meditating on the extraordinary piece of paper he held in his hand, in his heart he knew full well he was already totally committed to this risky, perhaps even foolhardy enterprise. His practical business-trained brain concentrated on the strictly factual problems, or what his insurance brokers called risk management. How could he minimize them? How to secure his own life and safety—and his sheer personal comfort, a factor which always rated high with him—in the event of things going wrong?

He made some notes and acted on them as he wrote: carefully wrap this letter and its envelope in tissue paper and give to Jo Liebmann for fingerprinting and identification examination. Work out and write down a detailed movement plan including all timings and mileages for his journey and leave copies of it with the chief security officer at the British embassy, Jo Liebmann, and Captain Gottfried in Munich. Have Gottfried make special arrangements to check him out at the Hof crossing and be alert for his estimated time of return. Yes, and leave a plan with Tommy Thompson, too, after having received his promise that he would not tell Sandra—not until afterward, anyway.

And if even after all that it still goes wrong? Well, Schwarz and the Ruttgers could be picked up by the police in short order. The press? Yes, good idea: leave a copy of the plan with Johnny Schuster, head of the Vienna PA bureau. He would ensure it was blown high, wide, and handsome in all the Western papers, and surely the highly placed gentlemen who fixed all those phony visas for Gerda would feel mighty uncomfortable. Rupert added all this up and found it reassuring. He had several good cards to bargain with and some trustworthy friends who would know the right sequence in which to play them.

He finished his note-making, paused to fill and light a new Charatan, which his nephew and niece in Wales had sent him as an Easter present, and as he gently breathed in and exhaled the first cloud of delicious gray-blue smoke, he gave the characteristic deep sigh and slight shrug of the shoulders that was his unconscious way of registering an irrevocable decision to himself.

Now, what had the East German commercial representative to say for himself? There were two sheets in the envelope: the first letter from the commercial representative in Vienna himself, full of official jargon and respectful assurances of the goodwill and peace-loving intentions of the workers of the GDR, and his own declaration of determination that his office would do everything possible, or even things impossible, to expedite the business of such great international importance at present being conducted between the Herr Doktor's esteemed artistic establishment and the people's own managed printing works in Dresden, et cetera, et cetera . . . but somewhere along the line there appeared to have been some small hitch. That would, of course, instantly be put right and, of course, was in no possible way the fault of the people's et cetera, et cetera. All bull and blarney, Rupert thought, but at least this man lets you down a little more gracefully than the man in the Chicago City Tax Department. What it all amounted to was: read the enclosed telegram just received from Wilhelm Tautz and you will know what the trouble is.

Rupert did as he was bidden. This kind of pompous officialese was even more cumbersome to read when reduced to telegrammese, but after three readings he concluded that the message boiled down to an admission that in the preparation of a negative for Plate Number Thirty-seven, a lab technician had accidentally made a scratch on it for which they were very sorry. It appeared there were three possible courses open. One: could the negative be replaced? That would require Max going to the Cairo museum and taking another photograph; at least a week or more of precious time would be lost; it couldn't. Two: would the Herr Doktor entrust Altenburg's to repair the negative themselves, realizing that he might not be satisfied with the result? They certainly know more about the technique than Max or I do, was Rupert's first thought. Or three: would the Herr Doktor please make another journey to Dresden himself to watch over and supervise the repair work? The telegram made it very clear that the Tautzes, father and son, would be much happier to shift the burden of this responsibility onto his shoulders, if at all possible.

Rupert put down the telegram and picked up the carefully wrapped sheet of tissue paper into which he had sealed Henesch's letter. He held it up to the light for a moment and stared as though through it out of the window. Then he put it down and telephoned the commercial representative. That helpful officer assured him that, due to the importance and urgency of the business, and in these exceptional circumstances, and in view of the high regard in which all the authorities of the GDR government services held the Herr Doktor, his visa would be ready by five o'clock this evening.

14

ON Wednesday morning, Rupert paid calls on the GDR commercial representative, the British and American embassies, and had a long telephone call with Captain Gottfried in Munich, whom he agreed to meet at a country inn near Freising that same evening. He had a drink at the Club Rennverien with Johnny Schuster and then walked across the Schottenring to see Liebmann. As he was rising to leave the police councillor's office, Jo Liebmann handed him a small parcel. Rupert opened it in silence and thoughtfully removed the contents.

"Neat," he said. "Never saw one like this before."

"Czech," Liebmann replied. "Made especially for the thugs of their Department Thirteen. You have gloves, of course?"

"Of course."

"I hope to God you don't have to use it, but if you do . . . well, get rid of it. The KGB don't know we have them."

They shook hands and parted without another word,

but as the door closed behind Rupert, Jo Liebmann passed his hand across his forehead and mumbled, "God help me; the things we do for that man!"

Rupert and Charlie took the Salzburg-Munich Autobahn as usual, turned north at Roenheim and pulled up at the small hotel outside Freising at ten minutes to six. By six-thirty, when Gottfried arrived, Charlie had been drained, exercised, fed, and was happily asleep in the parked Jensen; Rupert was sitting quietly in a corner of the *Bierkellar* puffing his pipe and enjoying a large stein of real home-brewed Bavarian beer. He ordered the same for Gottfried and, as there was no one within listening distance of where they sat, they were able to talk freely.

Rupert handed the police officer a copy of his meticulously worked-out travel schedule; a map had been clearly marked showing all routes and his timings worked out to within plus or minus ten minutes—one did not have to worry about traffic jams in East Germany. The only unknowns were the exact time he would have to stay at Altenburg's and how long he would need at Schloss Frauenstein. After Dresden two alternate schedules were shown, one based on half-hour stops as a likely minimum and the other on two hours as maximum. If the delay at the printing works exceeded two hours, he would somehow get a telephone message through to Max, who would notify Liebmann at once.

He planned to cross at Hof at nine A.M. tomorrow, and his latest estimated time back again was midnight. It was agreed that if he had not checked through by two A.M., the officer in charge would phone Gottfried, who would immediately call Jo Liebmann. Liebmann knew what to do after that; Schuster would put his first tentative story over the wires at four the same afternoon, and the British embassy would make direct contact with the ambassador in Berlin.

Gottfried wiped the delicious froth from his moustache and commented. "You have not forgotten your police training."

"I've given it more thought in the last week than in the previous twenty-five years," Rupert replied.

Gottfried said, "I had a call from Claud Lebel only this morning." Rupert put down his stein and concentrated. "The French police in Marseilles intercepted a tramp steamer bound for Tangier last night. It was a routine drug raid, but they also found two crates of pictures which we can definitely trace to Poland." He sipped his beer. "The tramp's cargo manifest had them entered as shipped from our friend Ruttgers in Munich."

"Does he know yet?"

"No. The tramp's radio equipment was pretty unsophisticated, and the radio operator was on deck when they boarded. Everyone is being held at sea and out of sight of land."

"What can you pin on Ruttgers?"

"Only the export of works of art without a license. We want much more than that. That's why I'm so interested in what you may find at Frauenstein. Now we know the lady goes there, we know what she does there, and how they dispose of the loot. We still have no clue as to why the GDR police let her get away with it. There must be a very big fish indeed at the other end of this net somewhere."

"I don't know that I'll find very much to help you."

"In this work every little bit helps. Keep your eyes and ears peeled every damned second." Gottfried took a deep draft of beer, burped, and gazed meditatively at the ceiling. "Of course, if they did pick you up, it might force a lot of things out into the open."

"Thanks very much."

"I'm only thinking out loud. You've got a perfect cover

story; I'd say your chances are pretty good. In fact, I'd like very much to go with you."

"Well, I wouldn't mind your company."

"Wouldn't work, though. They would never give me a visa, and it would take weeks to cook something up." They ordered more beer.

"Any more developments in Munich?"

Gottfried put down his stein and laughed. "Nothing important, worse luck. Remember I told you we picked up a Polish nun last week? She turned out to be a small-time agent. I'll never understand how the Communist mind works! She was operating with a Trotskyite student group in Munich; her boyfriend defected to a Maoist group and when she refused to change sides he denounced her to them. Our contact with the Maoists picked that up. We got a search warrant and went through her flat. Know what we found? Lenin's essays, five back copies of *Pravda,* and three containers of microfilm."

"Anything interesting?"

"Interesting?" Gottfried snorted. "A lot of pretty pictures of BMW's body plant, the Olympic stadium, and a beauty of the local Russian commercial consul coming out of a brothel."

They finished their beer and Rupert drove on to Hof, where he slept like a child. At exactly nine o'clock on Thursday morning, he passed through the frontier post, gave the agreed code word, and swept on through the valley and up the hill past the concrete guard towers to enter the Democratic Republic.

In order to pass through Ludendorff at exactly five o'clock, and to give himself time to navigate winding country roads, Rupert had calculated that he should leave Altenburg's by three, which in turn meant that he did not want to arrive there before one. All in all, he had comfortable time in hand—rather more than he had expected, because the frontier guards seemed to be in an unusually genial and cooperative mood that morning. They only kept him waiting half an hour, and the officer brandishing the usual revolver actually wished him a pleasant trip.

He had given that extra time in hand careful thought, however, and wanted it to test a little theory that had been buzzing round in his mind these last few days. Owing to the sudden appearance in his life of the elusive Herr Henesch, his quest for grandfather Eisenbath's stolen art collection had progressed far beyond the point that seemed to concern Jacob Schwarz and his questionable friends, the Ruttgers. The Schwarz-Ruttgers partnership was perfectly explainable in the context of the statute-of-limitations theory, and while it interested him enormously, it was now only incidental to his main objective. The Henesch story . . . Well, he had been over that time and time again; neither he nor Jo Liebmann had been able to fault it. The clue he had been searching for ever since 1945 had at last come his way; even if he could get nothing out, the proof that even some of the property stolen from his family and their friends so many years ago still existed—that it could be identified, claimed, and possibly one day recovered—that alone would be the fulfillment of a lifetime's dream for Rupert.

If it turned out that Schwarz and the Ruttgers were really the crooks they appeared to be, well, he would be happy to help the police secure their conviction. But . . . There were still a lot of *buts* that kept bothering him. Gerda, for a start. Her nonexistent mother. Did it make any difference how many villages there were called Frauenstein? The one he had seen was grim enough, but was there any connection between the two? Certainly none that had suggested itself up to now. He wanted to test something, just to satisfy his own curiosity.

It was almost eleven o'clock on that fine, sunny spring morning when Rupert came in sight of Karl-Marx-Stadt. The traffic had been building up a little these last few miles, and it began to look as though there might be some obstruction on the road ahead. Two miles farther east and just over a slight rise in the road he saw that there were two. A large convoy of Russian army missile carriers, at least fifty enormous vehicles, was making its ponderous progress just ahead of him, and there was already a considerable tail of civilian trucks and vans tagging along behind. Whether it was *verboten* for mere German civilians to pass the armed might of the imperial power or not he didn't know; it was clear nobody felt like trying it. He joined the end of the queue and proceeded at thirty kilometers per hour. After only three more minutes, he saw what he had been looking for, the turn off the Autobahn to enter Karl-Marx-Stadt itself. Besides the usual highway direction signs, there was a series of large, red temporary wooden frames that he remembered from his previous journey two weeks before. "Achtung!" they proclaimed. Men at work. The main bridge carrying the Autobahn over the local road into the city was being widened; the whole of the clover-leaf interchange was dug up.

Only a single lane was open, on the north side. In order to turn south, one had to exit on the north ramp and then complete the two hundred and seventy degree turn on the lower level. Rupert slowed down and signalled his left turn. Traffic here was down to a crawl, and the surface of the interconnecting road was nothing but a churned-up mud heap. He moved forward cautiously, and suddenly there was a great thump where the mud thinned out and the wheels of the Jensen dropped a good six inches onto solid rock.

The instant the front axle hit that spot, Rupert looked at his carefully adjusted gyroscopic compass. It pointed straight north. He completed the circuit very slowly, passed under the Autobahn, and drove some sixty meters onto a grass verge where he stopped to consult his map. He was confident he knew it, but his heart was beating faster and he had to be absolutely sure. The road in front of him went straight into the city. Just a few meters ahead of where he had parked was a crossroad and a sign pointing east which said "Freiburg." With a small transparent plastic kilometer scale, he measured off the distance down that road, through Freiburg, and along a tertiary road running south from there. The exact distance recorded on the bug which Gottfried's men had attached to Gerda Ruttgers' car, and which had been unaccounted for by the failure of the directional circuit, was precisely twice the distance from where he sat to Frauenstein. The security police's Frauenstein.

Rupert noticed in the rear view mirror that the Jensen was attracting the attention of a policeman leaning over the bridge of the Autobahn eyeing him intently. Why did ordinary traffic policemen need rifles? He quickly opened the door, stepped out onto the grass verge and invited Charlie to do the same. He knew full well Charlie could be relied upon to do the obvious; he promptly did against the nearest four trees. Rupert waved to the policeman, who smiled back and turned away. They got back in, turned round, and climbed up onto the Autobahn again heading east, exchanged another cheerful wave with the young policeman, and drove on toward Dresden. For the first time, Rupert was quite sure that he was involved in something more sinister than just smuggling valuable works of art.

He dawdled along contentedly, enjoying the rapidly changing views as the heavily wooded hills that lined the northern border of Czechoslovakia gradually petered out in the vast plain of the Elbe, which stretched out on his left all the way to Berlin itself. His first reaction of excitement at proving Gerda's direct connection with Frauenstein—as he felt he had—was quickly tempered by the thought that, really, we've known it all along. Someone in Frauenstein must be the source of all those visas she seems to get for the asking. Someone in Frauenstein ensures she can smuggle "state property" without risk. All his new information really did was to put beyond doubt that she had some positive relationship with the East German security police. Captain Gottfried had probably guessed that already. But they still don't know what it was —or why.

He drew up at one of the few service areas, near the small town of Nossen at the intersection with the Leipzig Autobahn. He was still running well ahead of schedule, and this was one of the few places where someone driving a very obviously foreign car could loiter and relax a while without inviting unwelcome attention from officialdom in some guise or other. He stretched his legs, gave Charlie a walk, topped up both fuel tanks, and had the mechanic check the oil, water, and battery even though he knew there was no need. At a quarter past twelve, he drove off leisurely to Dresden. He even had time to notice how superbly reconstituted was the façade of Dresden's famed opera house and how the daffodils sparkled in the Grosse Garten, once again beyond doubt one of Europe's most beautiful civic parks. It was only five past one when he reached the Altenburg printing works, and the staff were just returning from their noon lunch break.

The GDR commercial representative in Vienna may have treated Rupert as though he were a senior member of the Politbureau itself, but the Herr Planning Direktor Kamerad Greitz in charge of ideological purity at the People's Own Managed Printing Works was clearly no proponent of detente. Rupert was kept waiting alone in the cheerless and almost totally unfurnished reception hall; instructed to hand over his papers in the same surly, disinterested fashion as before; and then left for ten minutes to cool his heels after the "receptionist" disappeared and locked the door behind him. As before, he had to demand the return of his papers before agreeing to proceed to business; and as before, he got them without protest, explanation, or comment of any kind. The only change, an unhappy change, was to find upon entering the conference room that Wilhelm Tautz was not present. Johannes greeted him even more formally and stiffly than before and apologized, without giving any coherent explanation for his father's absence. Kamerad Greitz did actually shake hands, but it was his customary limp and vaguely unfriendly effort.

The third man present was a plump, broad-shouldered, typically peasant-faced fellow with enormous hands, wearing the distinguishing white coverall of a skilled technician. He turned out to be Hans Wlaka, in charge of the operation. Rupert quickly decided that in other circumstances, like sitting at an inn over a stein of beer, Hans would be excellent company. For the moment, however, he looked and acted as miserable and incoherent as the rest of them. Rupert was instantly and deeply conscious of the strained atmosphere. The obvious explanation was that the world-famous and work-proud house of Altenburg had made a bad mistake on a purely technical job at which they were supposed to excel—they were embarrassed about it, as well they might be, and did not attempt to hide their feelings. Rupert understood all this at a glance, but his second thought, typically British, was, rather overdone, isn't it?

On the conference table were the usual layers of fine white tissue paper in which the Tautz family still carefully wrapped their handiwork, a one thousand-watt negative projector, a series of microscopes, bottles, and what looked like surgical instruments. First, they showed him the good news: since their unhappy communication of last week, they had pressed ahead with the remainder of the work and would finish completely in another four to five days. All the sheets laid out before him were superb, and his only problem was to avoid wasting too much time exclaiming on the excellence of every single one, so that they could get down to dealing with the trouble. Hans Wlaka clearly wanted to be absolutely positive the customer made it certain beyond all argument to Johannes and Greitz that he thought the work of Hans and his team was perfect, superlative, marvelous, and worthy of all possible praise—before they came to the awful moment of having to examine his one ghastly mistake. At least, that is how it appeared to Rupert, and as he had taken an instant liking to Hans, he gave him the benefit of every doubt. It was fully half an hour before he was able, tactfully but firmly, to get them round to showing him what he had really come for.

The offending negative, some six by ten centimeters, was handed to him. Held up to the light, it was certainly obvious there was a small scratch almost in the center of it, across a confused tangle of human bodies that appeared to be in advanced stages of mayhem. Placed under a microscope, one could clearly see that someone had let drop a minute quantity of a powerful etching acid onto the surface of the negative and then, presumably hastily, endeavouring to remove it, had smeared it about five or six millimeters. Seen under the microscope, therefore, was a scratch not much bigger than a quarter-inch hairline with a slight fan-shaped wedge at one end. On any normal amateur's contact print one would scarcely have noticed it. As Hans Wlaka pointed out every detail of the mark with a fine steel needle, his voice became more and more agitated. Once again, Rupert gathered the impression they were making rather too much fuss about very little.

Then, they placed the negative in the projector and blew it up to the forty-by-thirty size of the printed sheets for which it was ultimately destined. They turned down the other lights in the room so Rupert could get the full effect, and the three of them stood round in solemn silence, while he stared unbelievingly at the screen in front of him. The picture, of one of the most valuable pieces in the collection because it was among the best preserved and containing more than usual detail, thereby telling modern students more about the culture of the people who had originally created it, and the people depicted in it, was a battle scene. From top to bottom of the frieze and from end to end, it was one solid mass of writhing bodies, many of them completely naked. In the foreground stood the massive figure of the obvious hero of the occasion, a fierce, bearded chieftain waving a spear in the air above his head in some kind of victory gesture, while his right foot was planted firmly on the back of a decapitated, naked victim. It was a stirring scene, the way the unknown artist had drawn it some five or six thousand years ago. The way it appeared now would be sensational. Protruding downward from the conquering chieftain's short, padded skirt was a streak that even the most prudish minds could only interpret as a monstrous penis.

Rupert's primary reaction as he took in this extraordinary scene would normally have been to burst out laughing. It was not pornographic; it was so bizarre as to be very funny. The dour solemnity of Johannes, Greitz, and Wlaka, however, and the heavy-handed atmosphere of the whole interview forebade any expression of levity. Greitz would be sure to report it as a symptom of Western decadence. Rupert's next thought was the possible loss of many thousands of dollars any ensuing delay might cost.

The urge to laugh faded instantly.

They turned the lights up and all looked at him in gloomy expectation. Rupert needed his pipe and all Kamerad Greitz's withering looks of disapproval were not going to stop him. He was delighted to see Johannes take out his package of small, fruity Greek cigars, and even more pleased that he offered one to Wlaka, who accepted at once. When they all had had time to breathe a little more deeply and the scowling Greitz had removed himself to across the table, where he could still supervise all the action and doubtless tape all the sound but get as far away as possible from the rapidly rising cloud of tobacco smoke, Rupert spoke.

"Yes, I can see your problem, Johannes. But you are the expert. What do you suggest?"

"You still say there is no time to replace this negative, Herr Doktor?"

"Only at the expense of quite unacceptable delay. What I must know is, is there any workable alternative?"

Johannes looked pensively at Hans Wlaka before he spoke. "Yes, there is. Negatives can be retouched. Hans here is one of the best technicians in Germany. Negatives of this quality and designed for this fine definition of printing are very delicate—they are not just photographic negatives, they are a whole complex prismatic system, reduced to the greatest possible degree of miniaturization. Once one starts to interfere with that system, the risk of completely ruining it is very high. Hans can touch up that negative—he has successfully carried out even more delicate operations than this requires. But the risk is high. Only you can accept the responsibility and give the order for him to try."

Rupert had no difficulty in deciding that one. "How long will it take?" he asked.

The reply astonished him: "Ten to fifteen minutes."

"Ten to fifteen minutes! I thought you said it was a delicate and complex job?"

"Enormously so. Like that of a surgeon removing a bullet from a human body. But it is not the actual deed of the removal that takes all the time. Hans has done his preparation—he has studied every stroke that will be required. All the instruments and inks necessary are there on the table. I deeply regret the situation, but as I have explained, the decision to run the risk must be yours. Should Hans fail . . . then the negative would be ruined beyond repair."

Rupert puffed on his pipe and looked across at the plump, furrowed face of Hans Wlaka. He was a type Rupert had learned to like from his earliest years living in middle Europe—a man of humble background and upbringing, patently honest, dedicated to his craft, as his peasant ancestors had been for centuries to their land. They looked each other straight in the eye. Wlaka picked up the first glimmer of Rupert's smile and showed just a touch of relaxing a little.

Rupert stood up. "Come on, Hans. Let's have a shot at it, shall we?"

In exactly fifteen minutes the operation was successfully completed. As Rupert climbed back into the Jensen, the clock on the control panel showed four minutes past three.

15

ONE of the many sophistications of the hand-built Jensen was a map board, which at the touch of a button slid noiselessly out from under the control panel at exactly the right height and to exactly the right extent adjusted to suit the driver, and focused an even spread of light over its whole surace. Rupert had Kummerly and Freys one-to-a-million scale map carefully set in the frame to give him the best picture of his target area that was possible. He consulted the map for a brief moment to refresh his memory and then slid it back out of sight. He had not memorized a piece of ground so thoroughly since the day he had led his company of Welsh Fusiliers around the eastern edge of Monte Cassino, straining to keep his men protected by the meager cover of rocks and rubble from a murderous cross-fire of machine guns, which shortly after had put an end to his fighting war. The map he relied on from here on was photographed in his memory.

Since his time schedule was running within a few minutes of plan, he stuck to his decision to drive back west through Dresden, joining the Autobahn at the north edge of the city, but then turning east rather than west. One of the many stray pieces of useful information that Tommy Thompson had mentioned was that the area around Bischofswerda, on the direct route from Dresden to the Polish border, was a favourite training ground for the Russian army, and there was no sense in running the risk of getting entangled in some unpredictable military exercise. He drove uneventfully to the end of the Autobahn at Bautzen and his turning took him directly past the People's Own Managed Railway Electronic Equipment factory, where Karl Henesch had worked for so many years before the fateful visit to Hungary that had brought him blundering into Rupert's life. By a similar process of reasoning, he had determined to avoid the direct road from Bautzen to Görlitz, where the main highway crossed over the Neisse onto Polish soil. Instead he swung northeast. If he was going to have to pretend to some nosey official that he had made a wrong turn and gotten lost, he might as well appear to be well and truly lost. At this moment, it suddenly crossed his mind to reach out and deliberately turn the compass some thirty-five degrees off its true magnetic bearing—a touch of misplaced science could add an impressive touch to any required alibi. Besides, the twist of country lanes would take him down to Görlitz through the little valley that led straight past Schloss Weesenstein. Not that he dared get out and ask if anyone there remembered the late Dr. Hans Reger and all the Hitler archives —or a pretty young girl called Gerda Wolfburg who'd worked there nearly thirty years ago.

He took another side road bypassing Reichenbach and, at exactly five minutes past five, came to the tee junction of the Görlitz-Rothenburg road, three kilometers south of Ludendorff. There was no traffic about except for a few farmers' carts and light trucks, all apparently heading home after a day's work in these fertile and well-tended fields. There were few signs of life at all in the village of Ludendorff, and Rupert reflected how inauspicious and unlikely a place it was to carry the name of the mighty and dreaded field marshal whose painstaking planning and iron discipline had so very nearly carried Kaiser Wilhelm II's armies to victory over the Allies in the spring of 1918. He drove through carefully, but not too slowly. He saw no uniforms, and nobody appeared to pay any attention to his rather unusual car; it crossed his mind that taking the back, unpaved roads had given him an added dividend he had not thought of before—even the sleek Jensen did not look very impressive under its present heavy coating of dust and mud. The difference between Austrian and East German license plates was little enough to pass unnoticed under a good covering of Saxon dirt.

As he left the unpretentious village behind him, he could see the river Neisse parallelling the road only a few hundred meters away on his right. The land was flat and open and, as Henesch had told him, there was not a house in sight. He heard the rumbling of railway wagons not far off and saw a freight train coming down the Polish side of the river heading for the junction at Piensk, only a few kilometers off to the northeast. In the gathering gloom, he could just make out Piensk's church tower and see the first few glimmering lights coming on across the border. The road started to curve westward away from the river, and he got his first glimpse of a large farmhouse set back from the road just ahead. There was no light showing anywhere, and no sign of life except two farm horses grazing in a field. He slowed down and came upon the entrance to the farm: two yellow and white stuccoed posts, in a sad state of disrepair and obviously long since missing the impressive gates they had originally been built to support.

As he turned in the drive up to the house, a dog barked; Charlie sat up and took notice for the first time in miles, sniffed, and growled. A stray mongrel ran across the drive and disappeared into the trees on the far side.

There was still sufficient light to pick out all the main features he was looking for without turning on his headlights. Approaching closer to the house, it was clear that it had once, long ago, been a handsome manor house, but now its windows were either broken or boarded up. It showed years of neglect, but nothing worse. The thrust of Hitler's drive eastward and the Russians' onslaught back to the west had been almost entirely far to the north and the south, along Europe's main arteries of transport linking the Nordic and the Slavic countries. Unlike in northern Bavaria, few conquering armies had ever bothered to fight pitched battles in this area—Frederick the Great of Prussia had taught military planners two centuries ago that whoever held lower Silesia controlled the central German plain.

The drive led right up to the house, but the last thirty or forty meters of it had long been lost in the derelict ruins of what had once been a formal garden and now was just a jumble of overgrown weeds, occasional piles of refuse, and the rubble of what might at one time have been a fountain. It was a melancholy picture. As Karl Henesch had explained in his letter, it was just at this point that a cart track—it was nothing more—swung off to the right and disappeared under a gabled archway that adjoined the house to a series of barns and outbuildings. The car was only moving at ten kilometers an hour, and Rupert, with every sense alert, instinctively moved his right hand to reassuringly touch the devastating little Czech 3.8 snugly secure in its shoulder holster. Even Charlie seemed to feel the air of strangeness and menace about their surroundings. He made a faint, plaintive whining noise, and Rupert murmured, "All right, old chap, all right."

He pointed the nose of the Jensen just into the opening under the arch and quietly slipped out on the driver's side, leaving the engine running. He stood for fully half a minute with his body wedged between two strong wooden posts, his eyes and ears straining for any sign of movement in the fast-fading light. In front of him was a typical farm yard, apparently completely enclosed on all four sides; a range of buildings of various dates and styles; a row of horse boxes on his immediate right; the old kitchens, pantries, storerooms and service areas of the main house on his left. Fifty meters straight ahead, at the other side of the cobbled stone yard, was a low single-story wing that a century ago had probably housed the blacksmith, the estate carpenter's workshop, and a hay barn and a somewhat higher edifice with huge broad doors, the coach house. The whole place was a patchwork, old and gloomy, part rough stone, part heavy timber beams, and here and there—as around the horse boxes and the doors of the coach house—the crumbling remains of what had once been decorative panels and tracings in the traditional white and yellow stucco. But there were plenty of signs that men still worked here.

From the far corner opposite him, there was a click as the top half of a wicket door swung slowly, gratingly open on its iron hinges, and a man appeared carrying an oil lantern. He showed no surprise whatever at seeing the nose of the muddy Jensen pointing into his domain. Very calmly he said, "Come in. I've been expecting you." He spoke German, but with an accent that was unmistakably Polish. The man walked out into the middle of the yard as casually as anyone expecting a visitor might.

Rupert waited a few more seconds to assure himself they were alone. Then he got back in the car and drove it slowly forward, stopping just where the man was standing. He said very quietly, "Are you Anton?"

"Yes, I am."

"Anton, Karlie is safe. He asked me to collect his mother's ring."

"I know, I know. There is no one else here. The farm workers have all gone home. Come in. Come in."

Rupert pocketed the ignition key and, feeling a little more relaxed by his reception, he got out. He still kept his right hand close to the automatic and the width of the car between himself and his new companion.

Anton seemed to display no apprehension, or even caution. Without another word he turned his back to Rupert and walked toward the open wicket door. He went in and again invited Rupert to follow him. Anton went straight to two other oil lamps, which seemed to be the only form of illumination available, and busied himself with lighting them. Rupert took his time getting through the broad door and had a good look around inside before actually passing through it. It was a bare, simple stone-floored room, but not without its homey touches. There was a log fire burning invitingly, two worn but comfortable upholstered chairs, and there were curtains pulled over the two outside windows, giving complete privacy. Rupert noticed two things that particularly surprised him: there were books, serious books in at least three different languages, resting on every possible table surface, and a faded photograph over the fireplace, in a silver frame. It showed one middle-aged man and two youths, all of them wearing the uniform of Polish cavalry officers. Anton was not the usual sort of "old family retainer" Rupert had expected to find.

Anton opened a large, heavily carved black oak dresser and asked, "Do you prefer wine or beer?"

"Whatever is easiest."

"They're both right here, but frankly I recommend the beer."

"Beer it is, then. Thank you."

It was good beer. "Prosit," said Anton. "Prosit," Rupert replied. They both sat down; they both lit up pipes. Rupert began to feel the whole encounter was a dream. Seated in the heavy armchair, for the first time there was enough light on Anton's face for a closer examination. He was of indeterminate age—an old retainer, Henesch had called him. Quite possibly, but the sufferings of the Polish people had been such that a man of forty was often indistinguishable from one of seventy. His hair was gray but still thick on top. His fine, clear-cut, wrinkled features did not seem to square with being an old family retainer either. As Rupert listened to Anton's voice, he became convinced it was that of an educated, cultured man. He looked directly at the photograph on the shelf above the fireplace.

"That you?" he inquired matter-of-factly.

"It was," Anton replied pointedly. "With my father and my brother. I am the only one left."

The pattern was not all that unusual. Rupert had known many Poles in London and in Vienna, men and women of high education, some of them the bearers of names famous in European history, who had been left penniless and stateless outcasts in 1945.

Anton rose and went to refill their glasses. Rupert began to feel that he had better come to the point, or he would be getting out of time cycle with that all-important schedule sitting on Gottfried's desk in Munich.

"Thank you very much for your hospitality. But I expect you know why I have come here?"

"Yes, I know. And I understand. Forgive me for delaying you, but it is lonely here for me." He indicated the many learned books scattered around the austere room.

"I can only work as a farm labourer—that is the law here. In Poland"—he waved an arm in the direction of the Neisse flowing across the bottom of the neighbouring field —"things are no better. Not for my kind." He put down his beer. "Come. I will show you what you want to see."

He went out another door that Rupert had not noticed, set in the side of the room and partly hidden by the oak dresser. Rupert followed this disheveled, gaunt, yet strangely dignified figure carrying the oil lamp above his head as though it were his last symbol of hope. They went down a long corridor and through another door, which took them into the coach house. It now contained two tractors, an assorted jumble of farm implements, ploughs, harrows, and three heavy carts. Across the back of the large lath-and-plaster chamber was a workbench, and beside it a strong iron barred and heavily locked door. From the look of the dust and debris and the number of bits and pieces Anton had to shift to open it, Rupert concluded it was little used. Anton seemed to read his thoughts. "Only two or three times a year," he said. Karl Henesch had said every three months. Maybe it just seemed longer to Anton.

Rupert was about to broach the subject of their mutual friend, acquaintance, and co-conspirator, but at that moment there was a definite shuffle of feet from just the other side of the wall. Rupert froze, and his hand went to the gun. Was this an ambush? Anton looked back at him and shone the lantern on his face. Then the spark of recognition and understanding crossed his lined, friendly countenance, and he said gently, "Cows."

Rupert took a sharp sniff. Yes, of course. Unmistakable. He must get a better grip on his nerves. They climbed the rough wooden staircase and came to another, even stronger, more heavily secured door at the top. Anton handed the lantern to Rupert, this time saying, "Here, hold this for me, please." He took out two more keys and, after some intricate maneuvering and pushing, the big door slowly yielded and swung inward. They went inside and Anton closed the door after him.

"Karl told you to bring a torch, I think?"

Rupert nodded.

"You can safely use it in here. There are no windows—and no cracks, either, I can assure you." Rupert looked at his somewhat sardonic smile. "Madame saw to that many years ago."

Rupert found himself torn between his intense desire to get on with exploration of whatever might lie ahead, and an overwhelming curiosity about the extraordinary Anton. Neither his manner, his bearing, nor anything he said seemed to shape up into any pattern Rupert could make head or tail of.

"Forgive me," he began. Anton stared him straight in the eyes with the calmness and assurance of a man who had no secrets.

"What's worrying you?" he asked.

For one of the very few times in his life, Rupert felt inadequate to the occasion. "Well . . . you." he said. "I just can't make much sense out of all this."

Anton laughed gently. "Don't waste your time trying, my friend. That photograph told you something of my background. I'm a Pole. I'm not a Communist. I must live. Leave it at that.

"Here," Anton continued. "You have not much time." He looked at his watch. "I don't know whether you will find what you are looking for in here, but I can only give you thirty minutes, so I suggest you do not waste it in idle conversation."

"You will wait here?" Rupert felt a slight surge of anxiety.

"Right here," Anton replied. "But there is no use asking

me any questions. I know nothing about anything. You understand?"

Rupert understood.

He took out his torch and started a preliminary general look around. They were in what appeared to be a huge loft—it was over the coach house, but it was clearly very much larger. He remembered the cows. The back side of the same buildings must be the cow barn, and this loft covered the entire area. Furthermore, since it was built into the gables of the enormous roof and had no windows, from the outside one would not even be aware that it existed at all. Yes, just the sort of hiding place many of the postwar looters must have been looking for—and, being way off the beaten track, miles from the nearest troop concentrations, about as safe and undisturbed a spot as anyone would be likely to find. Anyone? Who found it? Gerda? Did she have any connection with Henesch? Henesch said it had been his old family property, but he had only been allowed to return here—when was it, nineteen sixty something? No time to waste on this speculation now.

At first glance, the loft seemed to be one solid mass of large, wooden packing cases from end to end, indiscriminately covered with straw and dust. Was Rupert about to share the incredible experience of the MFA&A officers who first broke through the false wall in the Alt Aussee salt mine and found an Ali Baba's cave of some of the world's greatest art treasures awaiting them? Hardly likely, after all these years.

The first few cases he looked at depressed him beyond measure. They were all empty. Whatever had once been packed in them had probably been shipped through Tangier to South America years ago, he thought. Patience, patience. He moved slowly along the first row. Disappointment. Disappointment. But the fifth crate had something in it. He leaned over and shone his torch inside. There was a series of smaller cardboard boxes, each one wrapped in what appeared to be old linen towels. What a job it was before they invented polyethylene, he mused.

He took up the first parcel and carefully removed the wrapping. What he saw was not what he had expected, but the thrill was just as great. In his hand he held a royal blue, morocco leather case about fifty centimeters long, twenty wide, and four deep. On the top, chased in gold leaf, was the coat of arms of some noble family. Around the coat of arms was the easily recognizable chain and sacrificial lamb, denoting that the owner had been a Knight of the Golden Fleece.

Rupert opened the case with a sense of awe, and he was rewarded. The inside of the case was of thick blue velvet, and set into a series of regular recesses were twelve exquisite miniatures, each hand painted on ivory, signed and dated by the artists, and each one surrounded by a heavily garlanded gold frame. In the light and the time available, he could not positively identify the subjects, but from the plethora of red and white sashes, the numerous emblems of the Golden Fleece, and those firm, determined lower jaws, there was no doubt that these were Habsburg portraits. They certainly had never belonged to the Hofburg state collection, but there were still plenty of archdukes around central Europe in 1939. These would have come from somewhere not far from Vienna.

Time was desperately short. Anton had said only thirty minutes. Why only thirty minutes? There wasn't even time to argue or try to find out why. Rupert just felt the rest of the packages in that case and moved on. The next two cases were still sealed. No time to waste trying to pry them open. The next one was open. Indeed it was nearly empty—but not quite.

There were seven smaller boxes lying in the bottom of

the crate. Rupert nearly shouted out "Eureka!" Here was a range of objects which were unquestionably the works of Fabergé and other great nineteenth-century jewellers. Diamond tiaras with pearls like small pears hanging all over them. Definitely Russian. A set of gentleman's evening studs, buttons, and cufflinks, each piece supporting a cabochon sapphire the size of an American dime. He recognized them at once—they had been made by Cartier of Paris, and he could remember seeing them worn at his grandfather's dinner table by Max Weingarten in 1936, another Gestapo victim. There were no less than seven cigarette or jewel boxes, all exquisite, in semi-precious stones like malachite, jadeite, jasper, and rock crystal; all wreathed in gold tracery and decorated with diamonds and emeralds. A large dark green nephrite box actually had Karl Meulheimer's monogram worked on it in rubies—red and green had been Karl's racing colours. Wrapped separately in linen cloths were hand mirrors, ladies' lorgnettes, picture frames, a barometer and thermometer bearing the cypher of the last king of Bavaria, opera glasses, perfume bottles, and fan holders—all of the most superb craftsmanship, all made of metals and stones of the greatest rarity and beauty. There were velvet boxes of eggs and animals of such incredible design and imagination as to dazzle even so experienced a dealer as Rupert. There was a tin box, probably originally made to hold biscuits; now lined with a silk cloth, it contained something like twenty bracelets, and it needed no dealer's eyeglass to tell at a glance all the stones were real. Easy to see why none of this lot had appeared on the market before. All they had to do now was feed it out patiently, a little here and a little there; don't hurry and don't be too greedy and they'd be millionaires before long.

Rupert glanced at his watch; time was running on. The

next crate was carefully stacked with pictures, and he was relieved to see that whoever had hidden them had gone to plenty of trouble to see they were carefully preserved. They were all unframed, but firmly mounted on strong wooden stretchers, and each one was covered with a cloth of some kind—some of it looked like old curtain material—and in between each cloth were small wood blocks to prevent warping. The first one he picked out he recognized at once. It was a distinctive and outstanding representation of the Holy Family's flight into Egypt by Giacomo Cozzarelli, painted in Siena in the late fourteen hundreds. He was sure that had been on his MFA lists but could not immediately recall the owner. The next two were by Matteo di Giovanni, of the same style and period. He did not remember them but assumed they must have come from the same collection. How he prayed for more time! This old loft may not have been Alt Aussee, but it was certainly a fine "modest" treasure trove. Some person or persons unknown, in the legal phrase, must have worked to a very carefully thought-out plan for a very long time to assemble this warehouse of so many fine "minor" collections.

There was so much that was familiar, so many clues, but nothing yet exactly what he was looking for. Only another six minutes to go. Rupert walked firmly past the next three cases, came to the end of the row, and started down the other side. Unlike many Celts, he did not entertain illusions about possessing more basic senses than other people. He just happened to notice that the lid of the fourth case he passed in the second row was open, and he shone his torch into it. More small boxes, more linen cloths. The case appeared to contain mainly what dealers describe as "family silver"—not great works of art, but examples of finely wrought silver tableware, salts and peppers, teapots, and assorted trinkets, which at current silver prices were worth considerable money. There were baize-lined trays of knives, forks, and spoons, all engraved with some unfortunate dispossessed owner's crest. There was a miniature wooden chest of bits and pieces, a ladies sewing kit, three different-sized but beautifully matched pairs of scissors, some snuff boxes, a variety of chains and crucifixes, and a simple silver locket. Rupert snapped the locket open. His heart skipped a beat, and he slipped it into his back pocket.

There was something else familiar in that tray of miniature picture frames. What was it? Those ornate tangles of scrolls, cupids, and extravagantly unnecessary ornamentation so popular at the turn of the century never appealed to aesthetes of Rupert's upbringing. He passed the beam of the flashlight quickly over the tray again, hoping to find a monogram, coat of arms, or some telltale symbol that might provide hard information. Nothing but disappointment. Look again, he murmured to himself.

The pale beam of light caught a flash of colour. Not silver. Not cold metallic reflection. He felt it more than saw it. For the first time Rupert was conscious that his hand was trembling. He rested his wrist on the edge of the packing case and ever so slowly, unbelievingly, moved the beam back a few inches. It was colour all right—paint. To his practiced eye, very special paint—the unmistakable reds and blues of a Florentine artist of the fourteenth century.

The silver frame, which might be worth a few hundred dollars, faded from his vision like a ship over the horizon. He picked up the remarkable little object. Within its few square centimeters, here lying in the palm of his excited, sweating hand was a picture he knew from his childhood —a picture not only of superb beauty, but to him of the most profound significance. A tiny square of sheer, lovely, mysterious beauty—a madonna and child by that unknown genius whom the world's greatest art galleries had only been able to identify as the Master of the Castello Nativity. As though in a dream, Rupert turned it over, worked open the intricate catch on the back from long-forgotten memory, and gently rolled up the treasured little devotional canvas that used to adorn his grandmother's dressing table at Semmering.

There was a move from the other end of the loft and Anton came forward slowly, holding his lantern aloft. Rupert thought he looked like a symbolic replica of the Statue of Liberty.

"Sorry, my friend. Time's up. I have my orders."

Rupert didn't waste time asking "From whom?" As he put down the box of assorted silver, he noticed the lid of a red leather case next to it open. He couldn't help seeing the contents, and a quick flash from his torch left him in no doubt at all what it was. Inside the red box were five neatly stacked rows, lying on end; each row consisted of something like twenty original Maria Theresa twelve-ducat golden thalers. They were dated 1744. At current prices, each one was worth at least five thousand dollars. The thought of five thousand dollars brought Rupert's mind back with a jerk to his agreement with Karl Henesch. At a quick reckoning, he figured just one would be sufficient to arrange and finance that unhappy refugee's trip to Canada. He slipped one into his inside coat pocket and straightened up to face Anton. They just stared at each other. All Rupert said was "Most interesting."

They went back in silence the way they had come, and at each door Anton handed the lantern to Rupert to hold while he secured the heavy locks. After dealing with the big door opening into the coach house, Anton spent nearly two minutes pushing refuse and odd bits of timber back in front of it and then bent down to pick up handfuls of dust and dirt from the rough stone floor, which he scattered at random all round him. He borrowed Rupert's torch to scan the floor closely and satisfy himself there were no especially noticeable footprints to indicate anyone had used the door.

Funniest damn setup, Rupert thought. He seems such a decent fella; I wish there were time to find out exactly who does what and to whom around here.

There wasn't. They made their way back along the dark passage to Anton's quarters and walked straight out into the courtyard to Rupert's parked car. Charlie was certainly glad to see him, but the gloomy oppressive air of the whole establishment had dampened even his exuberant spirits. He wagged his tail to indicate pleasure, but nothing more.

It was almost dark now, and the decaying outline of the old buildings was a graying silhouette against the evening sky. Rupert opened the car door and turned to shake hands with Anton, who was silently motionless, just standing there holding his lantern. They both might have preferred an evening of long and interesting discussion; there was not time, and neither could really find the words.

Rupert put out his hand and said, "Thank you. I'm very grateful."

Anton took it and mumbled, "That's all right."

"If you ever get to Vienna . . ."

"I know. I know . . ."

Anton stood quite still while Rupert climbed into the driving seat and wound down the door window preparatory to a final parting greeting.

Suddenly, from just a few meters behind the car and on the driver's side, came a gruff, authoritative, and clear command. "Keep both hands on the wheel and don't move a muscle or I'll blow your brains out!"

Neither Rupert nor Anton moved. But Rupert could move his eyes far enough to see the rear-view driving mirror just in front of his elbow on the door. In the gloom, he could not see much—but enough. Standing not two meters immediately behind him was a man in uniform. It was too dark to identify either the cap or the greatcoat—might have been police or military—but the smartness of the cut of both made it pretty clear the man was an officer. And the pale glimmer of Anton's lantern caught a metallic gleam in the officer's hand, which made it quite clear he was perfectly equipped to blow Rupert's brains out if he chose to.

"Sit perfectly still, Mr. Conway, and you won't get hurt. We are going for a little drive. Anton, put out that lantern and get in the front seat beside this man."

Anton walked round the car and did as he was told.

Rupert heard the steps as the officer moved a bit closer.

Then the voice spoke again, just behind him. "Do not look around, Mr. Conway. I am going to sit right behind you." The man fitted the action to his words, and Rupert heard the door open. There was a momentary pause, which must have been the moment the officer and Charlie first stared into each other's eyes. The officer gave a slight grunt and said, "Not too dangerous, I think."

To emphasize just where the danger lay, he gave the back of Rupert's head a gentle prod with his revolver. "I shall sit right here behind you. You will drive precisely according to my instructions. If you make one false move or attempt to turn round, I shall shoot you. Is that quite clear?"

"Perfectly clear," Rupert responded.

"Good. I assure you I don't want any unpleasantness. Now. You will start the car, Mr. Conway, and you will drive back to the gate. No more than ten kilometers an hour. Turn your headlights on. That's right."

Rupert navigated as directed, out through the arch, along the track, and stopped at the gate.

"Turn right and proceed at twenty-five kilometers," was the next order.

They drove for about five minutes in total silence, and Rupert could see the road was gradually winding eastward until he noticed they were travelling right along the bank of the river. In another minute, they came to a small bridge. This was the first time Rupert had ever seen what the Warsaw Pact powers boasted of as the "peace frontier." He knew from the map that on the other side of that bridge was Poland, but sure enough, there was nothing more than a large painted sign to mark the border. No guards, no watch towers. As the will of the Soviet army is law on either side, I suppose they don't really need anything else, Rupert thought to himself. But audible comment would have been tactless, to say the least.

Rupert noticed an old truck parked by the bridge. There was not another vehicle or light of any kind in sight.

The next command came clear and sharp. "Draw into the side and stop here."

The car stopped.

"Do not switch off, and keep both hands firmly on the wheel." Rupert's mind was racing, trying to anticipate what might happen next. Could he ever get the 3.8 into action; would he have a chance to use it? If he did, would that mean escape or simply guarantee his own execution? He heard the rear door open and the officer got out on the road.

"I still have you covered," he heard the officer say, and as the voice came not more than a few inches from his left ear, Rupert had no doubt he spoke the truth.

"Anton, get out and come around here."

Without a word, Anton did as he was ordered. Rupert could catch snatches of the conversation, and made out the word *accident* quite clearly several times. Anton walked over to the truck, started the engine, and drove it onto the bridge. He left the engine running and walked back to where the officer still stood, pistol aimed at the back of Rupert's head. Rupert heard them exchange a few more words.

Then there was a shot.

For a moment Rupert thought he was dead. But he felt nothing—no pain, no shock. He sat frozen in his seat, his hands glued to the wheel. Funny the odd thoughts that crossed a man's mind in a moment of acute crisis. The only thing he was conscious of was that his hands were cold, sweaty, and trembling on the wheel, and he remembered how he had experienced the same blood-chilling sensation when he had regained consciousness lying in a mudhole on the slopes of Cassino to discover that his right leg was a bloody mass of flesh. One lost all sense of time when the glands were pumping adrenalin into the veins at this rate. Was he unconscious? Had he been unconscious?

It was Anton's calm and unruffled voice that broke the spell. He said, "Get out of the car a moment, please."

Please? Rupert had no idea what was going to happen next—nor what had happened. He opened the door very slowly and deliberately with his left hand, moving his right hand just a little closer to the shoulder holster.

"Turn out the lights," Anton said.

Rupert leaned back toward the control panel and pressed the necessary switch. He immediately realized that it would take a few seconds for his eyes to adjust to the deepening darkness and moved even slower than before. Anton just stood there and said nothing. When Rupert was clear of the car door and for the first time could see behind him, what he saw was Anton holding a pistol. The uniformed officer was lying, face up, on the road. There could be no doubt he was stone dead.

"Use your torch if you want to look at him," Anton said. There was no emotion or sign of feeling of any kind in his voice. Any Polish soldier of his age was well accustomed to the sight of dead men.

Rupert noted that Anton was holding the pistol quite relaxed, his arm hanging straight down, the muzzle pointing into the road. He certainly showed no sign of intending to use it again. Rupert took the torch from his overcoat pocket and shone it directly onto the face of the dead officer.

"Good God! Henesch!"

"Henesch?" Anton pronounced it as a question. "That was the name he gave you?"

"Yes, Karl Henesch." Rupert stood and stared at the face he would have recognized anywhere. Henesch had been shot from the back, straight through the heart, and so quickly, so unexpectedly that there was no sign of fear or anguish or anything registered in his face at all. Not even surprise. He switched off the torch and looked at Anton with a bewilderment he made no attempt to disguise.

"He used many names." Anton said. "It was part of his job. In recent years he had officially been called Rolf Heinrich." That name meant nothing to Rupert. He continued to look Anton straight in the eye. After a moment Anton said, "His real name was Ludwig Wolfburg."

Gerda's brother!

All Rupert said was: "Do you mind if I light my pipe?"

"There is no time. You must leave at once."

Rupert took a deep breath; his eyes were quite accustomed to the dark by now. "I think you have saved my life. Thank you. But, please, you must tell me why?"

He saw Anton square his shoulders; he seemed to grow a full two inches in height, and a tired smile creased the taut skin and lightened his sad, gray eyes.

"Herr Conway, I know very little about you. Just what the Security Police chose to tell me to play my part in tonight's little operations. An accident had been ordered for you." Rupert did not try to conceal a shiver. Anton continued, "Not a fatal accident was the order. God knows what they intended to do with you. It was not my business. But I know you were a British officer. I was a Polish officer. However lowly my lot in life, I shall always be a Polish officer.

"In 1943, Ludwig Wolfburg was in charge of the S.S. detachment behind the German lines at Lowicz, where I come from. With his own hands he murdered my mother and both my sisters. Through concentration camps, Russian salt mines, and thirty-three years of poverty and degradation, I have been waiting for the opportunity to kill that man. I found him in this district several years ago. Oh, I have had plenty of chances to kill him since then—often. But never with any chance of safety for myself. Perhaps at heart I am a coward, but I do not want to die, even now. When Wolfburg came here a week ago and ordered me to assist in arranging your, ah, accident, I thought at last my time may have come. Everything I have done tonight has been exactly according to his orders. Except for that one shot."

Anton stepped closer to Rupert and thrust out his right hand. "Here, take this gun." Instinctively Rupert accepted the weapon handed to him butt foremost. As his fingers closed around the grip, he noticed that Anton had been wearing gloves. Another kind of trap?

"I can only give you four hours to get back across the border. If I don't find the body and report it before midnight, it will compromise my own safety. You must leave at once."

"And what do you expect me to do with this?" Rupert held up the revolver. As he did so, he noticed it was still loaded.

"I suggest you throw it in the Elbe," was Anton's reply.

They shook hands in silence. Rupert drove off and, looking back, saw the shadowy figure of the Pole trudging back down the dark, lonely road toward Schloss Frauenstein. It was a silhouette he would never forget.

"That must be one of the bravest men I have ever met," he said out loud to Charlie.

Rupert did not need to consult the map again. Drive another few kilometers north to Rothenburg, turn left, and take the secondary road through Neisky on to Bautzen and rejoin the Autobahn. There was just one small village before he hit the junction south of Rothenburg. It was not marked on the map, but as he drove through it he noticed the signpost. It read "Leipensche."

16

THE night was clear and the traffic light. Rupert made good time, except for the traffic tie-up outside Karl-Marx-Stadt, where the new bridge was being built. It was just eleven minutes before midnight when, without incident, he cleared the East German checkpoint north of Hof. One and a half minutes later he drove into the car park on the West German side and walked briskly over to the police post. Two young officers at the duty desk were engaged in anxious discussion while studying a document in front of them. As he crossed the room a telephone rang, and one of them picked it up. He heard his name spoken. "I am Herr Conway," he said abruptly, and the two policemen looked up startled and unbelieving. The one on the phone said, "Hold on."

Rupert handed his passport and travel documents across the desk, where they were speedily examined. They handed him the phone. Rupert found himself talking to Gottfried in Munich.

"You all right?" was the captain's opener.

"Very much so, but tired," Rupert replied cheerfully. "And I've one hell of a lot to tell you."

"We've got some news for you, too. Why don't you drive straight to Munich. I'll book you in at the Bayerische Hof and we can talk first thing in the morning."

"Good idea. Just one thing: phone Jo Liebmann and let him know I'm back, will you? And ask him to phone my flat and tell them I'll be home some time tomorrow. I wouldn't like them to worry about me."

He rang off. The young policeman made an entry on the papers in front of him, and Rupert and Charlie were on their way again.

The night manager of Munich's world-famous Bayerische Hof was momentarily surprised by the unexpected arrival of Charlie, but he would not have held that delicate and important job had he not been a resourceful man. He quickly assigned them to a room with a balcony, just in case; both Rupert and Charlie slept without a care in the world.

At seven A.M. the phone rang to inform Rupert that Hauptmann Gottfried and party would be arriving in half an hour, and breakfast had been ordered to be served in the bedroom adjoining Rupert's for five people. While he was dressing, he could hear waiters moving furniture about, and at seven twenty-nine an assistant manager arrived to hand him the key to the connecting door. As he unlocked it, Gottfried and party came in from the corridor. There were, indeed, five of them.

Gottfried dispensed with names, but for the sake of clarity indicated each member by their function: his own deputy, a secretary equipped with tape recorder and note pad, two senior officers of the Bundespolizei, and a dignified official from the chancellor's private office, who apparently had just arrived by helicopter from Bonn. Rupert was impressed. He had done a lot of thinking for himself during the drive last night, but his figuring had not reached as far as the head of the West German government. As early morning greetings were exchanged and everyone shook hands with Rupert, the deputy gave the room a careful examination and exchanged words with a uniformed policeman who suddenly appeared out of the bathroom. The waiters were dismissed and the man in uniform joined another patrolling the corridor outside. They helped themselves from a series of hot-plates on the heavily laden sideboard, poured their coffee, and settled down to a working breakfast.

The senior of the two Bundespolizei officers chaired the meeting, Gottfried acted as local anchorman and *amicus curiae* for Rupert, and the gentleman from Bonn maintained very nearly total silence with such an air of authority that he seemed effortlessly to dominate the whole proceeding. Everyone deferred to him, explained to him. Fortunately, Rupert was not a big breakfast eater, as the first half hour was entirely taken up with his detailed account of yesterday's experiences, while the rest of them stuffed themselves with eggs, bacon and six different kinds of sausage, toast, plain rolls, sweet rolls, and coffee by the bucketful. He only managed to wedge in an odd mouthful between sentences and slip one sausage under the table to Charlie. The whole story was taped, and from time to time the secretary made a note as instructed by one of the officers around the table.

The coincidence of the two Frauensteins did not seem to interest them, but Rupert's calculation that Gerda Ruttgers must have travelled to the security police headquarters in eastern Saxony was regarded as highly significant. The chancellor's man nodded his head in a manner that was clearly meant to convey, "Didn't I tell you so?" And the secretary scribbled like mad.

The episode at Altenburg's caused some brief ribald comment but was passed over as inconsequential. Rupert was surprised, indeed a little disappointed by their apparent lack of any noticeable excitement on hearing the details of his discoveries in the farm loft. The story of the mysterious appearance of the security police officer, his few terse but threatening comments, the strange drive to the bridge at the Polish border, and the sudden and totally unexpected somersault in the whole situation brought about by his murder bound them in such rapt attention that every coffee cup on the table went cold.

The statement that the murdered man turned out to be Karl Henesch brought open expressions of excitement, and the revelation that Henesch's real name was Ludwig Wolfburg was a sensation! The man from Bonn fired off a series of staccato comments for the secretary's note pad; the number two man from the Bundespolizei rushed to the telephone; everybody talked at once. Rupert still had no idea what they had been up to in the thirty-six hours since he last met with Gottfried, but clearly he was fitting large pieces into their jigsaw puzzle in some highly critical places. He took the occasion of the diversion to help himself to a fresh, hot cup of coffee and light his first pipe. He also received a well-understood signal from his four-legged friend under the table, as a result of which another policeman arrived to take Charlie for a walk in the hotel garden. Everyone stretched his legs, the secretary disappeared into the loo, and the waiters brought fresh coffee and cleared away the dirty dishes.

It was a quarter to nine when they settled down to the second session. This time the man from Bonn took complete command. "Gentlemen," he commenced formally, "we are very grateful to Herr Conway. His information takes us several steps forward in our inquiries."

He paused to light a cigarette, while Rupert thought, but did not quite say out loud, "What inquiries? They seem to be off my art looting track altogether."

"But the explanation to the tangle still eludes us."

The senior police officer said, "His evidence about the Ruttgers woman certainly confirms all our suspicions that she is a secret agent working under cover for the GDR."

"It would seem to, but suspicions are not facts. What do we now know we did not know yesterday? We now know her brother was an officer in their security police. We know he played a major role in some elaborate plot to lure Herr Conway to an obscure village along the Polish border. Why? Why did they go to so much trouble? What had they planned to do to Herr Conway?" Rupert shuddered at the thought. "They are a ruthless and often brutal crowd, but they are not corrupt. Herr Conway, if you will forgive my saying so, all this business about jewelry and coins and so on is very interesting—very interesting indeed—but it is what you English call, I think, a red herring."

Rupert said, "Perhaps if I knew what you were looking for, I might be of more help to you?".

"Oh, you have been, you have—of great help. Frankly—and in the secrecy of this room, you understand—what we are concerned with, Herr Conway, is not art, but affairs of state, matters of defence which concern not only the Bundesrepublik, but all the NATO powers. Your inquiries about the mysterious Frau Ruttgers brought a number of other—what should I say—threads to our attention.

"Hauptmann Gottfried told you about the ship the French police intercepted en route to Tangier. Yesterday an expert from the Bayerischemuseum positively identified some of her cargo. As you had led us to expect, in her hold were items that had disappeared without trace during the last war. Our expert was absolutely certain they had not been lying hidden in Western Germany. Much of the packing was old newspapers, sheets from the *Dresdener Zeitung*—not conclusive, of course, but suggestive. You also provided us with the information that the reason always given by Frau Ruttgers for her visits to see her aged mother were false reasons. That faced us with something else we did not know: why did the East German security authorities allow her to get away with it?"

Rupert put his pipe down. "Naturally I thought a lot about this last night, in the car. Frau Ruttgers' connection with the GDR security police was, of course, then quite clear to me. But I also felt clear in my own mind that the kind of favoured treatment she received must be for some much greater reasons than just being the sister of a comparatively junior officer. Over a period of years, there must have been dozens of officials involved with those phony visas. Strange that nobody ever spotted something."

"So what conclusiòn did you come to?" the senior officer asked.

"My conclusion—and I must admit it is pure speculation—is that she must be a very important spy, and in return for the information she brings them, they allow her to help herself to certain property whose location is known only to her and a few close associates. They must include senior security officers, of course. You may remember, she did work with Reger at Weesenstein, cataloguing material for the proposed Führermuseum at Linz. It would seem perfectly possible that, when the Nazis were evacuating that area, she was involved in the operations—probably took part in some of the hiding. It is also well known how short they always are of hard Western currency, especially Deutschmarks. It crossed my mind that what she gave them must come pretty pricey, but they get it for free."

He looked carefully round to survey the effect of his own theorizing. The exchange of glances seemed to indicate that the great minds were all flowing in the same direction. The man from Bonn muttered something to the second Bundespolizei silver-collared officer, who put a small envelope on the table and spoke for the first time.

"We are trusting you completely, Herr Conway. You realize this is all highly secret, of course?"

"Of course."

"The Ruttgers have a country house at Weilheim," he continued. "We have had it under close surveillance for some days now. Yesterday one of our officers was able to gain admittance and make a thorough search. He found just two things of interest. The first was some very sophisticated high-powered radio equipment—transmitting as well as receiving. It proves nothing. Nearly all of it is of Japanese manufacture and bears American labels—but, again, significant. He also found this." The officer carefully opened the envelope and slid out onto the white tablecloth a tiny aluminum tube, which he picked up with a small pair of stainless steel tweezers. The gentleman from Bonn leaned forward, looked at it intently, and nodded knowingly.

The officer continued. "It might have been designed for a wide variety of pills, but it is exactly like a container the East Germans often use to carry microfilm. The officer found it empty at the back of a drawer filled with small radio parts, fuses—all that sort of thing. His suggestion is that someone who would not notice the disappearance of one of these little things must be someone who uses them frequently."

"Fingerprints?" inquired the man from Bonn.

"Yes, certainly, Herr Doktor. There are good imprints

here of thumb and forefinger. In due course we can compare them with the Ruttgers'; but we must get those very carefully. I don't think we are ready to move yet."

"Quite right. Quite right." The man from Bonn turned to Gottfried. "Have you got a photograph of this woman, Ruttgers?" he asked.

Gottfried opened a leather briefcase and took out a file from which he produced a very clear full-face and excellent likeness of the strikingly chic and immaculately groomed Gerda. He handed it across the table. The recipient studied it carefully. "The new Mark Seven pocket camera?"

Gottfried replied, "Jawohl, Herr Doktor. One of my men took it just as she walked away from her car. She had no idea it was taken."

"Very good. Very good," the Herr Doktor commented. They sat in silence for a moment while he scrutinized the photo. He said quietly and to no one in particular, "I've seen that face somewhere. Somewhere. Where was it?" He seemed to disappear into a revery of his own.

After another long silence, the senior police officer said, "The pattern is absolutely complete. Except that there is not a single piece of evidence that would prove anything in court."

Rupert spoke. "May I ask a question?"

"Certainly."

"Have you anything at all to connect all this with Jacob Schwarz in Vienna?"

"Nothing whatever. Our mutual friend Josef Liebmann has scraped the bottom of his barrel. Lebel has been helpful, as always. Other than the fact that they must all have known each other in 1946, we have found no link at all."

Rupert thought for a moment. "Mind if I go and talk to Karl Ruttgers again?"

"Not at all—provided we can rely totally on your discretion, Herr Conway."

"You can. I just have an idea. It may lead to nothing."

There was another pregnant silence, which was abruptly shattered by the man from Bonn, who dropped his coffee cup back on its saucer with such a bang the contents splashed all over the table. "That face! Of course I know that face!" He jumped up from the table and rushed to the telephone. From the way he barked his orders into it, Rupert realized for the first time that the other end of that line was also being manned by a policeman. All Rupert could make out of the telephone conversation was that the speaker was showing uncommon excitement for an official of his obvious authority, and he twice caught the phrase "the missing witness."

At the table, the senior officer was questioning Gottfried about Ruttgers' establishment and his movements. It seemed Gottfried knew for certain that Ruttgers was at that moment in his own office—his every move was being watched and recorded.

An hour later, having packed his overnight bag and checked out of the Bayerische Hof, happy with the assurance that his bill had been "taken care of," Rupert ambled casually into the aggressive modernity of Kunsthaus Ruttgers on Sendlingerstrasse. The charming young man with the long, wavy hair registered no marked surprise at seeing him, and five minutes later he was ushered into the massive office to be greeted affably by the apparently quite contented and self-assured owner of this luxurious establishment. If he had any inkling that Rupert had within the last few hours been a witness to his brother-in-law's murder, he certainly showed no sign of it.

"What brings you to Munich, my friend?"

"Just on my way back from Nuremberg," Rupert replied. He settled himself comfortably in a deep leather armchair, and they chatted amiably about the paucity of good art dealers in northern Germany and the remarkable success of Messrs. Sotheby and Christie in surmounting unhappy Britain's increasing economic anemia by their invasions of other countries' art markets.

After a sufficiently decent interval, Rupert brought the conversation a little nearer to home by remarking how much he admired Ruttgers' new advertising campaign in *Weltkunst.* He marvelled once again how a man of Ruttgers' unquestioned toughness and shrewdness was so susceptible to flattery. This time he had no difficulty in suppressing his mischievous instinct to try to needle him about those ghastly abstracts. Just to play on his vanity was Rupert's single purpose on this occasion.

In due course, and with fateful inevitability, the name of Peter Karl Fabergé entered the conversation. Ruttgers obliged him by mentioning it first, and Rupert even managed to look surprised. When a suitable opening arose, he inquired innocently, "Thought any more about that pink elephant I told you about?"

Ruttgers' reply seemed completely casual. For a moment Rupert thought a look of wariness suddenly appeared about those hard, unfeeling eyes, but he could not be sure.

"Oh, that?" was the rejoinder. "No, I can't say I have. An odd story. I don't really believe it, you know."

"It's true enough." Rupert could not help saying that, but he followed it quickly with an absolutely blatant return to flattery. "Of course," he continued, "you know much more about that line than I do."

Now that was the kind of talk Ruttgers just couldn't resist. "As a matter of fact," he said, "I think I was wrong on one point." Rupert waited, but decided not to help him out. "The fella you said it belonged to. What was the name? . . ."

Rupert was certain that didn't ring true, but now maybe he could gain a trick by being helpful.

"Schwarz," he said. "Jacob Schwarz."

"Yeah, yeah. Schwarz. I did remember afterwards. Knew the guy during the war."

"You were in the same squadron." Rupert egged him on just a little.

"Yeah, that's right. He tell you that?"

"Oh, it just came out. Casual conversation at a cocktail party—something like that."

Ruttgers appeared to be thinking he had said all he need on that subject. Rupert saw he was going to have to move carefully to keep this dialogue going.

"Remarkable story. You were his master sergeant, I believe?"

"Yeah, that's right."

With Ruttgers talking only in monosyllables, Rupert was sure he was getting worried. Have another shot. "At Kronach. I wish you would tell me about it."

"You seem to know so damn much. What the hell are you playing at?"

Now that definitely indicated the first real touch of fear. Fear and vanity, Rupert thought, the best possible combination of human emotions to get a man to trap himself. If I can just find the right key. He smiled his most engaging smile. "Well, Schwarz told me he won the thing in a poker game. I just couldn't believe he ever won any poker game you were in."

It worked. A man who under any other combination of circumstances would have been a model of hard-boiled cynicism rose straight to the bait.

"Damn fool!" he snorted and bit on his cigar. "He never won a poker game in his life! Worst rotten poker player in the squadron."

"That was what I thought," Rupert said encouragingly.

"What really happened?"

Without a moment's hesitation, the answer came straight back. "He *lost* it in a poker game."

Now we're getting someplace, Rupert thought. His great fear at that moment was that Ruttgers would dry up again. He need not have worried. The ex-master sergeant become wealthy art dealer and bon vivant, accustomed to all the accolades bestowed on the successful in this world, was just getting the bit between his teeth.

"Do you know where he got it from in the first place?"

"No. No idea. You were in Europe at the end of the war. You know how things were. Black markets, those poor damn D.P.'s wandering all over the place. There wasn't a building in most of Europe wasn't looted by somebody. But I know damn well how Schwarz lost that elephant. I was there." Vanity triumphed again.

Rupert changed gear instantly. "Who won it?"

"Fellow called Gleason."

"Gleason, who was Gleason?"

"One of our technical sergeants. Fat little guy. He was banker in the sergeant's mess. When we broke up to go back to the States, Schwarz was broke, as usual. He couldn't pay Gleason what he owed him, so they settled for that fancy elephant."

"That's fascinating. Any idea where Gleason is now?"

"Sure. I know exactly where he is."

"I'd very much like to talk to him."

Ruttgers snorted again. "You can't."

"Why not?"

"Damn fool's dead."

"Dead?"

"Like mutton."

"When did he die?"

"As I remember it, just a day or so before we were due to sail back to the States. March 1946 sometime."

"A few days after Gleason had received the elephant from Schwarz?"

"Yeah, that would be right."

"Very convenient of him. And how did Sergeant Gleason choose to die at such an obliging moment?"

"Got knocked off in a motor accident."

"How fascinating. Knocked off, or knocked down?"

"Both, maybe. I don't know."

"And who did the knocking?"

"You tell me."

"Sergeant Schwarz, of course."

"Of course," said Ruttgers with an audible sigh of relief. He lay back in his big desk chair, gazed at the ceiling, and poured out a cloud of cigar smoke like a man who had at long last gotten something off his mind and felt worlds better for it.

Rupert, with his usual slow, methodical gestures, refilled his pipe and took his sweet time about lighting it. Then with studied deliberation, he very gently started the process of bringing Ruttgers back down to earth. He said, "And you knew all this?"

Ruttgers couldn't un-live the last ten minutes. "Yeah," he said hesitantly. "Sure. I knew it."

"And you were master sergeant of the squadron?"

"Yeah, I was."

Rupert just sat quietly and looked at him. For the first time, Ruttgers showed unmistakable anxiety in his face. He thanked God Gerda was safely back home in Weilheim. She would have given him hell if she had heard this. He had no idea whatever of the hell that at that moment was rapidly catching up with Gerda.

Rupert still just sat there. He had no desire to sound any fire alarms for Karl Ruttgers. By the look on his face and the darting of his eyes, his own imagination was hard at work on the job and needed no help from anybody. Rupert's next question was almost a whisper.

"Shouldn't you have charged Schwarz?"

However gently applied, the knife went straight to its target. Ruttgers sat quite still for several seconds. It was Rupert who relieved the tension by rising and walking across to the desk. He thrust his hand out across it and said smilingly, "Strange bloody world we live in, Karl. Must run. Take care of yourself." And he was gone.

17

THE following night, over a quiet dinner at 5B Stephansplatz, Rupert told Sandra just enough about his adventures of the last two days to satisfy her curiosity without also arousing fears and apprehensions of physical danger to either of them. So far as events in Munich and their dramatic potential were concerned, he was of course pledged to secrecy. His conscience was a little tender about keeping Frauenstein's amazing loft from her, but he salved it by saying he had found further "trace" of their grandfather's collections; exactly what was there to be found, he had still no idea—which was true.

She had nothing out of the ordinary to tell him, only that Max's lecture to the postponed meeting of the American Ladies Club had been a great success, except for the unfortunate fact that on leaving the dining room Max had tripped over the carpet and ended up on the floor with a bloody nose. Neither event was really out of the ordinary. Frau Kröner had excelled herself with her creamed sweetbreads and garlic noodles, one of Rupert's favourite dishes, and he had discoursed at length over the quality of the Chateau Montrose 1966 they had washed it down with. As usual in that household, no point of interest that arose was allowed to pass unverified, and over coffee after dinner, Sandra found herself plying through the pages of Hugh Johnson's monumental *World Wine Atlas* while Rupert caught up with three days' copies of the London *Times.* The stereo was playing Brahms' Double Concerto for Violin and Cello softly in the background, and Charlie was curled up sound asleep by Rupert's chair. As so often happens to so many scenes of domestic bliss in real life, the whole idyllic picture was shattered by the telephone ringing.

With a mild "damn," Rupert put down his paper and reached out to answer it. Sandra paid little attention—at first.

"Oh, righto. Put him on." And after a few seconds pause, "Evening, Jo. Yes, thanks. They gave you the full story? What! A lady? Munich license plate. Yes, that will be it. Let's stick to the original plan, Jo. I'll be there in ten minutes. Right. See you later."

Sandra said, "What lady?"

Rupert chuckled. "I'm pretty sure I know. And I doubt if she's going to behave like a lady. Come on; let's go for a little drive." He slipped quickly into his dressing room and changed his coat. Glad I didn't have time to give that back to Jo, he said to himself, as he slipped the shoulder holster into place. If she knows all there is to know, she'll shoot me as soon as look at me.

Sandra was puzzled and intrigued. Charlie was always wildly enthusiastic about going for a drive after dinner.

Exactly ten minutes from putting the phone down after talking to Jo Liebmann, the Jensen drew up in Reisnerstrasse and parked alongside the Italian embassy. Just across the road a black BMW was parked under a lamp-post that had no light in it. As Rupert and Sandra crossed the street to the entrance of the apartment block at number 61, its headlights flashed for a split second and were answered by a similar flash from another BMW parked just around the corner in Rennweg. Right in front of the door to 61 was a red Porsche with a Munich license plate. As they reached the door of the building, it was opened by a man in a raincoat standing just inside the darkened lobby. He and Rupert grunted to each other, the man disappeared into what might have been a broom closet, and Rupert and Sandra headed for the elevator.

A few seconds later they rang the bell of Jacob Schwarz's apartment on the sixth floor. There was a long pause. Then Schwarz opened it. He looked at Rupert in startled disbelief and attempted what was probably meant to be a spluttering, mumbled protest. He certainly was not expecting guests, and his look and his protestations made it abundantly clear that none were welcome. He had no chance. The moment the door had moved, Rupert got his foot well inside and was effusively pouring out his most determined and aggressive charm. Completely ignoring Schwarz's obvious embarrassment and annoyance, he talked and acted as though it were the most natural thing in the world for them to pay an unannounced social call at this hour of the evening, marched straight in and took his overcoat off, talking all the time as though he had just been received by a welcoming committee complete with flags and brass band. Short of physical violence, there was nothing that could be done to stop him, and Schwarz was not capable of violence in his present state of health or mind. Sandra quietly brought up the rear, unbelieving but fascinated. Without being asked, they both sat firmly down in Schwarz's living room, and Rupert promptly lit his pipe. Schwarz looked so miserable Sandra really felt sorry for him.

Rupert kept on talking about everything and nothing. By word and gesture, and without actually being outrageously rude, he even bullied Schwarz into bringing them both a drink. He drank scotch as usual. Sandra, like Schwarz, was a bourbon drinker. He noted there was an unfinished whiskey glass on the table beside Schwarz's chair—and another one on the sideboard.

When Schwarz finally subsided into his seat with the air of a man who has recognized there is nothing else to do, Rupert started his inquisition. It was about the inevitable subject. He simply refused to accept that Schwarz would not consider a deal of some kind for the Stirislavski elephant. Whether it was the intrusion, his ulcers, or whatever the serious disease he had recently been suffering from, their unwilling host was in no condition to cope with Rupert Conway at his most exuberant.

"Look, Mr. Conway, I don't want to be rude, but I've told you: that's out. The elephant is not for sale." Rupert had already noticed that it was not in its previous place on the console table either. "Now, I'm sorry, but I have my own problems." His voice trailed on increasingly unhappy. "Will you just please leave me alone." He looked as though he was on the point of rising to show them the door, but Rupert's gale of conviviality blew him down into his chair again.

"Of course, Mr. Schwarz. I know exactly how you feel." If he did, he certainly gave no sign of it. "But you know us dealers. The more I think about it, the greater my longing. I just felt I had to come and renew my offer."

His whole attitude and response seemed unreal to Schwarz; he just couldn't figure out how to cope with this exasperating man. "You're wasting your time," he said irritably.

It was quite clear *he* was wasting his breath. Continuing

completely unperturbed, Rupert said in his friendliest tones, "I made you a firm offer for it, you know."

Schwarz gulped with undisguised disgust. "One hundred dollars!"

"What's wrong with one hundred dollars?" Rupert came back without batting an eyelid.

"Are you out of your mind? What is this, some kind of a joke?"

"All right, then. Fifty dollars."

"You must be out of your mind." Schwarz looked across at Sandra as though to appeal for assistance, for some glimmering of an explanation of Conway's incomprehensible behaviour.

But before he had a chance to put any intelligible words together, Rupert cut him off with, "You have a visitor, Mr. Schwarz." It was an announcement, not a question. Schwarz stared across the room at his tormentor with a look that changed from simple anger to sheer incredulity. He followed Rupert's line of sight—they were both staring at a bright red crocodile handbag sitting on the floor by the corner of the sofa.

"A lady," Rupert said rather loudly, "from Munich."

Schwarz could only stammer out, "What the hell are you talking about?"

At that instant, every trace of friendliness, of charm, of good humour disappeared from Rupert Conway's face and body as though he had suddenly turned to ice. Sandra watched the split-second transformation as though she were hypnotized by it. Even the colour of Rupert's eyes seemed to change—it was as though an Arctic gale had suddenly swept across a tropical island. This was an aspect of her indulgent cousin's character she had never even suspected.

"I'm talking about theft, Mr. Schwarz. And murder." The words came out like icicles.

Schwarz was incapable of moving or saying anything. He, too, seemed to be frozen solid in his chair.

At that moment, Gerda Ruttgers walked out of the bedroom. Schwarz remained frozen. Sandra looked astounded. Rupert said very politely, "Good evening, Frau Ruttgers. I don't think you have met my cousin, Sandra Fleming, from New York."

Both women attempted a half-hearted smile, and both stared at each other in undisguised curiosity, until Gerda turned to pick up her handbag and looked across at the unhappy Schwarz.

"I heard what he said, Jacob," she said in her usual, unfeeling, glacial tone of voice. She took out a jewelled cigarette case. Rupert was at her side in a second to light her cigarette for her.

Her presence stimulated Schwarz into an attempt at some kind of manly response. He rose somewhat shakily from his chair and started, "Now look here, Conway, you can't—"

"Sit down."

No sergeant in the United States Marine Corps ever barked out an order with more vigour, volume, or total assurance of authority. Schwarz rocked on his heels, as though he had been hit in the face.

"Wha . . . what did you say?" he stammered.

With only token politeness, Rupert replied, "I said, sit down, Mr. Schwarz." As he turned to Gerda, his voice somehow managed to acknowledge her femininity without losing more than a fraction of its tone of command. "And you, too, Frau Ruttgers. Please." To the slight flickering of resentment in her revealingly expressive eyes, he condescended, "I feel sure this will interest you." They both sat down.

Rupert walked over to the sideboard and picked up the almost empty glass Gerda had obviously left on departing to the bedroom when the doorbell rang. He sniffed it. "Scotch, I think, Frau Ruttgers?" Her face showed anxiety, but just the touch of a smile told Rupert she was still unaware of what had happened to her brother—assuming, as he did, that when she found out about it she would be perfectly aware he was involved in it. He refilled his own glass while he was at it. As a gesture to emphasize his now total control of events in chez Schwarz, it was effective, but superfluous. He walked over and stood with his back to the window, from where he not only had the best view of his audience, but could most impressively fulfill the role of state prosecutor, which he now intended to do. To all three of them so assembled, his opening line was delivered with unexpected gentleness.

"Now, Mr. Schwarz, tell me just exactly how you acquired the Stirislavski elephant."

The few moments of peace had allowed Schwarz time to recover some of his savoir-faire. He answered quietly. "I told you that the first day we met. I won it in a poker game."

"No, Mr. Schwarz, that won't do. You see, I happen to know you *lost* it in a poker game."

Schwarz's hard-tried savoir-faire reeled against another shock wave. The turmoil going on in his brain was very nearly audible. The problem of trying to cope with his inquisitor was now multiplied by his natural, glandular urge to assert his manhood in front of Gerda. He reverted to an angry approach. "Why the hell should I tell you anything?" It was not intended as a question, but rather as a declaration of defiance.

Without moving a muscle, Rupert reverted to the tone of icy menace. He virtually spelled it out. "Because I have already heard Karl Ruttgers' version of the story, and if what he told me is true, I know enough to hand you over to face a murder charge."

Rupert was more interested in Gerda's reaction than Schwarz's. It was clear this statement did not come as any surprise to her. Maybe that was why she was here. For the second time in five minutes, Schwarz fairly choked on the word. "Murder?"

"Yes, murder, Mr. Schwarz. The murder of Sergeant Gleason. You might have got off with manslaughter, had it not been for the elephant."

"But that was thirty years ago!"

"Mr. Schwarz, in American military law the statute of limitations does *not* apply to murder."

The victim choked. The vortex of a whole world of tension and fear swept back over him. He slumped forward in his chair and put his head in his hands. Rupert was quick to note that Gerda Ruttgers showed no glimmer of emotion of any kind. He turned off his icy manner and said very softly, "Take it gently, Mr. Schwarz. I'm a good listener."

There was total silence in the room for more than a minute. Schwarz raised his head and took a final gulp from his whiskey. By way of further encouragement, Rupert went to the sideboard and refilled his glass, too. Schwarz looked across piteously, pleadingly at Gerda Ruttgers for some kind of support—any word or gesture, the merest smile or look of reassurance. That intrepid lady remained relentlessly impassive. She just ignored him.

She stood up and said quite calmly to Rupert, "If you wouldn't mind holding the drama for a moment, I would like to use the telephone." It was, of course, Schwarz's phone, but he was lost in another world at that moment.

Rupert, having assumed the role of host, smiled graciously at her and said, "In the hall."

She walked out of the room, and in the silence they could hear her dialing. To Sandra's further astonishment —she was reaching the stage of feeling that she would never be surprised by anything again—Rupert moved three quick, short paces to the corner of the sofa, reached down and opened the red crocodile handbag, took some small object out of it, and slipped it into his inside coat pocket. Schwarz was entirely unaware of that, too.

Gerda's words over the phone were only barely audible, but it was clear she was reporting something of the recent events to her husband, Karl, who appeared to be back in Munich. It crossed Rupert's mind that it did not now much matter where he was—one or more of Gottfried's men would be within a few meters of him. Gerda came back from the phone, sat down without a word, and everyone resumed their places for the next act. The last act? Or was it the first act?

Agonizingly, at first slowly and haltingly as though he scarcely recognized the sound of his own voice, Schwarz began to tell the story that had reached its climax on that wild winter's night near Kronach, the 20th of March 1946. He spoke of his love for Gerda, of their love for each other, of Ruttgers' continued bullying and browbeating, and how it had ended with Ruttgers getting the girl.

Yes, he had for a few weeks owned the pink elephant. He had acquired it illegally—but fairly, he insisted—from a D.P. in return for smuggling that unfortunate, hunted individual out of the military zone in an army vehicle and delivering him to friends and safety somewhere across the French border. What Ruttgers had said about the poker games was true: he usually lost. When Gleason closed his bank three nights before the squadron was disbanded, he had owed over a thousand dollars. He just didn't have it, and Gleason had settled for the jewelled elephant—it was the only thing of value he had to offer. Everybody left in the sergeants' mess knew about the transaction; others settled in similar ways. Everybody knew Gleason was collecting that sort of stuff.

What happened on the night of March 20th? Ruttgers had told him Gerda was sorry about jilting him; if he wanted to say goodby to her, she would be waiting in a truck parked across from the scientific instruments storage shed. He remembered every detail of that as if it had been yesterday. He had gone to the truck. They had talked for over an hour. Then suddenly Ruttgers had come leaping into the truck, pushed them both across the seat, and over the next nightmare of an hour, he had never opened his mouth nor done anything. Schwarz had just sat there, having no idea what was happening nor what was going to happen. He was scared to death of Ruttgers, who had hit him and beaten him up before this. He had no idea who or what was in the van they were following—until the next morning—and he hadn't dared ask. All he knew was that Karl Ruttgers rammed that van into the ditch—he heard the smashing of glass—and when Ruttgers ordered him to help shift those cases, he did see a man's body lying in the snow. He ended in a state near to collapse.

"That's the truth, Mr. Conway. I swear it is," he said exhaustedly.

"Interesting, Mr. Schwarz. Very interesting. But you have omitted to tell me how you got the elephant back?" Rupert was gentle but relentless.

Schwarz gave Gerda another anguished look and was met with continued stony silence. All through the grisly story she had not shown a glimmer of emotion or even interest. The only indication that she was not made of marble had been an occasional, minimal movement to sip her drink. Schwarz took another large gulp from his glass and mustered up just enough strength to complete the epilogue.

"After we left the accident, Ruttgers drove to a house in Coburg. I was too dazed and scared to notice just where. We went into a garage, and he ordered me to help him unload the crates. One of them had burst open—when the van crashed, I guess. The elephant—my elephant—was lying right on top. Ruttgers took it out and shoved it at me. I don't remember exactly what he said—something about being paid for my night's work, and if I ever opened my mouth about it, he would have me on a manslaughter charge." He paused for a moment and with a trembling hand lit a cigarette.

"With my accident record and his authority, well, I couldn't see any military court believing me."

The silence in the room was complete. Then Rupert said, "Just one moment." He walked into the hall and they could hear him make a phone call. Sandra just caught the words "Jo" and "nearly finished." Rupert came back and took up his prosecutor's stance in front of the window. He also resumed his harsh prosecutor's manner.

"Yes, Mr. Schwarz. A very interesting story. Now just tell me one more thing."

Schwarz looked up like a drowning man grasping for a lifeline. It was immediately snatched brutally away from him.

"Why the hell should I believe one word of it?"

Sandra, whose sympathies had been pulled about unmercifully for over an hour, gasped. Even Gerda Ruttgers, for the very first time, showed signs of interest. Schwarz groaned as though he had been poleaxed.

"It's the truth! I swear it's the truth. That's exactly how it happened. Karl Ruttgers killed Gleason. *He* killed him!"

In the same frigid tone as before, Rupert said, "You haven't answered my question."

Schwarz looked hopelessly, pathetically at Gerda. "I've told you the truth. I swear it is." The sight of the sphinx-like Gerda saying nothing, nothing at all, seemed to multiply his misery by ten. His voice, never strong in masculine timbre, shrilled almost to a scream. "For God's sake, Gerda, tell him! Tell him it's the truth. You know the truth." The tears of despair began to well up in his eyes again.

Gerda remained still. Then the muscles of her face tightened—just enough to be visible to an acute observer of human frailty like Rupert. She had made her decision. She reached down and picked up the red crocodile bag. Very slowly she rose from the deep easy chair from which in comfort she had watched her lover's ordeal. Without registering the faintest trace of emotion or reaction. Very slowly and calmly she turned away from Schwarz and looked straight at Rupert.

"Herr Conway, I don't know what business this is of yours. But since Jacob insists I tell you the truth, I will." Her eyes moved back to the trembling, expectant Schwarz. "A very ingenious story, I think Herr Conway called it, Jacob." Schwarz sat staring at her like a rabbit hypnotized by a rattlesnake.

Then she let him have it. "Without a word of truth in it!"

She almost spat the words out. If indeed she had ever been poor Jacob's lover in any sense of the term, her voice, her whole face, now registered nothing but contempt.

If she had hit him, the blow would have been less painful. Schwarz slid off the edge of the low sofa like a dying man. On his knees he looked more wretched than ever. "Gerda!" His voice degenerated to something between a scream and a whimper. "Gerda, what are you saying? What are you doing to me?"

"I've done it," she said, if possible with more malice than before.

"Gerda! How? Why?" By now he was crying and shaking like a terrified child cornered by bullies. "We love each other." He could not have chosen a worse line on which to appeal for mercy.

"Love! Love!" she fairly shrieked at him. "You think I could ever reject a real man like Karl Ruttgers for a weak, stupid fool like *you?*"

It was no question.

Schwarz was finished, anesthetized. Gerda Ruttgers turned on her heel.

"You wanted to know the truth about Jacob Schwarz and his precious elephant. Now you do. Good night, Herr Conway."

She was gone.

Sandra needed that bourbon now. The confrontation had been fascinating, but somehow she felt unclean, as though she had just been forced to watch a fully grown Alsatian tear a spaniel puppy into pieces—for the second time. She went straight to the sideboard right next to the window and poured herself a stiff drink.

Schwarz would have been better off if he had been unconscious. He was still hunched up, half on the floor, half grasping at the seat of the sofa for support. All he could do was keep mumbling in a whipped, bewildered monotone, "Gerda knows the truth. She knows the truth." Weak, pitiful, broken as he was—contemptible even—very probably a man who had committed cold-blooded murder at one time, Sandra was no Gerda Ruttgers. No one with her kind of warm feeling for fellow humans could help but feel sorry for the poor devil now. Slowly becoming aware of his humiliating situation, Schwarz painfully dragged himself onto the sofa and sat there with his head in his hands, sobbing and groaning to himself.

Through all this, it was Rupert who had not moved. No facial expression gave evidence of what might be passing through his brain. From the time he had flicked the last torturing verbal electrodes to bring about Schwarz's final collapse, until several seconds after Gerda Ruttgers left, his only perceptible movement of any kind was to suck his pipe—he never even once had to relight it—and take an occasional sip of scotch.

He walked quietly over to where Schwarz sat slumped in the corner of the sofa, reached down to pick up the glass of bourbon, which fortunately had been just out of reach while its owner was doing his grovelling act, and handed it to him. "Here, I think you need this." The tone was gentle again, even friendly.

Schwarz looked up as though he thought Rupert was about to throw it at him. After a second or two his befuddled brain got the idea that this really was meant to be a kindly gesture. Rupert's smile was once again benevolent, reassuring. Schwarz took the glass in shaking, faltering fingers, sipped a little, and spilled some of it down his still-quivering chin.

"She knows the truth," he stammered out again.

"Yes, I'm sure she does," said Rupert in his most relaxed manner. "And so do I."

Schwarz reacted to a very different kind of electric shock.

"You . . . you know?"

"Yes, I know. I believe you."

Schwarz thought he must really be going insane. His impression was immediately heightened by a shriek from Sandra, standing at the window.

"Rupert! Look! Those men! They're arresting her!"

If he had been in any state to think about it, Jacob Schwarz would have been astonished at the speed with which a breath of strength came back into his tortured body. His mind was still numb with fear, with heart-breaking sorrow, with the bitterness of rejection. But it was just capable of connecting the words "arresting her" and Sandra staring down at the street as though she had seen a ghost. He stumbled to the window and threw it open to look.

Rupert sipped his scotch pensively and never moved.

"Rupert, what's happening? The police. They're shoving her in a car. She's being kidnapped!"

"No," said Rupert. "You were right the first time. They are arresting her. Is Josef there?"

"Yes, he's talking to two other men in uniform. She's in the car now."

"Good."

"But wh . . . why?" Schwarz found words at last.

"Because the Munich police have requested it."

For the first time in over an hour, Rupert sat down and visibly relaxed. Inevitably, he refilled his pipe. "Now, Mr. Schwarz, we still have some unfinished business to discuss. Do sit down."

Schwarz was, if possible, more bewildered than before, but Rupert's words and his manner seemed to have removed all immediate danger at any rate.

"Unfinished business?" His brain wasn't ready to comprehend such words yet.

"You said you believe me?" That was—or sounded like—salvation to Schwarz.

"That's right," Rupert replied in his most avuncular manner.

"Thank God for that. But . . . but . . . why? What's happened?"

"Quite simple, really." Rupert had now completely reverted to his normal urbane manner. "Frau Ruttgers supported her husband's story, right?"

"Right."

"Well, I knew that he was a liar. So obviously she was, too."

"But, I still don't understand. Gerda loved me?" The words hurt and came out in spluttering jerks, but he still seemed to believe them.

"Sorry to hurt your vanity. No. I'm quite sure she didn't love you."

"But she said so—often," he protested.

"I don't doubt that for a minute. It suited their purpose at the time."

"Their purpose?" Sandra asked.

"Yes indeed. Hers and her husband's. They were quite a team." He looked at his watch. "The Munich police will have picked him up by now."

The atmosphere was calmer, at least by comparison with the last hour. Rupert thoroughly enjoyed the surprises he continued to produce like rabbits out of a hat. It was time for some explanations, and Rupert was in the mood to enjoy giving them.

"The key to all this is simply that this is 1976 and that you chose this, of all times, to move to Vienna. You will remember my telling you that U.S. military law does not apply the statute of limitations to murder. Nor does it. But the statute does apply in international law to stolen property, and we agreed long ago that it applied after thirty years. The Allied judges at the Nuremberg trials decided that the critical date for claiming looted property started to run from January first, 1946. So the thirty years were up on January first, 1976. Our friends, Karl and Gerda, waited a long time for this. And they were set to make a real killing."

"She was arrested for dealing in stolen property?" Sandra was loving this.

"That will be part of it. We can now prove many things they sold years ago were stolen. Gleason's loot got them started. And they did well. But the real big haul was lying hidden in East Germany all these years. They dared not bring anything out—there are still too many people like me about who would have spotted something. The first time a known missing piece had come up at Christie's or Sotheby's the game would have been blown. Now, it doesn't matter any more. All legal claims to possessions have come to an end." He relit his pipe. Then continued, "Once the police in Munich got on their trail, and once I found out that Gerda's dear old, white-haired mother in Frauenstein did not exist, all sorts of interesting things started turning up. The charming Ruttgers will be locked up for many years when all the charges come out."

This was the best news poor Schwarz had heard for a long time. "But where did I come into all this, Mr. Conway? I never dealt with them."

"No, not until you made the mistake of coming back to Europe. The police know that. You could have endangered all their operations. They're not the kind of crooks who go in for murder personally, though I'm sure they considered it when they found out you were careless enough to let me see the elephant. But they had to watch you closely. Gerda knew exactly how to keep track of you, to know exactly what you were doing."

"But what was so special about the elephant? Fabergé made thousands—greater pieces than that."

"The elephant was important to me. I told you it belonged to Karl Meulheimer. He was a friend of my grandfather's. It was the sort of clue I've been looking for since the end of the war.

"You know my background, Mr. Schwarz. For thirty years I've been trying to trace the treasures stolen from my family and my friends here in Vienna. That was the main reason I settled here. By an outstanding fluke you suddenly provided that clue. Thirty years is just a year too long for me to do much about it, but I've solved the riddle —and got a small dividend. Your friend Gerda was a very sharp girl. I wonder how much you really know about her?"

Schwarz's blank look was answer enough; he was the kind of man whose emotions easily override his reason.

"She had been a Nazi all through the war, but she worked fast, and she used all the weapons nature gave her very effectively. By July 1945 she was a Communist. She carried on working as a clerk for the Russians at Schloss Weesenstein in Saxony mostly as she had for the Nazis.

"We were always sure the loot from many Viennese families had been stored in that area—as far back as 1938. It was handy to Linz, where Hitler intended to put it all once he had conquered Europe. Being just over the German border and close to Dresden, where Posse and Reger were working in those days, it was convenient and safe from prying eyes—until, of course, the Russian army came on the scene."

Sandra said, "You mean all this priceless stuff has been sitting there ever since?"

"No, not a lot of it, I'm afraid—but enough to interest the Ruttgers. And me. The larger pieces—pictures and so on—stayed there when Reger moved out. Many of them were destroyed in the fighting. D.P.'s and marauders of all kinds wandered freely through central Europe in 1945 and '46. Outside the big towns and military centers, there was little law enforcement of any kind. One can't prove it, but I'm certain that anything they could get their hands on disappeared into Russia years ago. When the Red Army crossed into Germany and Poland in the winter of 1944–45, Reger moved everything he could—the smaller pieces—to an old house near Frauenstein."

Schwarz was looking almost human again. He didn't understand half of this, nor did he care. Karl Ruttgers was off his back; that was all he could think of.

"However, East German spies and Weesenstein are not your concern, Mr. Schwarz. From your point of view, all that matters is that you are really a free man again. The threat Ruttgers had hanging over your head is all past now."

"Karl Ruttgers." Schwarz couldn't quite say his name without a shudder of fear.

"What exactly were your relations with those two?"

"Ruttgers was master sergeant of my unit. How you found that out, I don't know. I was the youngest and most junior sergeant. He bullied the hell out of me from the moment I arrived; I really believe Gerda did love me once." He could not help reverting constantly to that subject. "She was the first German girl I ever met. She arrived in Kronach the same week we did. I was the first American she had ever met. We became lovers then. We even talked of marrying and going back to the States together. Then Ruttgers met her. He took her away from me. I guess that's why he was always riding me. Then when he threatened to frame me on the manslaughter charge, well, with my driving record and his authority, no court martial would have taken my word against his. What could I do?"

There was no answer to the question.

"It was not until years later, when I came back to live in Europe, that I found out he and Gerda had married. I met him at a diamond merchant's in Munich—must have been about, oh, 1968, I guess. From that moment, he's never really been off my back. And later on my affair with Gerda started up again. Or, I thought it did. I guess I just had too bad a case of overactive glands to think she had any other reason to want to see me."

Facing facts, like confession, is good for the soul. Another stiff gulp of bourbon helped, too. "I can't tell you how grateful I am, Mr. Conway," he said, his tone almost matter-of-fact.

Rupert's mood and humour went through another rapid switch. "Oh yes, you can. Our unfinished business, remember? I've done you a great favour, you know."

"Yes, you have. All I can say is thank you."

"Oh, come now. There need be no feeling of ingratitude hanging on your conscience. I left my bid in for the elephant."

"You still want that?" For an instant Schwarz gave one glimmer of being able to stand on his feet again.

Without a moment's hesitation, Rupert responded.

"I insist on it. Will you sell it to me? Or do you want to hear some other things I've dragged up?" That was pure bluff, but it worked.

"Oh, no. Please, Mr. Conway. I've had all I can take."

Resuming his customary polite but firm manner of giving orders when he felt they were necessary, Rupert said, "Go and get it."

Schwarz had no choice, an experience he had learned to understand and endure. Reluctantly he got up and unlocked a drawer in his desk. He put the desired object on the table, removing layers of protective white tissue paper.

"Beautiful," Rupert said. "Quite beautiful. My last bid still stands."

"You mean you expect me to let you have it for . . . a hundred dollars, you said?" Schwarz passed from one bad dream to another.

"No, no. My final bid was fifty dollars."

"Fifty dollars! But it's worth thousands!"

"I'm well aware of that," Rupert replied. "But I'm not bidding anymore, Mr. Schwarz. I'm dictating my terms. I advise you not to forget it." How could a man pass in a few seconds from being so brutal to being so nice—and back again even faster? It was all a matter of practice and, above all, of never losing sight of the ultimate objective. Rupert had learned that lesson years ago.

Schwarz looked at the lovely jewelled carving. He hesitated, shook his head, thought about Ruttgers, picked it up, put it down again. Could this Conway know about the D.P. he had literally stolen it from? What else did he know?

Rupert sometimes looked like a statue of himself—the army had taught him to stand perfectly immobile. He knew there was no need to say anything more. Fear and irresolution were written all over Schwarz's face again.

With a last, despairing gesture, Schwarz picked up the Stirislavski elephant, blinked, and thrust it into Rupert's hands.

"Thank you. A very satisfactory piece of business for both of us," Rupert said. He held it in one hand, put his always handy jeweller's glass to his eye, and examined the diamond eyes. "Yes," he said. "They are the originals alright."

A man whose mind was more alert than Schwarz's at this moment would have been insulted. Rupert emptied his glass. He didn't relight his pipe, but carefully knocked the burned-out ash into a large glass ashtray. He turned towards the door. Schwarz just stood dazed; nothing registered any more.

"Oh, yes. Sorry, I owe you fifty dollars." Handing the precious object into Sandra's hesitating hands, he searched in his trouser pockets.

"Here you are. I took the precaution of bringing a fifty-dollar bill with me—good American money." He passed it over to Schwarz, who gazed unbelievingly at the crumpled green bill in his palm.

"A very satisfactory transaction," Rupert repeated.

"I hope we never do business again," Schwarz said bitterly.

"Quite," said Rupert. "Sandra, my dear, I think Mr. Schwarz is tired. We must not outstay our welcome. Good night, Mr. Schwarz."

Rupert stood politely aside, as always, while Sandra passed out into the small narrow hall. The building was dead silent. At 1:55 A.M., it was a fair bet that no over-curious neighbours had been watching from their front windows; there were no signs of gossip or scuttling feet anywhere to be heard.

Sandra clutched the precious elephant as though her life depended on it. Unhurt in any way, nevertheless she was almost as breathless and confused as poor Schwarz. Now she really did feel sorry for him. She wondered if he might by any chance have passed out cold as soon as his apartment door had closed behind them. She contemplated the oddity of the situation that might arise if Schwarz's cleaning woman were to find his body lying on the sitting room floor tomorrow morning. What a story for the sensationalist press. "American art dealer found dead in mysterious circumstances. Favourite treasure stolen. Fingerprints in apartment prove to be those of world-famed art dealer, Rupert Conway, and the girl he was living with, Sandra Fleming." What an American tabloid could do with that one! Then she remembered that Jo Liebmann was waiting downstairs and knew everything that had happened.

There was a soft whirring noise, and a little green arrow lit up over their heads. A door slid silently open, and Sandra and Rupert stepped into one of those very well-known transportation machines that was one of the very few things they could never agree on. She said it was an elevator; he insisted it was a lift. Anyway, it worked; that was all that mattered. In a few seconds, the door slid effortlessly open again and they walked through the small front hall door into the street.

All was quiet and dark. Rupert's beautiful, sleek, deep-blue Jensen stood just where they had left it, a few yards down Reisnerstrasse and right under the lamppost. Behind it was parked a police car, from which Jo Liebmann emerged as though activated by an electronic switch. There was no one else about except the police driver—the street was deserted. Under the lamppost there was sufficient light for Sandra to show Jo the famous animal that had started all the fun and games. The police officer and Rupert exchanged greetings. They were not just old friends—they were frankly very pleased with themselves and each other.

"Well done, Jo. That was quick work."

"The boys in Munich didn't waste any time. We'll have no trouble dealing with the extradition proceedings. I've arranged to have a judge sign the papers first thing in the morning. Munich has all the information I need."

"What news from the other end?"

"I've been talking direct to Munich on our noise-box here. They picked up Ruttgers an hour ago—on the smuggling charges. They are searching his office now."

Liebmann leaned his head in through the car window. "Any details yet, Sergeant?" He spoke to the police car driver, who turned up the speaker a bit louder. The radio gave out squawks intelligible only to those who are expert on these matters. To Sandra it sounded as though police officers on at least three different frequencies were playing some kind of numbers game. It might have been chess.

The sergeant leaned over and spoke to his chief.

"Sounds useful," Jo said. "They have got into Ruttgers' strongroom and found code books, copies of secret NATO documents, and cabinet papers—up to date."

"Good. Good. Great night's work. Tremendous fun."

"Do you think I had better go up and interview Schwarz now?" Liebmann had a well-developed sense of duty, but his tone still invited the right response from Rupert.

"No, no. I'm sure that's not necessary now. He's had a rough evening, has friend Schwarz. I'm sure he won't run out; he'll make more sense after a good night's sleep, too, though, frankly, I don't think he's really involved anymore."

"Munich may want him as a witness at some stage."

"I don't think he will cause you any trouble that way. I can promise you, Schwarz wants to see that lot locked up just as much as the Bonn government does!"

The air was suddenly rent by a series of wild, unrestrained yelping. In the back of the Jensen, Charlie had suddenly awakened, heard his master's voice, and finding himself alone in a strange place, started to bark his head off. Rupert said a hurried good night—there were very strict anti-noise laws after midnight in Vienna. He and Sandra wasted no time in unlocking the Jensen and responding to the extravagant enthusiasm of the terrier's welcome. He kept leaping from one end of the car to the other, falling off the seats, jumping up and down like a mad dervish, but at least they were able to persuade him to desist from trying to wake up the whole neighbourhood.

The police car drove off with friendly waves all round. Rupert, calm and unhurried as always, inserted the ignition key, reached down the steering column and flicked over the antiburglar cut-out. Sandra sat beside him, took a deep breath, and tried to secure the elephant inside her fur coat, where there would be minimum risk of Charlie knocking it out of her anxious grasp. But Charlie was perfectly happy now. He made himself part of the coat as well. Like all really high-class dogs, Charlie appreciated good mink as well as the girls who wore them.

The car slid silently into motion. Rupert drove slowly along Reisnerstrasse, turned right into Rennweg. He had, of course, relit his pipe while talking to Liebmann. Quietly humming some mysterious melody to himself, he had the air of a man who had just spent a quiet evening with friends, wined and dined well, and had not another thought in the world besides the happy prospect of a quiet night's sleep with a clear conscience.

Sandra's brain was still working flat out. "The Ruttgers, smuggling, spying—all that I've got. But the elephant . . . you virtually stole that! Fifty crazy dollars. Really! The cheek of you Englishmen!"

Rupert benignly took no offence, but such a remark could not pass unnoticed. "Welsh, my dear. Welsh."

"I stand corrected. But don't evade the issue."

"I'm not evading any issue."

"What are you going to do with it?"

"Sell it, of course. It's beautiful, but not my line."

"It's not your property either!" She could not help feeling just a little bit reproachful. Up to now she had never doubted for a moment that Rupert was always on the side of the good guys.

"Legally, it is."

Sandra, generous, honest soul, was shocked. "But not morally! Really it belongs to Fraulein Meulheimer."

"Indeed. But what would poor old Fraulein Meulheimer do with this in her pathetic little boardinghouse back room?"

Sandra was shocked again. Or was he teasing her? "Can't she prove it really belongs to her?"

"Doubtful, but even if she could, it would do her no good. Statute of limitations, remember?" He braked gently and the car came to a stop as they met the red traffic light at Schwarzenburgplatz.

"No, I have a much better plan than that. The best place to sell this is in Bonn. Ludwig Friedkraus has a good market for Fabergé, and prices are higher in Germany than anywhere else right now. With luck, we'll get something like fifty thousand dollars there."

"Fifty thousand dollars! And you paid fifty!"

"That's right." The light turned green, and they headed for the Ring. Rupert's tone changed again. "It isn't remotely enough to compensate the old lady for all she has lost, nor for all she has suffered. But it will be enough to get her to her beloved Israel, where she can live in more comfort and happiness than she has known for many, many years."

Sandra swallowed hard. How could she have just been thinking such unkind thoughts about him?

They sat in silence waiting for the stoplight at the Ring.

"Tell me more about this spying business," Sandra asked.

"I told you: Gerda became a Communist in record time as soon as the war was over—all very easy for her. During the war she had worked for the Nazis at Weesenstein, in Reger's office. She helped compile all those famous catalogues of art treasures. I can't say exactly what happened in '44 or '45, but the pattern seems pretty clear. Reger disappeared; Gerda must have been left behind at Weesenstein. She must have known all Reger's secrets, and with her charms and nimble brain she must have bedded down some commissar almost from the beginning. She had a lot of things they wanted and information as well. They must have made a deal, and she was recruited straight into a Communist spy network—I don't know which one, but it will all come out at the trial, no doubt. By January 1946, she had moved into the American Zone, where she made up to the American Air Force boys by the usual method. She has worked for the East Germans ever since."

"But how did all this come out?"

"Because when I told the Munich police that Gerda had no mother and they checked the record of her border crossings, at last we all knew the right questions to ask."

"Why were the East Germans so accommodating to her?"

"You can't bribe those boys."

"Gerda had influence?"

"At the highest level. Do you remember reading about Gunther Guillaume?"

"Rings a bell, but I can't say where."

"The spy who was caught in Willi Brandt's office in April two years ago. There was a terrible scandal about it. Ruined Brandt's career."

"Was Gerda involved in that?"

"She was one of their star couriers. She had no apparent connection with the Communists. Her family had lived in East Germany, so she had reasons for going back and forth across the border that no one but the East German authorities could check on. She carried all the intelligence reports, microfilm, and so on to the Commies, and in return they left her loot alone until she was ready for it. It saved them a lot of money. The right time for the more easily identified pieces was not until January this year. That's how I got onto it, when you told me about the elephant. The West German counterintelligence people have been trying to round up the whole of the Guillaume gang ever since Guillaume and his wife were caught. The fact it has taken nearly two years to catch Gerda just shows how good she was."

"Was her husband a spy, too?"

"I really don't know, but he must have been deeply involved. Not from the start, probably, but they can't have worked together for long, let alone been married, before they found out they deserved each other. We know he's crooked, unscrupulous, and a murderer. He must have known she had no mother living in Frauenstein. Suited his book just fine."

The traffic in the Ring was heavy, even at that hour. They made slow progress and got stuck behind three taxis unloading late party-leavers at the Bristol.

Rupert reached into his coat pocket. "Cigarette?"

"Thanks, I need one."

She took it from the case he held out to her. She didn't stop to look at the brand or anything else. A nerve-soother was all she had in mind. She took a long, deep breath and exhaled slowly. Then it was her turn to shriek. "Cigarette! You never carried a cigarette case in your life."

"I never had a case like this to carry before," was all he said. He put the case down on the seat arm, swung the steering wheel, gave a touch on the accelerator, and they moved into the right-hand lane to be in a position for the next turn.

Sandra just stared at him.

"Take it," Rupert said.

She reached down and picked up the case. He pressed a switch in the control panel and a small flexible light slid noiselessly out, almost into her hands. The case she was holding was made of solid gold—she could tell that by the weight of it. The edges of the case were mounted with gold scroll woven into a pattern of garlands and flowers. Its top was an intricate and exquisite pattern of green and white Russian enamel, criss-crossed with gold threads, the whole making a sunburst pattern that emanated from a garlanded monogram in the center, which at first sight seemed to be a solid mass of emeralds. It was superb, and she had no need to ask who had made it.

"Magnificent, isn't it?" Rupert said in his quiet, most matter-of-fact manner.

"You took this out of Gerda Ruttgers' handbag," she said.

"That's right. She won't need it where she's going."

"You are incredible!" She was not going to risk accusing

him of stealing a second time. "What are you going to do with this, may I ask?"

"Me? Nothing. I've done it."

"Done what?"

"Given it to you. I said, take it."

"But I can't take stolen property."

"You can take that with a perfectly clear conscience, I assure you. Have a closer look."

Sandra lifted the beautiful object a little closer and moved the map-light so it shone directly onto its center. The cluster of emeralds formed a ribbon, tied in a bow about four centimeters in diameter. Inside the ribbon, in old German script, were two most delicately formed letters with some figures underneath.

"You can read it?" Rupert asked.

Sandra looked very carefully. She read: "J.E. 9.3.08."

"That's right."

"What's it mean?"

"Sandra, my darling, your brain really must be tired. It means Julie Eisenbath, 9th March 1908."

"Grandmother!"

"That's right. Grandfather gave it to her on their twentieth anniversary. She always carried it. I recognized it the first time I saw Madame Ruttgers use it—in Ruttgers' office the day I went to Munich. That was the second great clue. But I couldn't do anything about it until tonight."

"You want me to keep it?"

"Of course. You have a far better right to it than anyone else. You are her only living granddaughter."

They drew up at the entrance to 5B Stephansplatz.

"Heinz can put the car away in the morning, before those damn meters start operating."

Now it was really all over. Even Rupert allowed himself the rare indulgence of feeling tired. All the standing had made his bad leg ache a little. Rupert flicked over the burglar cut-out, they got out, and he turned the key in the door lock. Charlie stretched and ambled a few yards down the sidewalk.

Rupert, with his usual meticulous care, turned the two big keys in the front door, deactivating the alarm system and opening the door. As he turned to let her pass, Sandra paused, still clutching the elephant in both hands, then said abruptly, "Here, hold this."

Rupert looked a little surprised, but did as she asked. He was rewarded with the biggest, most loving kiss a middle-aged cousin had ever received.

They didn't even notice Charlie paying his last respects for the night to the long-suffering cardinal.